I0659304

RIVERBOAT BILL 1961

RIVERBOAT BILL 1961

ED MIDDLETON

Copyright © 2019 by Ed Middleton

This book is a book of fiction. Names, characters, places, and incidents are a product of the author's imagination or are used fictitiously. Any resemblance to actual events or locales, or persons living or dead, is coincidental.

All rights reserved. No part of this publication may be reproduced, stored in a retrieval system, or transmitted in any form or by any means—electronic, mechanical, photocopy, recording, or any other—except for brief quotations in printed reviews, without the prior written permission of the publisher.

Published by Skipjack Holdings LLC

ISBN: 978-1-7330258-0-5

Also by Ed Middleton
Skipjack Maddox 1859
Mr. Maddox 1953

For Deanna

THE CREEKSIDE SAGAS

RIVERBOAT BILL 1961

CONTENTS

CHAPTER 1

STORM

I was soaked to the bone, and I was scared. Scared silly like a nightmare, with the sheets all twisted and me lying in a pool of sweat or worse. I felt I was too old to be scared, and I felt stupid on top of it. I was fourteen and I wasn't lost or anything, but now it was dark except for the traces of lightning that were moving downriver. Everything became quieter, and I could hear the creek swirling past and the water dripping down through the leaves of the tree I crouched under. I was soaked, but mainly I was scared and I hated that.

The storm had been a monster: loud as bombs and mean as Frankenstein. Home wasn't so far, maybe a mile or so, but a mile can seem like forever through brush and fences and stuff you can't see except when the lightning flashes.

And this storm had a brother. I felt like the air around me was standing up to welcome him as he marched toward me across the sky. Too early to tell how mean he was. He just crackled and teased and rumbled.

Seemed like they were talking: one saying "hurry up" and the other just taking his sweet time, saying, "I'll be there directly."

The creek was coming up, not fast, but rising and I was thinking that if it came up too much more, I wouldn't have much choice. Either head into the storm and take my chances or climb a tree.

Down the creek a way was a shanty boat that I could make out when the lightning lit up everything. Some old drunk lived there, all red faced and scaly. I'd seen him before, drinking his beers and sitting on some kind of bench. He pumped gas sometimes at the boat dock, but mainly he just sat around and drank. His voice was weird, like a scratchy growl.

I was cold as frog skin and then the storm that was leaving kind of called back to his brother who was following, and that bastard roared back an answer and lit up the darkness like the Fourth of July. The debate was about over. When he answered again, just a tad louder, I decided to call upon Riverboat Bill. There was no way in hell I was going to walk into that storm.

I started scrambling down the muddy creek bank and, thank God, it was spring and the bank wasn't all grown up with weeds. It was bad enough climbing over drift and roots and junk. I wanted more light, and then the thunder would boom, and I figured that dark wasn't all that inconvenient after all. Then it seemed like I got all the damn light in the world and, just when I would think that, and make a lot of headway and get excited, then there would be a pitch-black-stumbling dark and a poke in the eye and a turned ankle.

At least it wasn't raining yet. The wind was blowing drops out of the trees, and then it blew like hell and thundered so loud I was afraid to cuss, and then the storm poured more rain than the last one. This monster dumped a hundred buckets and it didn't matter anymore. I would have tried to run through a tree trunk. To hell with roots. I fell over stuff that wasn't even there. I stepped in something (a paint can, it turned out later), and when I couldn't shake it loose, I took it along with me. I was on my way to see Riverboat Bill.

There was a bit of a problem. Something I hadn't really considered. I mean, I knew it, but I hadn't really thought about what it meant. The boat, if you could call it that, all waterlogged and hashed together, was tied up across the creek.

It wasn't that far. I could have hit the old tub with a rock. But the creek was all swollen and running fast. Besides that, although I was from Kentucky and used to 'em, this storm was the kind of noisy that shushes like an angry mother and then booms at you like a last-word father, and then all the rest of the stuff like all the brothers and sisters in the world.

"Bill," I yelled. "Bill!"

"Yo, hey! Who's there?" he growled in a voice that cut through the storm. "Who's out there? Who's there?"

The second time his voice was louder and it had even more of an edge than the first time. I could sort of see him standing under some kind of overhang that covered his deck. The glow from his cigarette lit up his face for a second, making his eyes shine, and then he flipped the butt into the water. "Who's . . ."

Just then, a bolt of lightning crashed nearby and the boom that came with it about blew my ears off. I spoke up then and loud.

"Me! It's me, Ed, the guy from up the hill. How are you?" I yelled.

"Not worth a damn! What the hell do you want?"

"Nothing, I guess."

"Nothing, you guess? Are you nuts? Stay just where you are. I'll be over in a minute. Don't move."

"All right." I answered as strongly as I could.

A few minutes and a whole bunch of storm later, he started putt-putting across the creek. He had to travel only about thirty feet, but the water was full of branches and logs and was moving so fast that he had to point way upstream and dodge through the junk.

The old skiff he was in looked about half sunk, and the old motor sounded clanky and smoked like a factory. When the lightning lit him up, the whole outfit looked like it was on fire, but the way the rain was coming down, there wasn't much chance of that.

"Over here," I yelled.

He never answered. The motor and thunder must have drowned me out. He was aimed upstream and the old motor was coughing and straining. The rain seemed to be pressing the smoke down so it couldn't get away; the black swirls were thick enough to make me gag.

And then here he turned, roaring down on me and he crashed

into the bank right at my feet. I just stood there and stared into the boat half full of water, with bottles and cans floating all around him.

"Get aboard, damn you! Watch your step."

I jumped in as carefully as I could and about busted my tail. There were around six inches of water in the bottom and I splashed him pretty good, but I guess it didn't matter. We were both waterlogged.

"Sit yourself still. You hear me?"

I could barely see him, but I could feel him staring at me, and I nodded. He nodded back and let the current drag us off the bank, and then he swung upstream and the motor choked out. I started to reach out for a branch and halfway stood up.

"Sit your ass, damn it."

"Yes sir," I said and plopped down low.

He yanked on the old starter rope five or six times, all the time saying, "Yes sir, my ass," and "Start, you son of a biscuit!" And finally, the clunker did. Caught real shaky at first, then grabbed hold and poured out all kinds of awful smoke and roared until I thought the thing might explode, but then it calmed down and we sputtered back upstream.

"Keep an eye out for logs. Yell and point if you see one."

We missed all kinds of stuff. I pointed out a couple of things that looked like they might be logs, and we dodged around them. Then I saw something that was sort of white and I couldn't quite make it out, but it was definitely coming our way and it was big. The shape might have been a log, but wasn't running right. Whatever it was swirled all solid and seemed to change shape right in front of my eyes. One minute it was big with a couple of branches sticking out and then flat or at least not so big, and then it was rounded and then straight. The swirling thing changed, zigged and zagged under special rules, but I couldn't decide what those rules were.

I started to point left and then to the right, and started to yell just as the lightning busted up something so close that the thunder about put my eyes out. I squinted out in the rain and saw the bleary old shanty about twenty feet away. I could see the boards and the paint all chipping and the mossy ropes tied to some trees. I could even see how the lines had rubbed the bark off and how the wood was white there, or yellow, and how the bark was gray.

We moved upstream in slow motion. I could reach out and touch the boat. Almost.

Faster.

Come on.

"Come on," I yelled. "Faster, come on, faster!"

I looked for the white thing and I couldn't see it. Suddenly, the crazy shape was going that way, and then coming this way, and I yelled out, but I didn't know which way to point. First, I pointed this way and then I pointed the other.

"What you want, boy? What the hell you want?"

"That way," I screamed, pointing at the scow. Then it came right at us and knocked me silly. Last thing I saw was this big old belly and an eyehole, then this white branch with a hoof, and then I took a very brief nap.

Mainly, I was just stunned. I was stretched out in the bottom of the boat. All the water didn't bother me much. The bottles and cans were a different matter.

"Holy bejesus! A stinking dead cow!"

"A what?" I exclaimed, as I struggled to sit up.

"We done just had a head-on with a cow."

I wrestled myself back up on the seat and, in our wake, there it was, all swollen and bloated and spinning around.

"Boy! How hell you miss that one? This just ain't your day, is it?"

We bonked into the side of the scow and Bill hollered for me to hold on. I grabbed the catwalk, and then my other hand found a cleat.

"I got it," I yelled, and Bill reached over me with a line he had snatched out of the mess at my feet and made her fast. The boat drifted back to the deck where I had first seen him. The current held her in tight.

"Now, you watch your step getting off here. Don't want to have to fish you out. Hear?"

"I hear you," I said.

I got out easy and stood up on the deck. The storm was still crashing, the rain pouring down. Bill just stood there looking at me and shaking his head.

"What?" I said, finally.

He clambered onto the deck on his knees, groaned, and stood up. He kind of shook himself like a dog, then stood there, grimly shaking his head and looking me up and down.

"Boy, you're a damn case, ain't you? I've never seen the match could hold a candle to you."

He kept staring at me, first my head and then my feet. I looked down. My foot looked funny.

"Look at you, boy, just look at yourself. Got a lump on your noggin the size of a Titleist, the beginnings of a first-class shiner, and a busted lip. Your shirt's all tattered, you're covered with mud, and you're drenched to the bone.

"I can buy into that. What I don't get, besides why you chose this particular night to come calling is this . . . what in the name of all that's holy are you doing walking around in a paint can?"

So that's what it was. I could see it now. I reached down and my foot was poked in. The can was rotten, I guess. My heel was poked out the side.

"Can't explain it," I said.

"You can't explain it?" he asked incredulously. "You got no clue?"

"No, not really."

"No idea at all?"

"This is a first for me, too," I said.

"I don't believe it. First, get kicked in the head by an old dead cow and then you're just lounging around with a paint bucket on your foot. Then you tell me, matter of fact, that it's a damn first. What you up to, boy?"

I shrugged. Man, I felt dumb. Then all of a sudden, he just reared back and roared and laughed until he wheezed and wheezed, then he coughed and coughed so hard I thought he was going to fall overboard.

But then, he caught himself up and kind of rearranged his bones, tucked in his shirt and shook his head.

"You ever smoke?" he asked in that rough old voice.

"Sometimes," I said.

"It's a bad habit, boy, but what the hell could you expect from the likes of you. Sit down and take off your paint can. I'll be damned if I'll have a man in my boat wearing a damn can."

"Yes, sir," I said.

"Cut the crap and come on inside."

He ducked down and went in through the little door. I struggled with the stubborn old can and finally managed to kick it into the drink. Gusts of wind blew the rain right into my face. Everything looked bleary, especially out of my right eye. I felt my cheekbone and eyebrow. Both were smashed and swollen. There was a big lump on my forehead. That didn't hurt much though. All of a sudden, I shivered hard and realized how cold I was. I stooped and stepped through the door down into the boat.

There was nobody in sight. It wasn't real dark. A lantern was burning and I saw an old jar with a lit candle sticking out of it. There was no place to hide that I could see.

The room was small. There was a table with three chairs and a couch crammed up against one wall. A door on top of an old log was in front of the couch. A wood-burning stove with a rusty pipe stood in the corner. There was no place to hide. The far wall had a couple of big maps on it, one of the United States and the other of the world. There was a big US flag nailed up floor-to-ceiling.

The rain pounded on the roof and splattered against the windows so hard that I half expected them to bust out. I strained to hear something, but all I could hear was rain, and then a flashing crash of thunder hit so close by that I wished I couldn't hear anything.

I guess the thunder had made me close my eyes, because when I opened them, Bill was standing right in front of the flag. He was all wrapped up in a green blanket.

"What are you making all those faces for?"

"What faces?" I asked. "And where were you hiding?"

"Who's hiding? You all right, boy? What you looking for, son?"

I was still looking around trying to figure out where he had been, but there was nowhere. Bill walked over to the stove, opened the firebox door, struck a wooden match, and stuck it in there. A little blaze started flickering. He shook his head and grunted.

"Damn wood's wet."

He grabbed a can of lighter fluid down off the shelf and squirted a liberal portion into the stove. A roar of flame curled out of the potbelly and licked at the ceiling. He grinned at me and made like he was going to do it again. Then he thought better of it.

"Naw, that ought to do it. Come over and dry out."

I didn't move. He put the can back on the shelf. The flame slowly eased its way back into the stove.

"What's with you, boy?"

"Where were you when I first came in here?"

"Oh, I get your drift." He started chuckling and shaking his head.

"Well, where were you?" I asked

"I was in the master stateroom taking a pee," he said, as he gathered his blanket around him and walked over to the flag. He grabbed it and it opened like a door. It *was* a door.

"What? You thought I was a magician? Poof!" he said and covered his head with the blanket. He was mumbling something, but I couldn't make it out.

"What?"

He opened the blanket and said, "I was saying if it was that damn easy to disappear, I would do it in the blink of an eye. Now, go get warm."

As I walked toward the stove, I tried to see past him into the next room, but he shut the door before I could see anything.

"That's my room. The captain's room. Private. You hear?"

I nodded.

"Good. Now, get warm."

The heat from the stove felt great. It popped and hissed. First, I toasted my backside and then the front. I stood right next to it and shortly steam was curling up off my pants.

Bill handed me some sort of towel with ice in it. He told me it might take down the swelling. The cold kind of burned and stung. My eye was almost swollen shut. I kept turning slow, trying to cook the rain out of my clothes.

Bill disappeared into his private room and came back a few minutes later with some potato chips, a couple of glasses, some beers, and a bottle of whiskey. He put them on the table. He opened a beer and stood next to the stove beside me.

"I suppose if you smoke sometimes, you probably drink some too, so help yourself if you want a beer."

I looked up at him to make sure that he meant it. Wet as I was, I was awful thirsty, but I wasn't accustomed to being offered a beer. Mostly I had to sneak them. He held out a pack of Pall Malls and offered me one. I took it and he lit our smokes. I figured he meant it, but I didn't want to seem too eager for the beer, so I smoked about half before I cracked one: a frosty Falls City Beer, cold and sour. Delicious! Things were turning out good.

Bill shed his blanket and tossed a couple of logs into the stove. The fire was rumbling now and was competing with the storm in the noise department. The rain seemed to be letting up and the lightning was hitting downstream mostly. I was about half dry from my knees to about my shoulders, so with a cold beer and a cigarette, I was close to comfortable.

When I had opened my beer, I put the towel packed with ice on the table and left it there. I hadn't thought anything about what would happen, but the ice melted and made a puddle. Bill saw the water oozing and that made him sore.

"I didn't mean to hurt your table. I didn't have enough hands, that's all."

"Might not be too much of a table to you, Mr. Richie Rich, but this here's a fine table and it don't need to be messed up no more than it is, you hear?"

I nodded. He looked pretty upset. It looked like a beat-up old table to me with burns and drink rings all over the top; one of the legs looked like a dog had cut his teeth on it. He was still looking at me hard. I had no idea why he was so upset. It meant something to him, I could tell that for sure.

"Look, I really am sorry. I'll wipe it up."

"What's the damn point?" he said and he swiped the whole business off onto the floor. He sat down and poured himself a glass of whiskey, a full glass. He stared at it and continued to drink his beer. The shadows jiggled on the ceiling and walls. I studied them and the flickering candle on the table. I wanted to say something. It was strange with nobody talking and the storm letting up. In fact, outside it was getting quiet and I could hear the water dragging against the hull. Bill sat there and said nothing, and I acted as cool as I could, but my insides were uncomfortable.

Now that the storm seemed to be over, I was thinking about how I was going to get home and about what I was going to say. To say the least, I was already screwed. I was in hot water when I left, slamming the door and screaming. I guess cussing was more like it.

Neither one of my parents liked cussing, even though they did it sometimes. "God dog it!" meant sort of mad. "God damn it!" was real mad. But "God damn it to hell!" meant head for the hills. That's exactly what I had done and down the other side into the bottomland and across to the river, then to the creek. I might have done it even if I had known about the storm.

Lightning and thunder were scary, but they usually missed—my father usually didn't. My mother never could control his anger; she seemed to be able to slow it down, but that just made it take longer. He almost never hit me after I was three or four, but he knew how to get inside and blow me up like an enemy bunker, leaving me twisted and speechless. He would ask what I had to say for myself, and when I didn't answer, he would swell up and insist that I speak out, and I would try. He would drown me out or just stare in a way that swallowed my words or jumbled them so that even I knew that they made no sense at all. Then he might say, "Pull in your lower lip." I wouldn't even know it was sticking out. I would want to explode, to blow up the whole place. My sister would be crying. My little brother would be shaking. My mother would try to be mother—on the one hand defending her brood, soothing my brother and sister, calming her husband, and yet being supportive, which meant telling me to listen to my father, which was ridiculous since it was impossible to do anything but.

I had exploded. I threw my math book at the wall, and I ran and slammed the door and screamed every four-letter word I had ever heard. I did that in the garage right off the kitchen. I stopped for a couple of seconds and listened to my voice, which sounded big and loud and nasty. But then, it sounded empty like an echo. I heard footsteps coming through the kitchen. I shot out of there and ducked into the woods. They were both yelling my name. My father's voice sounded loud like he was pounding in fence posts. My mother's pleadings were the barbwire strung between the posts. I tore out.

Bill just sat there, nursing his beer and smoking. He stared at the glass of whiskey like he was listening to it. The way he looked, I was afraid to speak, almost like I would be interrupting something. He grunted and nodded, which confirmed what I was thinking. I took a sip of beer and noticed he was looking at me, and then he nodded and went back to gazing at his whiskey glass. After a while, he coughed hard and spit into a handkerchief. He studied the wad of cloth, and then carefully folded and placed the handkerchief down on the table.

"I ain't dead yet. What about you, boy? What kinda jam you stuck in, hmmm?" He raised his eyebrows and I shrugged.

"Just caught out in the storm, I guess."

"Nice poetic way of putting things. You ain't no scholar like I've ever seen, but you never know." He paused and cleared his throat. "I'll ask you once again, what in hell's name were you doing tramping around in a storm like that? You from up the hill. That used to be a nice button-down shirt. The shoe that was in the can and ain't completely caked with river mud cost somebody some money."

He went back to staring at the whiskey. I didn't want to get into it all. I'd had enough of trying to explain myself for one day. I mainly just wanted to dry out and drink beer.

"Looky here, son, I ain't really into playing Fearless Fosdick with you. I just figure if a man is going to drink my hooch, smoke my cigs, and warm his ass by my fire, I got a damn square right to know a little bit about who that fellow is. What you think? Sound reasonable to you?"

I nodded.

"So you are in a jam, right?"

"Yes."

Bill shook his head and stared at the whiskey with that same look he had before, like he was listening or something.

"All right, I'll play then. You rob a bank?"

That took me by surprise and I kind of laughed.

"No. Maybe you chopped up your grandma with an axe? Naw, that's too old-fashioned and bloody. How about, did you steal a car and wreck it?"

"No, I didn't steal a car, and if I did, I wouldn't wreck it either, because I drive real good."

"Good, good. That might come in handy," he said, "but back to the business. Did you set fire to somebody's barn? Naw, that would have been a problem in this rain. Couldn't have if you'd wanted to. So maybe out of spite, you up and shot your daddy's prize bull?"

"My daddy don't have a bull," I insisted.

"No bull at all?" he asked, eyes wide with disbelief.

"Well, no," I said. "He's not a farmer."

"Well, young man, what does your daddy do for a living?"

"He goes to work."

"No fooling, but what does the man do?"

"He goes into work every day."

"No bull! Now, son, you already said that, and so for the last time,

I'm going to ask you, what the hell *does* the man do?"

"How should I know? He's a lawyer. He goes to work, that's all I know."

He stared at his whiskey again, but this time, he winked at it and chuckled.

"So that explains it," he said and nodded.

"Explains what?" I asked.

"You're just like your dad."

"What are you talking about?"

"Neither one of you can talk straight, and you're full of bull."

"What do you mean?" I asked.

"You said he was a lawyer, and you're his son, right?"

"Right." I nodded and shrugged. "But I can't help that, can I?"

"Son, never bullshit a bullshitter. I rest my case. Guilty as charged, amen."

My mouth sort of dropped open a little and then a lot, because he picked up the glass of whiskey and swallowed the entire thing in one gulp. His eyes got big and watery, then tight and glinty, and then he started to rumble, low at first and then louder and louder, then he seemed to hold his breath, and he shut his eyes completely for a few seconds.

"Ahhh! On Donner, on Blitzen, Earl Warren, and Nixon, away, away, away!"

I started to laugh. I tried not to. I covered my mouth with my fist.

"Go on, laugh out loud, you little pecker gnat! One day I'm afraid you'll understand."

CHAPTER 2

THE HAIL YOU SAY

The ride home was fun and strange. The fun part was that I drove. The car was a wreck. Even Bill admitted it. He called it La Bomb Flambé—a bright red '54 Ford coupe. One of the things it was doing without was a muffler and it roared when I fired her up. But the bomb was missing all kinds of things. It had a windshield and a wiper on the driver's side, but didn't have any other windows to speak of, except for the back one, which was shot through with a big old bullet hole. The backseat was nothing but rusty old springs. Bill told me there had been a slight fire back there, but he couldn't remember her name. He told me that a smoking woman was often a dangerous proposition that now and then was worth the risk.

The speedometer was stuck on some speed like a hundred. There was no horn. No turn signal. No glove compartment. No trunk. It had a taillight and a headlight. It had reverse, but no first gear; to get it going in second, you had to rev it up, but since the clutch slipped so much, when you popped it, the car had a real smooth takeoff like a Cadillac or an Oldsmobile. "Just your basic car" was the way Bill referred to it. No frills. Just a get-you-there-and-back. There was no emergency brake and no rearview mirror. Bill said just watch where you're headed. Keep your damn eyes peeled to the road up ahead, and what's behind would most likely take care of itself.

"What about the police?" I wanted to know.

"Money in the bank. I got him in my pocket," he said. Bill told me to stay on the right side of the road and we'd be damn near invisible.

Like I said before, the fun part was that the driver was me. The strange part was the way everything looked after the storm, and it was like we were invisible. We didn't see that many folks, just some men clearing limbs out of the road, but there was a cop there, lights flashing into the car, making everything look weird. The cop just waved us on like we were on our way to church. He even said good evening to Bill as I maneuvered around him, and didn't bat an eye when my wheels left the shoulder of the road and bounced over part of a tree. He just grinned and waved his flashlight.

"Watch the damn road, else I'll have to drive."

I wrenched the wheel and we bounced back up onto the pavement and roared away. Everything was dark. The little headlight was dim and the steam off the road was yellowish and spooky looking. There were patches of white here and there where the hail had rolled up into a pile and not melted yet. The air had a chill in it as it whirled through the windows, and up above, the dark clouds were breaking up and wheeling across what almost looked like two half-moons. I blinked and looked again and, sure enough, there they were, two half-moons. I was about to say something, but Bill beat me to it.

"Watch the damn road!"

I let off the accelerator and kind of eased away from a mailbox that was about to knock out the headlight. My pulse picked up and my palms got sweaty. I stared hard at the road, but it was dark and wiggly. I was afraid to look up at the moons, because all of a sudden, now there were two roads laid on top of one another and shifting around somehow.

"Close one eye, boy. You hear me?"

"Close which eye?" I asked. I figured I needed two more to see all that was happening, not one less.

"Just close one eye, now!"

I did and then there was only one road again. I opened my closed eye just to check up on things, but I slammed it shut again. Man, this was strange. I took the left fork and eased through the curve leading up to the one-lane bridge that crossed the creek. I wanted to look up with my eye and check on the moons, but I was afraid to. All I could think of was that there better be only one bridge. I shut my eye hard, but it was so swollen it didn't take too much effort. Then there it was—the bridge. There was just one and I sighed with relief, but then I saw how small it was, and the two diamond-shaped reflectors stared at me like pale yellow eyes through the dim mist.

"Just take her easy now, son. We ain't in no race. Just take dead aim right down the middle. Easy does it."

Then we were on the bridge and the exhaust roared off the concrete posts. I seesawed the wheel a little, but somehow, we crawled on across. When we hit the other side, the noise calmed down a bit and I missed it a little, so I gave it some gas.

"Now, just take it easy, Hot Rod. And don't even think about looking at the moon. There's only one up there; trust old Bill on that score."

"I know that, but I thought I saw two."

"You did see two, boy," he said matter-of-factly. "Good thing you passed on the whiskey. You might have seen a whole sky full of 'em."

I laughed. "And stacks of wiggling roads."

"Roads writhing like snakes in all directions except for the one you want, which is nowhere to be seen."

"I ain't doing too bad now, though, am I?"

"Naw, I reckon not, but you got your eye shut, don't you?"

He was right, I did, and I felt grand, marvelous, fantastical.

"The hail, you say," I said conspiratorially, referring back to a moment on the boat during the storm. Bill laughed.

"What the hail! The hail you say. Then that damn old lamp just guttered out right on cue. I couldn't have planned better if I'd tried," he said.

"Yeah, but what about the stove booming and popping and firing out those sparks?"

"Aw! The hail you say!" Bill said and laughed. I laughed too, and Bill laughed until he coughed, and he coughed so hard it shook the car. And I was laughing so damn hard that I missed my turn and had to go about a hundred yards past it before I could turn around.

It had been one hell of a storm. I should say *storms*, I guess, because there had been several, one after the other. The hail had come in the last one to hit, the one that had snuck up on us after it had quieted down and it had seemed like all was clear.

The way it happened was this:

After Bill had guzzled down the glass of whiskey, everything had gotten real quiet. You could hear the creek whispering by, and the stove was hissing and popping, but other than that, nothing. Bill sat there, staring straight ahead at some point over my shoulder. The way his eyes were fixed made me want to turn and look, but I didn't. I just stood there and soaked up the silence, until after a while, the kerosene lantern seemed noisy. It was almost spooky quiet. Then the flame in the lantern started dancing bright, and then dimly, back and forth, and that got the shadows jumping and weaving, almost like they were moving to music, but there wasn't any I could hear. Bill sat there, quiet as a mouse. Finally, I couldn't take it anymore. I had to say something.

"Well, I guess it's all over now, don't you think?"

Bill blinked and kept on staring.

"I'm just about completely dry now. Sure am glad that's all past, ain't you?"

Bill cleared his throat and licked his lips, but he didn't say anything. It seemed to get even quieter somehow, then the lantern got dim and the flame went out. The wick glowed reddish and smoke wriggled out of the chimney. Either Bill didn't notice it or he didn't give a damn. He just sat there, and the flickering candle was the only light we had, and his eyes looked dark. I couldn't tell where he was looking or even if he *was* looking. I wanted to say something, but I couldn't think what. Then he spoke.

"World without end," he said in a voice just above a whisper, so that although I was pretty sure I had heard him right, I wasn't one hundred percent certain.

"What's that you say?" I asked.

"Lawyers ain't nothing compared with preachers, although I suppose if you could breed the two together, they might come up with something worse."

While I was puzzling over this, not sure what to say, he sighed deeply.

"Teachers ain't no picnic either, mostly, but like as not, they're both good and bad. However, I must add, that if a man could breed a teacher into the offspring of a lawyer and preacher, odds would be damn good you would come out with one mean son of a bitch. Do you catch my drift? Do you?" He slapped the tabletop so hard it must have hurt. I jumped back a bit. I think I nodded.

"What the hell you think teachers got? Did you ever stop to think? And preachers? You looking so bug-eyed, I'd swear you're listening, so I'll tell you, so you'll know. Teachers got . . ." He paused and then lowered his voice. "Idealism and what they call facts to back them up. Preachers got idealism, but they crank it all the way up to heaven and all the way down to the dreadful hellfire and brimstone, and their authority comes from power so absolute and certain that doubt is an intolerable hell-born blasphemy. Do you hear me clearly?"

I nodded.

"Good. Now lawyers are untroubled by these things, except for how they balance on the scale of law and the law is the law, and the law is blind. Can you see what would happen if you crammed all of that into one head? The poor creature would never know for sure if it was giving a lecture, a divinely inspired sermon, or making laws to rival the Ten Commandments. Are you with me, boy?"

I think I said, "Uh huh."

"So then, as a scholar, you can plainly understand why this pitiful creature would be afflicted with an awful sense of responsibility?"

I nodded.

"You say yes, but do you really know what responsibility is? Do you?"

I didn't respond. Bill shook his head and closed his eyes.

"You look dry," he said. "Crack us a couple of beers."

The beer was ice cold and slid down easy. Bill motioned for me to sit down in the chair across from him and I did. He offered me a smoke.

"Son, responsibility is the buck-stops-here word. It means the outcome is you. No ifs, ands, or buts about it. You! You with me?"

I nodded.

"Now, if I told you there were all kinds of these weird creatures running around loose, would you believe me?"

I shook my head.

"Running around crazy with responsibility, divinely inspired, wrestling with forces from the depths of the underworld, teaching facts out of books whose texts are incomplete and forever changing, laying down laws, trying to stop water from running downhill. In fact, all at once using promises, logical arguments, and threats of jail and perdition to make that water run *uphill*—to make water defy nature and run up the hill like an altar boy in his Sunday suit. Water raging and running like the creek underneath us, a creek with no thought but for where it's going, except stronger than that. Can you imagine how you might feel if you found yourself with that job? Think about it. Think it might make you a little bit crazy? Do you know who's got that job full time, no joke? Take a stab at it."

I squirmed a little. I was thinking maybe politicians, but before I could say anything, Bill shook his head and said, "Nope, it ain't politicians. They get elected and they can quit. These ones can't quit, not really, though some try. Think. They're everywhere, and they're closer than you might realize."

Bill was looking at me hard, like he was trying to pull the answer out of my head. I took a swig of beer.

"Maybe principals. You know, school principals," I said.

"Pitiful," Bill responded, shaking his head. "Darkness has its place, but, son, turn on the lights. Drop the scales from your eyes, open your ears."

He paused and drank deeply and polished off his beer. He pointed at the cooler and I went over and cracked two more. Everything seemed slowed down, like the air was thick and heavy. It was strange, almost like an invisible hand was on me holding me down, and it was quiet. *Muffled* is the word that comes to mind. I put the beers on the table and sagged into my chair, and I felt the beer slosh around in my belly. Bill stared into my eyes.

"The police?" I ventured uncertainly.

Bill's mouth dropped open and his eyes bugged out. Then he threw back his head and laughed. It seemed like he was trying to say cops, but couldn't pronounce it, because he was laughing too hard. Finally, he just stopped, shook his head, and looked at me with his eyes all glittery and squinty. I shrugged and took a swig. He took one too, a real big one. He poured it down and pointed to the cooler. I went over and got him one.

"You say you can drive a car?"

I nodded.

"Good thing, too. I was wondering though, you seem kind of slow. Maybe I've misread you. Maybe you aren't the scholar I took you for. What's two plus two?

"Four," I said.

"Who is the president of the USA?"

"John Kennedy," I said.

"Very good. Now I'm going to ask you one more time. Who's got the job I've been hammering on? Who wrestles with devils and angels? Who teaches texts and is supposed to know everything that hasn't even been written, and all that *has*, even if it's horse manure that smells like a stinking dead fish? And who makes laws that nobody could live with? Who comes in the night banging on the door, and you have to open it or else, and they have to have something to say, and it must be right and big and true and unforgettable, but right most of all, and also full of helpfulness, truthfulness, and holiness?

And I ask you, because that one is near, nearer than you think, meaner than a junkyard dog, undaunted by anything you can imagine, more terrifying than Frankenstein with three brains patched together. More than that, right at hand, with authority unchecked, undaunted by any restraint whatsoever as long as the reaper, the grim grinning skull, is at bay. Nearer than your first whisker. Inside your face and speaking in your blood, unseen but always there, here, now. Can you hear me? Who can read your thoughts? Who knows the condition of your underwear? When you skip school, who makes your ears burn? What crazy, mean, and nasty demon sits in on your dreams and winks? Who loves you and has a voice that whittles through nonsense? Who has three heads times two, but only four eyes that mostly work as one, but sometimes work as two, unpredictably? And who hears what it wants to hear and says what it wants to say in any tone at any time, and is right when wrong and right when right and near, always near, nearer than you think?"

I didn't know what to say. He was staring at me hard and grinning sort of funny. Then he spoke in that voice just above a whisper.

"They're nearer than you think, and they're always there. Even when they're not, they're still there."

The way he said "still there" was spooky, like a man giving up his last breath. Then he closed his eyes and I guess I squirmed. Seemed some squisher was pushing me down into the chair and some other thing was pulling me up. I didn't know what was happening, but I knew I didn't like it. Something seemed to bang on the deck or hit the hull. Then there was that awful silence. Bill not moving. I couldn't even see him breathe. Out of nervousness, I took a big gulp of beer. Three heads times two and four eyes that worked as one or two if they wanted. What the hell was he talking about? What did he mean by "they're near"? Then he spoke again in that whispery voice.

"Near . . . They're near . . . near . . . near . . ."

I started to sit up real straight. I took another swig, a big one. I started eyeing the door. Bill just sat there. Then something was tapping on the door. Bill sat up straight, but not as straight as me.

My hairs stood up, my eyes got big, even the puffy one. I had a big grin on my face, but I sure wasn't smiling. I wanted to run, but I was frozen in the chair. Then the tapping got louder and seemed to be coming from everywhere, the ceiling, the walls, the windows. I looked from side to side.

"What the *hell*!" I exclaimed.

"Parents. Your parents, that's who," Bill said in his gravelly voice.

"The hell," I said, totally confused. Bill started laughing. I saw no humor at all. I must have glared at him. He laughed even harder.

"The hail you say!" Bill chuckled. "The hail. The hail you say! Har! Har!"

Then the stove banged and fired out some sparks. I jumped up out of my chair and then a crashing bolt of lightning hit so close there was nothing between the flash and the boom. I sat right back down, and there was so much racket I couldn't hear anything, just a roar and Bill laughing to beat the band. It was pouring down again— rain, hail, and catfish, probably with pitchforks and horns. Bill was laughing his head off and I felt like an idiot. Then the sirens up at the old firehouse sounded. They wailed and wailed and the thunder was crashing, and finally it just got so loud and wild that it was almost funny. There was nothing we could do.

At home, my mother was probably making everyone go down in the basement. My father would be acting like the whole thing was blown out of proportion. My mother would be deadly serious, just a hair from panic. Voices would be raised. Everything would be urgent, all except for my father, who would make himself a drink and then walk on down to join my brother, sister, and mother with candles and a flashlight, in case the lights went out.

"Too bad we ain't got a basement," I said, trying to make it light.

"Afraid my basement's kind of wet," he said. "Nothing to do but ride her out. If she's a tornado, we're pretty damn low as it is."

"I know," I said. "There's nothing we can do."

Bill pointed to the cooler. I walked over and got out some beers. The rain and hail were still tapping on the windows and roof, but not as loud as before. The thunder rumbled, but it sort of sounded good, strong and rich. I put a beer down in front of Bill and, just as I did, another blast boomed right overhead, and in spite of myself, I jumped about a foot. Bill started laughing and my ears turned red.

"The hail you say," Bill growled, raising his beer in a toast. I clanked my bottle into his.

"The hail you say," we said in unison. We both took a long drink. Then Bill looked at me like he was sizing me up, but I didn't mind. Everything seemed sort of cheerful and funny.

"I swear it's true though," Bill said. "It's parents. It's just too much sometimes, just too damn much responsibility. Makes them crazy."

I nodded. I could go along with that.

"You're probably right," I said. Bill raised his eyebrows.

"I *am* right. There's no probable to it," he said. "So you can drive a car?"

"Like a bat out of hell," I said.

"The hail you say!"

"The hail I say!"

"Well, sir," he said, "if and when this rain lets up, if the creek hasn't swallowed up the car and we can wade over to it, and if it'll start, maybe you can maneuver us over to your folks' place. I could use a change of scenery, and besides, your folks are bound to be worried about you. It's just an awful responsibility."

I nodded. I was just excited about driving. Driving at night would be something new.

———

The road back to my parents' house was about a quarter mile long. It was really a narrow lane bordered by brittle old locust trees. I half expected the road to be blocked by fallen limbs. That often happened during storms, but although there were a lot of branches down, there were no big ones across our path. My plan was to try to sneak in.

It was late and I hoped that everyone would be asleep.

My plan was to cruise the last hundred yards real slow. Just ease her through the final turn, quietly roll up the gentle rise, and then once on the flat stretch, back off the gas completely, shift into neutral, and coast up to the turnaround. Looking back on it, I probably should have hopped out back at the turnoff.

We crawled through the final turn slowly. The apple trees were in bloom and the headlight lit up the blossoms. The ones that had been knocked to the ground by the hail looked like big old snowflakes. One of the trees had been uprooted. The house was dark. Not a light on anywhere. I took that to be a good sign. Maybe I could sneak in. Slip in the back door, tiptoe up the stairs, gargle some mouthwash to cover up the beer. Maybe slip back down, dig out some leftovers, and have a quiet snack.

While I was thinking those thoughts, I had allowed the car to slow down too much, and it was lurching up the slight grade. I didn't want to, but I gave it a little gas, and she chugged and burped and then sped up and coughed and backfired. I pushed in the clutch to try to tame her down, and she did it again just for spite. Bill started chuckling.

"You sure are quiet all of a sudden," he said.

I didn't think it was too funny. I gave her some gas and eased out on the clutch and we lurched forward a few yards, and when I put the clutch in again, hoping to coast to the turnaround, she backfired again.

"I give up," I said. "This is ridiculous."

Bill laughed and took a swig of beer. I took one too. I felt like turning around in the yard and hauling ass out of there.

"Damn good thing you're a scholar. You'd make for one hell of a poor burglar, son."

I didn't think that was too funny either. I eased up to the garage, and then I saw the candle burning at the kitchen door and my mother behind it looking like a ghost.

"Son of a bitch," I said. "I'm screwed to the wall."

"Aw, ain't no point in making it worse than it is. As beat up as you look, you could tell her about anything, and she'll probably just make over you and thank the heavens you're still alive."

"Maybe, but what about my dad? He'll kill me."

"Aw, the hell he will. I tell you what. I bet your mother worried your dad to death. 'Where's my baby boy? Go find him! He might be killed' and all like that until he poured himself a triple and just conked out to get some peace. And if he ain't asleep, he'll just be glad you're safe and the ruckus is over."

There was no point in being quiet now, so I just turned the old cherry bomb around and gave her all the gas she required, and she roared, and I started laughing and couldn't stop.

"What the hell! I'm still alive. If they come after me, I'll take off again."

I put her in neutral and opened the door. Bill slid over and got behind the wheel. He revved her a couple of times and she backfired once again. I shut the door and glanced over my shoulder. The back door was open and there was my mother in her bathrobe holding her candle. The dog started barking. My father appeared beside my mother. He started walking our way and then he picked up a rake.

"What the hell is going on out there?" my father yelled, as he kept coming our way cautiously. "What in the name of hell is the meaning of this?" He picked up his pace and raised his rake menacingly.

Bill winked at me and revved the engine.

"Nice to meet you, son. I best skedaddle. Bonne chance," he said and he started to roll. My father was just a few paces away. I guess he hadn't made me out yet. He wasn't wearing his glasses and he was in his pajama tops and boxer shorts. He looked kind of funny, but his voice was murderous.

"Get the hell out of here," he boomed. He was coming at me, rake held high like an ax about to fall. I figured I better set him straight and quick.

"Daddy! Daddy, it's me, Ed, your son."

That slowed him some and then I said it was me again and he

stopped right in front of me. He looked at me closely, then turned toward the car, whose taillight smoldered through the oily exhaust. He shook his head like he was totally dumbfounded. He lowered the rake. Bill was taking off slowly, just barely moving, so it wasn't real loud.

"Get the hell off this property," my father yelled as he lurched after the bomb, which popped a small backfire, almost like an insult, and then Bill stuck his head out the window and looked back at us. My father started running, brandishing his rake. My mother started screaming his name, and that made my father run even faster He just about clobbered the taillight with the rake, but he missed and hit the driveway, sparks flew, and he fell over the dog, who started howling. It was a mess, and for some damn reason, I started laughing again. It was just too absurd.

"To hell with you," my father screamed.

"The hail you say! The hail you say! Har! Har! The hail you say!"

Then Bill hit the gas and roared away. He wasn't really going very fast, but it sounded like he was going a hundred miles an hour. My mother was beside me now, and she put her arm on my shoulder and turned me toward the house. My father was staring down the driveway at the slightly diminishing roar.

"Go up to bed now," my mother whispered. "*Now!*" she insisted. The way she said it gave me the feeling that it was going to be a long night if I didn't. I didn't say anything, afraid she'd smell the beer and change her mind. I just started walking toward the garage, thinking that maybe she could keep my father at bay. I figured that was her plan and I sure wasn't about to discuss it. All the laughter left me and a stealthy resolve replaced it. Get the hell upstairs and in bed quickly. I began to think of darkness as an ally. If the lights came back on, I was screwed.

As I passed through the garage, I heard my father call out my name, and then I heard my mother tell him that it was a school night, that he should keep it down or he would wake up my brother and sister, and that's all I heard, because I kept on moving. I climbed the back stairs two at a time, went into my room, peeled down, and hopped into bed. I could hear the back door slam and then the buzz of their voices rising and falling in the kitchen. I heard ice tinkling in glasses and I noticed my head hurt.

When I closed my eyes, the whole room felt like some big swirling ride at an amusement park, and I thought I smelled popcorn and peanuts and cotton candy, and it smelled awful. I opened my eyes and that helped a little, but I was thirsty as hell and my mouth tasted like metal. I was afraid to move, so I just stared at the ceiling. I thought about counting sheep, but math was what had started the whole thing. How in the hell could my father have expected me to explain problems to him that I didn't understand? He had wanted to know why I couldn't understand. I hadn't known where to begin to tell him, because I didn't. He couldn't understand that and had made me go back through the chapters until we could both find something that we agreed I understood. Well, that never happened, because either I understood and couldn't make him understand it, or else I didn't understand and couldn't convince him I did. Hopeless. He couldn't even understand why my book was some stapled together thing without a proper cover. He didn't understand why it was called New Math, and I really didn't either, and he really couldn't understand that.

I didn't want to relive that. I tried sleeping with one eye open, like the way Bill had taught me to drive, and it must have worked. I felt a hand on my forehead, cool and light, and the next thing I knew, it was morning.

CHAPTER 3

HOT WATER

orning. All hell broke loose. Everybody had to have a shower and it was funny. I was in total control. At least of the hot water. My father would wake us all up. First my brother, then my sister, then he would pad to my door and knock.

"Time to wake up!" he would say, and I would roll over and groan, and he would repeat the process and pad away. But what was funny was that I controlled the hot water. I still don't know why.

As usual, my father took the first shower. I staggered out of bed and into my bathroom. Before I had even peeked in the mirror, I hit the faucet—the hot water faucet—gave it a turn. Turned it and heard, "Turn off the *hot* water! Turn *off* the hot water!" I did and took a look in the mirror. I wasn't pretty.

Scars. I kind of liked scars. Some of my friends like Mac and Andy had cool scars. One guy had a scar from a burn that was wrinkly and neat, and I had been around some pretty good bruises too. But I didn't look good. There was no class—just black and blue with a tinge of reddish pink and maybe a bit of purple, or my sister's lavender, in between. It was swollen, for certain, half shut and bleary, and I was scratched up pretty good, but somehow it just wasn't right, and no matter how hard I looked, there was nothing heroic or grand about it.

You might have thought a cow, even a dead cow, might have done a little better than that, but it hadn't, and there I stood, facing the awful truth. How could I explain it to anyone, least of all Willie, or Mac with the ax chop, or Trimble with those terrible knees? I was ugly, and I felt bad. I had some dandruff too, and my teeth were yellow. My eyes were red, my stomach was churning slow-motion somersaults, but the rest of me wanted to be still. When I heard the water shut off from my father's shower and knew that my sister would try to get her shower ahead of my brother, I was so caught up in my colorfulness and this one wild whisker snaking out of my chin like a vine that I almost forgot to give her the treatment. I remembered at the last minute. When she piped in "Turn off the *hot water!*" I obliged and then considered my brother. Should I or shouldn't I? I studied my face and wondered how it would fare in the light of day.

By the time it was my turn to shower, the hot water was barely warm, and as I soaped up, it got cooler and cooler, then cold, but it sort of felt good, especially on the black eye and the lump. There was no steam on my mirror and when I looked at my face again, I figured I better try something to pretty it up. Of course, I had no makeup. But ah, ha! I did have flesh-colored pimple medicine, and I decided that would have to do. It went on okay, but then when it dried, it wasn't right somehow, sort of cracked and it was too pink, so I washed it off and dabbed it on a bit lighter. It worked a little better, toned down the purple, if you didn't look too close, but the eye itself was swollen almost shut. The pimple medicine didn't help that at all. I remembered my glasses. They were so weak that they did nothing. They were supposed to correct something or another. Probably my grades. I had worn them for a week and then stashed them in a drawer. I broke them out. They didn't help much, but they helped a little.

Then I remembered the game. This afternoon, we played Trimble County. I had brought my uniform home and washed it. I dashed back into my bedroom and there on the bed on top of my freshly pressed uniform lay the answer to my dilemma—my sunglasses and cap.

The sunglasses were new. Coach Hagman had suggested I get some after I lost a fly ball in the sun. I put them on, snugged my cap down over the lump on my forehead and peeked in the mirror. Perfect.

Of course, the family might find it a trifle odd that I would wear that stuff to breakfast, but I would just explain that the coach had ordered me to wear the glasses as much as possible so that I would get used to them. I finished dressing, gathered up my books, and sauntered down to breakfast.

My father was behind his newspaper. He didn't look up. My little brother started to point at me, but I shook my head. My sister just smiled and winked. My mother was in the kitchen banging around. My stomach was queasy and when I looked at the scrambled eggs through the dark green lenses, they looked god-awful. Not even the orange juice looked good, but I knew I had to eat, so I did. If I just didn't think about it, it wasn't too bad.

My father turned the pages of the paper and gave me a brief glance. I expected him to say something, but he didn't. In fact, as he drove us to school, he didn't say a word, not to me or my brother or sister. I couldn't really think of anything I wanted to talk about, especially not the night before, but still, it was weird, everyone being so silent. My mother had been quiet as well. When we pulled up in front of school, my food had just about settled, but then my father took care of that. Jauntily, I asked him to wish me luck in the game, and he did. Then he said, "We'll talk tonight."

Gulp.

My breakfast stayed with me until about third period, but his remark stayed with me all day. I had tried to wear my disguise to class, but that changed in first period. Mr. Grimley turned from the blackboard after writing down and pronouncing the word for the day—*arcane*—but before defining it, had glanced my way. He shook his head and said, "What's with the sunglasses and hat?"

"Nothing, sir," I replied.

"You will kindly remove them now."

There was no point in arguing with this buzzard. I complied.

He smiled and then craned his old wrinkled neck and peered at me over the top of his spectacles. I was in the back row, scrunched down at my desk with my hand against my forehead, trying to shield my black eye, but it didn't work. Everybody turned and stared at me. Several guys oohed and aahhed. I knew what was coming, but I didn't know what to say. The truth was too strange, but all of a sudden, all of the lies I could think up were even stranger. Why couldn't I have thought of something simple like falling off a bike, but no. I thought of sword fights, bronco busting, falling down a well, ridiculous stuff like that. My palms began to sweat. I squirmed.

"Please, lower your hand."

I did.

"What in Puck's name have you done now, you cyclopped knave?"

I shrugged. Nothing good would come to me.

"I demand an explanation, sir," he insisted.

"Maybe his little sister beat him up," brayed some wiseass.

I gave him a dirty look. The teacher hushed him. Then he pointed at me.

"Been fighting at school, young man?"

The room was abuzz. Mr. Grimley slapped his desk. Everything got quiet. He stared at me and raised his brow. *What the hell?* I cleared my throat.

"Last night on the creek in the storm, I got kicked in the head by a cow."

The whole room exploded with whoops and howls. The old buzzard bent over at the waist and snorted. I'd never heard him laugh before. He sounded funny, but didn't *look* funny when he slammed his hand on the desk again. The room got quiet. He surveyed it sternly and then returned to me.

"I will not be mocked, young man. Do you understand?"

I nodded. Then he nodded back and smiled icily and opened his hands in a way that suggested I give it another try.

"A cow in a creek in a storm?"

"Well, yes sir," I said. "I know what you're thinking, but it's true.

See, old Riverboat Bill had heard me call out, and he came over in this half-sunk old skiff, and we were running upstream in the storm, dodging old logs and drift and junk. I didn't figure what the thing was or where it was going, and then he just knocked me in the head and crashed me back in the boat into a whole bunch of bottles and cans that were floating there. Knocked me silly, sure thing."

He cocked his head and shook it side to side. A couple of guys laughed, but mostly it was eerily quiet. Everybody knew he was mad.

"The only part I believe is the silly part. First, you say it was a cow that kicked you in the head?"

I nodded.

"Then you say he kicked you in the head and knocked you into a pile of bottles and cans floating in the bottom of the boat."

I nodded.

"So I presume you have changed your story."

I shook my head no, but he kept right on.

"And that now you maintain that some character, probably a pirate in some future installment, some character with the unlikely name of Riverboat Bill, knocked you over the head?"

I shook my head no, vigorously. "No sir, it was the cow that did it. He didn't mean to, it was dead!"

The room exploded again and even Mr. Grimley was snorting. I tried to explain that the cow was caught up in the current and that Bill was running the boat, but I couldn't even hear myself so no one else could either. Then his look silenced the room.

"A *dead cow*?"

I nodded.

"A dead cow."

I nodded again slightly.

"Headmaster's office and not another word," he said and pointed to the door. I opened my mouth, but before I could speak, he wagged his head, smiled that icy smile, and mouthed, "No." I gathered up my books and stuff and shrugged.

Before the door had shut completely behind me, he continued,

"*Arcane*: from the Latin. It means secret or hidden. Last Friday's word was *prevaricate*. Who remembers that definition?"

I heard fat ass with the stupid voice pipe up. "To deal loosely with the truth, sir."

"Use the word in a sentence, please, young fellow."

I heard my name and then a whole bunch of laughter. My ears were burning. The bastards! My mouth was dry as paper and my hands were shaking so badly I could barely make the water fountain work. It squirted me in the face. I felt like screaming. The water dripped down my shirt. I felt sick. I walked as slowly as possible to the head dog's office.

I didn't know what to expect, but I decided to stick to my story. I was mad as hell, but I tried not to show it. The door to the secretary's office was open and I walked in. Mr. Fenway was standing in the doorway to his office, quietly talking to the secretary who was doing her nails. They didn't see me at first. Mr. Fenway had a habit of talking with his eyes closed. He always looked weary. He was puffing on his sweet-smelling pipe and mumbling. Miss Wooten saw me first.

"Oh, my goodness child, what happened to you?"

She jumped up from behind her desk, grabbed my shoulders, and looked into my eyes. She went on so that I didn't know whether to laugh or cry or do both. She smelled funny, so sweet that it made my nose itch. I think I kind of laughed.

Mr. Fenway asked me if I was all right. I told him I was. He raised his eyebrows. Miss Wooten let go of my shoulders, shook her head, and clucked sympathetically. I cleared my throat and summoned my courage.

"Mr. Fenway, sir, if you have a minute, I need to talk to you, sir."

He raised his eyebrows and motioned me with his pipe into his dark old office. I followed him in. He went behind his desk, sat down, and closed his eyes. He gestured toward a chair and I sat down too. He puffed on his pipe, then he opened his hand and pointed it at me. I was scared to begin, but I just jumped in and told him the whole thing, except for a few parts that I felt he didn't need to know about.

I told him about the storm. I left out the part about the math and the fight with my father. I told him about Bill, but I left out the beer cans and bottles. When it came time for the cow part, I carefully prepared him for it. I told him I saw a dead old bloated cow coming at me, but that it swung around and hit me before I could get out of the way. Naturally, I left out the paint can, the smokes, the beer, the ride home, and all that stuff. I told him Bill was a nice old guy who was a friend of the family and that his boat was first class and that he was a decorated navy veteran from WWII. Other than that, I left the truth to do her work and let the chips fall where they might.

When I ran out of story, I stopped. "So that's it," I said.

He smoked and said nothing at all. I started to look around. There were coffee cups everywhere, papers stacked up, and books on the walls and on the tables, even stacked up on the floor. There were no pictures except for one photograph on a bookshelf, a couple of army guys in the desert standing in front of a tank. They had their arms around each other and they were smiling. They looked young.

I ran out of things to look at, and Mr. Fenway just kept smoking. He took a swig of coffee and I thought finally he would speak, but he didn't. I was tempted to make a face. His eyes looked closed, but I resisted the urge. Finally, I felt like I had to say something.

"So anyway," I said. He nodded, allowing some smoke to leak out of his nose. "Well, so anyway, the reason I am here is that Mr. Grimley asked me to come see you, I guess because when I tried to tell him how I got my black eye, I didn't do such a good job of telling him and everybody laughed and nobody believed me. In fact, when I was outside the room, I heard somebody call me a prevaricator."

Mr. Fenway knitted his brows and puffed out a cloud.

"So that's it, sir," I said.

"Now, Ed, you have to understand that your story is indeed an unusual one." He opened one eye, nodded, then closed it. "I suggest you write the thing out, just as it happened. Keep it simple. Not too much thunder. Keep the cow part real easy to understand, just like you told me, and that part about Riverboat Bill . . ." He opened both eyes and shook his head before he closed them again. "Leave that part out or else you will be a prevaricator and we both know it. Bill's boat has a certain charm, one might say, but first class?" He chuckled. "Bill was decorated all right, but he served in the Marine Corps. Bill Maddox was decorated for bravery on Iwo Jima. Write it down and turn it in to me in the morning. I will see that Mr. Grimley gets a copy. That's all. Carry on. And by the way, go see the nurse."

He nodded and pointed to the door. Miss Wooten blew me a kiss when I walked past her desk. Either that or she was drying her nails.

I couldn't believe old Fenface knew Bill. I also couldn't believe that Bill had been a marine and a hero. He just didn't seem the type somehow, and what really made it strange, was that my dad had been on Iwo Jima. He had almost been killed there and he was a war hero, too. But how in the hell did Fenway know Bill? He had been pretty nice about the whole thing, but I figured if I wanted the truth, I better ask Riverboat Bill.

On the way to the nurse's room, I got a Coke. I thought it would calm my stomach. Miss Lockness made me lie down on a cot and she checked me out. She put her bony cold fingers on my forehead and smiled. Then she took my pulse and smiled again. She shined a flashlight into my eyes and told me sweetly that I would live. I wasn't so sure. She told me to stay put for a couple of hours and rest. Now that would have been all right, except for one thing. Her perfume. I don't know what it was, but it was so strong I felt like it was crawling on me, like it was climbing into my pores and walking around under my skin. It made the Coke taste funny. I prayed she would leave. But she didn't. She sat down at her desk and started typing. Every now and then, she would look over her shoulder and smile. After a while, I couldn't take it anymore. I told her I felt great and that I really needed to go to math class.

"Honey," she said sweetly, "now, honey . . ." The very sound of her voice and the mention of honey made me want to gag. "You just have to lie there till you're feeling better. You're looking a little green around the gills," she said with a giggle. I tried to smile and then I threw up.

She raced over with a pan, but she was too late. I tried to tell her I was sorry, but she hushed me up and gently pushed me back on the bed. She put a cold washcloth on my forehead. That wasn't so bad, but then she poured some Pepto-Bismol and made me drink a little, but I couldn't drink it all, and when she turned away to answer the phone, I poured it between the bed and the wall. It was awful in there. I don't even like to think about it, and she made me stay there till lunchtime. It seemed like forever. It sure made you want to stay healthy.

The rest of the afternoon was a definite improvement over the morning. I surprised myself at lunch. Don't know what the stuff was, but it went down okay. It even smelled good, but maybe that was some sort of reaction to what I had just been let out of.

Anyway, as we sat there stuffing our faces with the glop, sopping it up with bread, and guzzling milk, Ben and Albert and Andy wouldn't lay off me until I had told them all about it. This real funny Jewish guy named Jerry was sitting with us. He had a huge plate of food, and at first he didn't say much, he just shoveled the junk in.

Ben was real skinny and what little food he had on his plate lay undisturbed as he acted as the main interrogator. What was I doing out there in the first place? I wanted to get to the really good stuff. The car. That would get them. And the beer. But first, I had to tell them about the math stuff and the cussing, and then Andy wouldn't believe I cussed at my dad. Then Albert couldn't quite picture the paint can. Ben hushed him up and told him that he would get to that, but what he couldn't picture was how I could make this character hear me in the noise of the storm. I couldn't answer that to his satisfaction, so he Perry Masoned me on that one for a while, until Jerry allowed that Bill was probably listening real close for the beer delivery man. Everybody looked at him like he'd said something stupid, and he just smiled and lifted another fork full of goo. I thought it was funny he would say that, because I hadn't even gotten to the beer part yet.

Jerry winked at me and Ben waved him off with the back of his hand. He wanted to know about the cow. How did it get there? How did I really know it was a cow, if it was a cow anyway? And how did I know it was dead? I told him about the eyehole, and Albert thought that was sickening and pushed away his plate. He was skinny, too. Ben wanted to know how I could see it in the dark. Andy reminded him that lightning lit up things, and Ben looked annoyed and wanted to know if I had seen the eye socket before or after the dead cow—if that's what it was—had kicked me. When I had to think about it and swallow before I could answer, he said that he thought he had me and he smiled all around. But I told him it was just a split second before, and that I saw the hoof, too, at the last second, right before it clobbered me and knocked me back into the boat. Ben kind of shrugged and asked me to tell him about the boat.

"He gave you beer?" Andy asked incredulously.

"What kind?" Ben insisted.

"Five dollars says it was Falls City," Jerry said as he reached for his wallet.

Ben looked annoyed. Everybody looked at Jerry who pulled out a fiver and held it up daintily between his pudgy finger and thumb. His eyes twinkled and his grin was steady. He winked at me.

"What do you know about all this, Jerry boy?" Ben asked.

"That's for me to know, Mr. Ben. Five dollars on the shitty city. You can't win unless you take a chance," he said with a smile and another wink.

"Aw, he doesn't know anything. Bet him, Ben," Andy said.

The whole thing was kind of funny and while they argued about who knew what, I ate my lunch and Ben's too. Finally, Jerry laughed and said he didn't want to take Ben's money. Ben got fired up and wanted to bet. Jerry wouldn't bet him. Andy called him chicken and then Ben called him chicken. Jerry said he hated to do it and that he wouldn't do it, if he hadn't been insulted. So they shook on it and Ben asked me what kind of beer it was. I told him Falls City. Ben went nuts and asked me to prove it, and Andy called Ben a four-flusher. Jerry laughed and laughed, until Ben reached into his wallet and came up with three ones. Jerry called him a three-flusher, and Ben told him he would pay off the next day.

Ben wanted to know how Jerry knew. Jerry told him that he knew the man, because his dad and his uncle kept their boats a little upstream. Ben wanted to know what that had to do with anything. Jerry told him that Falls City was the only beer Bill would drink, and that a beer truck stopped there every once in a while and delivered a few cases to him. Ben shook his head in disgust. Jerry laughed. Ben said it wasn't fair.

Jerry told him that a bet was a bet and then he asked us if we wanted to know what his family's boats were named. The way he said it almost made you have to know. Everybody, except for Ben, nodded.

"HMS *Bullship* and HMS *Chickenship*," he said, deadpan.

"Aw, *bull*," Ben said.

"No way," Albert said.

"You're kidding me," Andy said.

"Want to wager, gentlemen?" Jerry asked, as he reached for his wallet. "A five and three singles say I speak the plain truth. Care to bet?"

No one would bet him. That shut everybody up, so I told the rest of my story just before lunch recess was over. I don't think Ben quite believed the backfires on the driveway, but he didn't say anything. What he really couldn't figure out was how I got past my parents without them knowing I was full of beer and after smoking. I could tell that bothered him. He figured they would smell something. I told him maybe oily exhaust smoke might have helped me out. He shook his head like something didn't figure.

"Sounds like a cool guy though, doesn't he?" Andy said.

"Maybe the car part sounds pretty cool," Ben said.

"You're just jealous it wasn't you," Albert said.

"Aw, the hail you say!" Ben said with a big grin.

Then we all said it together and shoved each other and wrestled around, and then the damn bell rang and we had to go back in for science.

Usually I liked science. It was sort of interesting. Sometimes we had movies. The classroom was bigger and built like a theater, with the rows of seats on different levels, and the space wasn't all cramped and stuffy. We were studying water. The water table, the aquifer, artesian wells, and stuff like that. It wasn't bad, but then the teacher asked Alex, who seemed to be dozing off, if he knew what an artesian well was. Alex started to explain in his slow kind of way that it was water that was pushed to the surface by the pressure of the water uphill, and that it needed no pump and couldn't be stopped. But just at that moment, as Mr. Hartly was nodding like he was weighing this response and preparing to pass judgment upon it, Ben cut a wicked fart. A truly wicked fart. It was rude, long-winded, and incredibly musical. It had a certain rhythm, strong base tones, mingled with high-pitched screeches, then a rat-a-tat-tat or two, a few pops, and finally, a whistling squeal that was completely original. It was a very fine fart, and those of us fortunate enough to be several seats removed from the source grinned and applauded, while those nearby coughed, groaned, and seemed to be falling out of their seats.

Mr. Hartly was not amused. His face was red and he shook his chalk stick at Ben, who made a face and shrugged. Andy started laughing and couldn't stop. That got Albert going. Then somebody cut another fart and someone else cut another and Mr. Hartly threw his chalk right at Ben, who snagged it cleanly on the fly.

Mr. Hartly loudly demanded order, but it was too late. The room resounded with laughter and farts. Mr. Hartly walked over to the fire door, which exited to the athletic fields, opened it, and took a deep breath. Of course, that led to more laughter and many more rude eruptions, both real and fake, which escalated the laughter to a roar, until old Hartly slammed the fire door shut and demanded order.

"Are you people animals?"

Of course, we thought that was funny, but our hands covered our mouths to hide our snickering, because we knew he wasn't amused. Mr. Hartly was furious. He stood at the fire door. He first threw Ben out and then all of us. He warned us there would be a test the next day and that it would count double. He sent us out to the baseball field and warned us if we caused any trouble, he would flunk us all. When Alex said that he didn't think that sounded fair, Mr. Hartly slammed the door shut and then reopened it and told us all that he was the one to decide what was fair. He pointed to the field and closed the door.

Well, we hadn't been out there ten minutes when the assistant headmaster started walking our way. He was a total jerk and we all hated him. Some of the guys who were giving Ben grief for getting us in hot water really started to get after him. Some of us stuck up for Ben, so it was pretty noisy when old Hatchet Head stalked up, but it got quiet quick. There was something about him, like he was dead or something. He was bony and skinny. His eyes were squinty and glassy. His gray suit hung on him like he was a hanger. When he pointed at us, his wrist stuck out of his sleeve like a skeleton. He didn't say a word. He just crooked his finger, wiggled it a little, and turned back toward the building. We followed, silently exchanging glances. We knew we were screwed.

He marched us right back into class. Mr. Hartly stood in the front of the room and nodded to Hatchet Head as we filed back in. Nobody said anything. We took our seats. Hatchet Head and Mr. Hartly nodded at each other.

"You gentlemen would be well advised to check the bulletin board before you leave the grounds today," he drawled. "You will find some important information concerning your weekend posted there." He grinned. "Oh, and by the way, there will be a small writing assignment due tomorrow. It is to be signed by those responsible for your presence here, namely your parents, and if the assignments are not signed, don't bother to come to school, and gentlemen, we will be checking signatures. Do you understand me?" He shut the door.

"Now," Mr. Hartly said, as he turned to the chalkboard, "we will have a . . ."

As he started to write, almost everybody in the room gave him the finger and made faces at him. He turned and smiled. His face looked greasy.

"We will have a small pop quiz. You have five minutes to read the next chapter and then I shall ask you three questions."

A couple of hands went up, but Hartly just shook his head and pointed to the clock. The bell was going to ring in about ten minutes. He smiled and shook his head.

"I decide what's fair," he said. "Now begin."

I opened my book. At least I had it with me. Willie didn't, so he was out of luck. Old Hartly wouldn't let him look on with anybody, so he was really screwed. I opened it up to chapter thirteen, "The Amazing World of Electricity," and dove on in. The words were talking about how water flowed and how, in a way, electricity was like water. It was a long chapter, so I flipped to the quiz part at the end, looking for clues, but by the time I had located a couple of answers that I didn't quite understand, time was up.

"Close your books. You have three minutes. Leave your quizzes on my desk as you quietly file out the door."

1. What is a volt?

2. What is an amp?

3. What is an ohm?

I wrote, "Units of electricity." I knew I was had.

It wasn't until the last bell rang that we had time to find out what old Hatchet Head had dreamed up for us. We crowded around the bulletin board and jostled for position. Saturday detention. *Probably some kind of dumb work detail.* Washing windows and scrubbing walls or else just sitting in the study hall reading and watching the clock tick from nine to twelve. Our writing assignment was about manners. Where were they learned? How did bad manners reflect a lack of respect for the school? The importance of respect and good manners in the classroom. And then the clincher: What could I do in the future to ensure that I reflected honor and respect on my parents and the school, as opposed to a slovenly and disgusting disregard for both? Three to five hundred words. Due tomorrow. D. Hatch.

The guys who were mad at Ben were really mad now. They didn't think it was fair. Ben was mad, too. He said he wasn't the only one. And somebody said that he started it, that he was the main one. Ben told that guy that he saw him blowing on his hand making all kinds of noise. Yeah, the guy said, but by then it was too late, we were already screwed. I looked at Andy and he looked at me. We grabbed Ben by the elbows and dragged him away. Albert formed the rear.

"Damn it," he said. "We've got a game to play. There's nothing we can do about it anyway. If you want to blame something, blame the stupid food. The crap ain't worth eating. And blame Hartly and Hatch. We got a game to play. Come on!"

All of the guys on the team chimed in. Then somebody said their parents were going to kill them. Then somebody said, "No shit, Sherlock." We started walking toward the gym. I was pissed. *Another damn essay.* I was doubly screwed and triply screwed, because I still had to talk about all that other stuff with my father. *How in the hell could I explain all this stuff? How could I explain the greasy lunch? How could I talk about farts?* My father never even burped. *And what about Riverboat Bill and the cow and all that? What did all of that stuff have to do with education? I could hear him already. What did that have to do with school and Saturday detention? What about that?* And a test in science too. All of it made me sick.

"I really couldn't help it," said Ben. "That was slop. I couldn't have cut that one if I had tried. I couldn't help it, I swear!"

"Bull," said Andy. "What about the last part? Don't tell me you haven't worked on that."

"It wasn't too bad, now was it?" he replied with a quick grin.

Albert rolled his eyes. I shook my head. Willie motioned with his head to keep moving. I glanced back and saw Hatchet Head peering out of his office. He looked evil. The guys behind us had all gotten quiet.

"I thought lunch was absolutely divine, as they say. Delicious. Simply wonderful."

We all looked. It was Jerry who had said that. He was the team manager. Close to his chest, so that no one but us could see, he held a pack of Lucky Strikes. Our pre-game smokes. He smiled and winked. I winked back.

"Let's give Trimble County hail," I said.

"All the hail in the world," Albert said.

"The hail you say," Andy said.

Ben said, "Hey, that's my line, Drew!"

"No, it isn't," Jerry said. "That line belongs to Riverboat Bill, doesn't it, Ed?"

"Who owns anything anyway?" Willie asked.

"Cut the crap, fellas," Andy said. "Hell's bells! Let's go smoke and stomp 'em."

CHAPTER 4

SLOW EASY CURVE

The ball hung in the air, stitches smiling. It floated, round no
longer, but pinched in the middle and glob-like at each pole,
spinning, sort of wobbling, dipping in a broad wide curve
and then becoming impossibly fat with those red threads smirking,
stretched comfortably against the chalky white leather stark against
the blue of the sky. I nearly ducked as it slowly spun toward me and
then it seemed to wink and then it just floated. I tensed, drew back,
tensed again and still it floated, slowly revolving as I strained back,
and then the bat took over and the ball stopped, but it was too late. I
cut loose with all I had.

It was three and two, bottom of the ninth. We were down five to
two, three on, two outs. Here it was, wobbling, the moment of truth,
my moment of truth, and everybody watching and holding their
breath so that the air was sucked in and what little remained stood
still. The ball hung there like the catcher was blowing and coaxing it
back to the mound, while it seemed like I saw everything that had
happened in the whole damn game.

That stupid pitcher was the first thing I saw, with his arm as long
as your leg and his skinny face like rubber with eyes staring hard. He
wanted to get me again. I was only one for three, but the last time
I almost blew it out of there—almost. The center fielder caught it.

Then Albert dropped that easy grounder and missed the throw to first. He never missed, usually. Then Alex threw one right down the pipeline to their best hitter and all you heard was *ohhhhh* as we all turned around and watched what was left of the ball roll into the middle of some girls' field hockey game. Mr. Hagman tugged on his ear and spit three times over that one. Then, after scooping up a line drive, I missed the cut-off man, and that ended up costing us a run. And so now this was it, and the pitch seemed to slowly start rolling in, directly at my head.

Right before I had gone on deck, Hagman had slapped my butt hard and given me that look. It was the kind of look that made you feel stupid before you'd even done anything wrong, a look that said, you'd better not, or else. Then I saw our fans, a few kids, old Hatchet Head, and a couple of parents, all standing on the first base line and behind the backstop. I walked to my spot and took a few swings.

When we came up to bat, it looked bad. It was the tail end of our batting order and we were weak there. The first guy struck out. Coach shook his head and spit. Then Ben, the next guy, popped up, an easy out. Hagman shook his head.

Then Albert, Andy, and I put our heads together. Albert whispered so the coach couldn't hear. "To hell with Hagface. Let's do it for us." Ben trotted into our little huddle, saying he was sorry, and Albert told him to shut up and he did.

"We're doing this for us. Not anybody but us."

Then Alex poked his head in and Albert told him what to do after he got on. He said, "Just advance me, got it? The rest of you will know what to do."

I had never seen Albert look this way. His skin was so pale you could almost look through it, but there was fire in his eye and his voice; his voice was dry and certain. The way he said it, there was no choice. He nodded at Andy and then at me. We nodded back and then, while Hagman made motions like he was pushing Albert toward the plate, Ben said, "The hail, you say!" The coach glared at us and Albert turned so that coach couldn't see him and winked.

Albert drew a walk. One of the pitches was in the dirt and another was so far outside that it hit the backstop. He tossed his bat and loped to first. Then Alex dropped a perfect bunt that nobody could have fielded. Then Andy slapped one into short right. Coach held Albert at third and it was a good thing he did, because the right fielder rifled one home and it smacked into the catcher's mitt about six inches above the plate. No way Albert could have beat it out.

My mouth was dry. My palms were wet. I wished it was the other way around. When I dug in at the plate, the catcher snorted. *Easy out. Easy out.* Coach had signaled for me to take the first pitch, and it hit the outside corner for a strike. *Easy out.* I backed out of the box, scooped up some dust, and rubbed my palms together. Coach signaled to swing away. Next pitch was a screaming inside fastball. *Ball one.* Then he scorched one right down the middle and it had my name all over it. I gave it all I had and missed it clean. I practically fell down. *Ooh wee! Easy, easy out!* I stepped out of the box and wiped my hands on my pants. I looked at my teammates, and they were all shouting encouragement, but mainly what I heard was that stupid catcher. *Hmmm, baby. Hmmm, baby. Easy out. Easy out.* Next pitch was high and wide. *Ball two.* Next one was inside and right at my head. I hit the dirt. The catcher walked out to the mound.

I tried not to think of anything, but I knew it was three and two. I tried not to look at the crowd. There weren't many people, but I didn't want to be distracted. I glanced over toward the road and the trees that lined it with new leaves, fresh and shimmering against the sky. Then I saw Fred Ruby standing all by himself, smoking his cigar. He must have seen me looking. He waved and I sort of waved back. The catcher brushed against me on his way back to the plate.

"That your daddy over there?" he muttered.

"What if it is, turkey?" I said.

"Play ball!" the umpire cawed.

I glared at the catcher and stepped back into the box.

"Blue plate special. Easy out, easy out! Blue plate special, hmm, baby, hmm, baby!"

The windup seemed to take forever, but the pitch itself seemed to float somewhere outside of time, and I was so pumped up and angry that I had made up my mind that I was going to take a cut at anything I could reach, even if I had to jump across the plate to do it. Then the damn thing seemed to stop (and wink at me) just as I started swinging, before slowly floating away across the plate and slanting just out of reach and then picking up speed. I extended every straining tendon, and managed to sort of nick the thing with the tip end of my bat, which sent the ball scooting down the first-base line right at the first baseman.

I ran like hell, filled with a raging sense of doom. I tried to beat it there. The ball got there first, but it skipped and glanced off the guy's glove and dribbled about ten feet past him. Everybody was running on the pitch, and since the damn ball had taken so long to arrive, I was not too surprised to see Alex rounding third with Andy in hot pursuit. I half expected to see them sitting on the bench. Everything went crazy. I just kept on running, digging it out for all I was worth. The throw home went wild and both guys scored. I dug out for third; I saw the catcher throw and it was wide. I just kept pouring it on and headed for home, and everybody was jumping up and down and the catcher crowded the plate, so I hit the dirt and slid right under him and knocked him flat. The ball clanged into the backstop.

They pulled us apart before anything really got going.

"Nigger lover!" he sneered as he tugged on my shirt.

"Idiot! Son of a . . ." I said between clenched teeth as we were pulled apart.

He kept glaring back at me as his teammates hauled him away. Mine were surrounding me and jumping up and down.

"We won! We won!"

Coach stood off to the side, arms folded across his chest. I felt real good about winning, but I felt sort of silly when all the little kids were hanging on me. Jerry made a big deal of putting my bat into the duffel bag. He waved it like a scepter and kissed it before gently stuffing it away. Albert gave me a big grin and shrugged. I shrugged back.

As I walked past, Coach motioned me over with a jerk of his head. He folded his arms across his chest and then scratched his stubbly chin with his hairy old hand.

"Don't mean to deny you your moment of glory, but son, don't let it go to your head."

I nodded.

"I mean, my three-year-old grandbaby could have met that pitch."

I nodded again, trying to hide my anger. I knew I was lucky. He didn't have to rub it in.

"By the way, whatever did that catcher say to fire you up like that?"

"Nothing," I said, but the truth was I really hadn't sorted it all out.

Fred was my friend; he was old enough to be my grandfather and he was sort of like a father, but mainly, he was my friend. Hell, he had taught me to ride a two-wheeler. And he was there for me even when nobody else was. The fact that he was a colored man, a Negro or whatever, didn't matter to me one way or the other. I started to realize that it wasn't that the SOB had insulted me that had lit me up. It was that he had insulted Fred. Fred had worked for us since I was eight or nine. He was the gentlest man in the world. My mother would tear into him sometimes about silver polish or something and then ask him to take our dog to the vet all in the same sentence. If Fred was mad, he never did show it. He was there always for all of us, even my mother. Once he dove into the pool with all his clothes on and saved my little brother from drowning. He almost drowned himself. He could barely swim. Like I say, he was there for all of us. Hard to explain why. The catcher made me sick and I realized that my stomach was still a little knotted up.

"Nothing really. I just don't like the guy. He got to me, that's all."

He winked. "Did you aim those spikes like I taught you, right at the back of his hands?"

"No, I got his shins, I think."

"But you got him?" he asked and winked again.

I nodded. "Yes sir, I nicked him up a little, I think."

"Well, the slide was done close to the book, son, and made me right proud, but that hit, son, was out of the comic strips, plain bush league pathetic. Don't practice that, you hear?"

I believe he would have talked and talked. He started in on smooth easy swings, none of your lurching and jabbing and reaching. He started to demonstrate the proper stance and he spread his skinny legs and put his furry hands together like he was holding an imaginary bat. I told him I had to pee, and he took an imaginary cut and smiled with satisfaction as the visualized ball climbed out of sight.

We nodded, man to man, like we both understood.

"A win's a win," he said with another nod, this one very serious, accompanied by a furrowed brow. Then with squinted eyes, he raised his arm and pointed toward the locker room. When I was about halfway across the diamond, he called out, "Don't let it go to your head!"

I looked back. He took another swing with a bit more gusto than the first, as if he'd had a bat long enough, he would have smacked me back to the showers. I waved my glove to signify that I had heard and understood.

Then I saw Fred pointing at his old bug-green Buick. He raised his other hand, made a fist, and shook it victoriously. I raised my glove and did the same. Then I thought of my father and our upcoming talk. *What the hell was I going to tell him?* But before I could worry about that too much, Jerry, huffing and puffing, sidled alongside. I took the duffel bag stuffed with the bases to lighten his load. He thanked me. He told me he had won another dollar off Ben on three and two. He told me he knew I could do it, that it was a very fine hit. I gave him a look and shook my head.

"Well, we won, didn't we? Didn't we win? Well, didn't we?"

"We sure did, thank God," I said, and then I saw Albert, the way he had looked, glowing like something you could see through and it made me feel good and uneasy all at the same time. "And Albert," I added. "Thank God and Albert. I guess we needed them both today."

Jerry gave me a big grin and an inquisitive look. "What are you talking about, God and Albert? Albert walked. You're the one who drove them home!"

"Yeah, I guess I did at that."

We trudged past Fred. The damn old bags were heavy.

"Be out in a minute, Fred," I shouted.

With cigar stub poking out of the side of his mouth, he grinned his big old round-faced grin and pointed at the pocket watch that he held in his hand. I couldn't remember right then where he had said he got it. It was important to him; I remembered that. It was a gift somehow. He pointed to it and a cloud of smoke furled around his head, gray and wispy, like fog off a river that his eyes sparkled through. He wasn't, of course, but he looked like a gnome.

"I'll be quick as I can," I said.

As we passed him, he smiled and released more smoke, which parted on each side of his stogie and curlicued on both sides of his broad face like some temporary harp.

"Who's that guy?" Jerry wanted to know.

"Well, that's Fred Ruby," I answered. "He does yard work and stuff for my mother."

"Some bomb that is!" he said with an expression hollowed out with wonder. "Did you ever drive that one?"

I had to laugh. So bad it was good. "No," I said. "That's Fred's pride and joy."

———

Cigar smoke smell rose out of Fred's car seats, which were as soft as cushions should be, and dust swirled and twirled in the golden glow of the late spring afternoon. I slammed the door and it thudded, solid and pudgy all at the same time, just like Fred. He sat there at the wheel in a white shirt and a threadbare gray sweater that enveloped his body; come to think of it, he was shaped sort of like his car—big thick curves, sturdy, substantial, but a bit tattered and dated.

He winked at me and the stub of cigar nodded up and down to confirm his good humor. His face was broad, wide set. His hair was salt and pepper, mostly salt, and in the light, it looked tinged with gold. I smelled whiskey. He winked again.

"You done made a mess out of those boys. I never seen you run so fast. Like the devil was behind you and you were running for your life, and that slide was a doozy. I swear you knocked him five feet and dropped him flat."

He shifted into drive and we oozed off. I waved at Andy, who was jostling with Ben beside the road, but they didn't see me. All these kids waiting for their rides, and fancy cars lined up with nervous mothers beeping—hurry, hurry, hurry—but Ben and Andy didn't care. They lived close enough to walk home. Before we could go home, Fred and I had to pick up my brother and sister at their music lessons. That was the Monday routine.

"I got him pretty good, didn't I?"

He nodded.

"Well, I had to after what he said. I mean that hit was sickening. The guy razzed me. I almost completely blew it. I had to. I just had to."

Fred missed our turn and headed toward home instead of heading for the music lessons. I started to point to the park, but Fred held to the long broad curve that led home. He passed the turn and burped. I did point and he shook his head.

"No, not today," he said with an unexpected gravity.

"What?" I asked, sensing that something was amiss. "What?"

He winked at me, but I knew Fred. Something was wrong. We didn't have to talk much to understand, but on the other hand, a wink and a look or a nod had to be placed just right or we knew something was up and something was up.

"What's going on? C'mon, Fred what's up?"

He smiled and asked me if I wanted a malt. I loved them and I nodded, but I knew something wasn't right. This wasn't like Fred. He was always straight with me. He wasn't like my mother or father.

I never had to second-guess him, at least never had had to before. I was thrown off. It was like he was treating me like everybody else, like a damn kid. Hell, Fred and I talked about everything. I stared at the tobacco flakes stuck on the windshield and dashboard. He took a puff on his cigar and flicked a few more bits off his lower lip as he exhaled. That was just like him. It brought me back. Maybe nothing was that bad, after all. I looked at him. He put the stogie back in his mouth and smiled, then he chuckled.

"You want that chocolate malt or not?"

"Who's buying?" I asked.

"Your mamma's buying," he said. "She's buying for us both." He winked again and poofed out some more smoke and tobacco flecks.

"Okay, so what's up? What's going on?"

Fred told me that nothing was going on. That my mamma was playing bridge, my brother and sister were going to stay the night with my grandmother, and that everything was just hunky-dory. But the way he said that last part made me suspicious. He wheeled into the Erhlers slowly, and I searched his face for clues, but all I could see was Fred as he carefully glided into a parking slot. He reached into his breast pocket and handed me a few bucks. He wanted a Coca-Cola. I nodded. This just wasn't like him at all. We never held anything back. At least I didn't think we did.

"I'll tell you what in a minute," he said and he winked.

Some other kids from school were there, but nobody said much and I just got the stuff and left. When I climbed back in the car, the whiskey smell hit me again, but I didn't say anything. That was his business and I wanted to know what was what. He took the Coke, drained half of it, and handed it back. I let the malted cool the roof of my mouth and tickle my throat, so good and cold it made my ears ring. *But what was he up to?*

He backed up slowly and it was a good thing, because some crazy woman in a station wagon full of kids careened into the lot and just about clobbered us. She shook her fist and blew her horn, but Fred didn't even touch the brakes. He kept backing up, until he just about tapped her, and then waved his hand, nodded, and dropped into drive. We eased into the traffic. The woman blew her horn and yelled something. Fred didn't even blink. We kept on cruising.

"Some folks are plain crazy," he said, then he hit the dashboard with the heel of his hand. The radio sputtered and came on, but it was the weather report and he looked at me, shook his head, tapped it a little differently, and the radio turned itself off.

"How do you do that?" I asked. It never worked when I did it. He smiled, burped, and excused himself. I burped back, hit the dash, but nothing happened. I shook my head and took a slug of malted milk. Fred laughed, then he chuckled, scratched his cheek, looked at me, shook his head, and laughed out loud.

"Watch out!" I yelled. He almost didn't stop at the stop sign, and the traffic on River Road was bumper to bumper. We would have been smashed. He just kept laughing as we squealed to a stop. I wanted to know what was so funny and he shook his head, like no, it wasn't funny, but somehow, he just couldn't stop laughing. I gave up. Suddenly I was pooped. It had been a long day and then I thought of my father. *One of his talks. Jesus!*

I gazed out onto the river, muddy and churning. Last night's storms had worked it up. It was angry and hauling all kinds of stuff—trees, oil drums, at least one dead cow, and God knows what else.

"What that boy say to you, get you stirred up like that?"

"What boy? Oh, you mean the catcher?"

He nodded and slipped into the traffic. He was sort of looking over his shoulder away from me so that all I could see was the back of his head and gray hairs that ducked in and out of the folds of his neck. I didn't want to talk about that. We had settled our score and I had got him good, but that was that, and I didn't want to talk about it. But Fred turned and looked at me and I guess I realized that what was fair was fair. If I wanted to know, I had to tell too, but God, I didn't want to. I mean, Fred was about the nicest man there ever was, maybe even nicer than Albert, and that's saying a lot.

"How did he fire me up?" I took a draw of malted milk. Fred motioned for the Coke. I handed it to him. He took a swig and smiled.

"Well, okay, but you're not gonna like it. I can tell you that much, but the rest of it's kind of hard to tell."

"Why is that?" he asked, looking straight ahead. I didn't even know what to say or where to begin.

"Okay," I said. "He called you a nigger when you waved. Actually, he called you my father. I don't know; I'm not saying it right. He called me a nigger lover, but that's not it either! He asked me if you were my father, and then I said, so what if he is? And he didn't say anything. I mean, he didn't really say anything more, but he makes me sick! Sick! Not because of you. You're not my father, but Fred— oh Jesus—Fred, it's wrong like always and I don't know how to say it! Damn it!"

Fred was real quiet. I felt like I might have insulted him or hurt his feelings. It had all tumbled out like something spilled. I was breathing hard. Out of frustration, I hit the dash and the radio came on, and we learned that Mickey Mantle had hit a grand slam in the bottom of the ninth. Fred chuckled and tapped the dash and the radio quit.

"I wonder what fired up ole Mick today?"

His eyes were giggling and I knew he wasn't mad at me, and I felt stupid thinking he was. He was bigger than that. So I told him again, just how it happened, from Albert to the coach. I could tell that Fred liked Albert and the rest of the guys, but that Coach didn't stand much higher than the catcher. When I told him about the cleating part, Fred shook his head and said that wasn't right. "The man ought to know better."

He said, "Shit," and the way he said it, like a slow easy breeze, made me study leaves and look upriver.

A big old towboat was pushing a bunch of coal barges. The spray off the scow bow splashed up into the breeze and fanned back, glistening. I saw a deckhand carrying some kind of large wrench, and although he looked tiny, he also looked strong and dashing. I wanted to be out there going somewhere, and then I realized how wet he must be and it was warm, but not that warm with the spray and the breeze and all. I pointed him out.

"Glad I'm not that guy," I said. "I bet he's freezing."

"I reckon so," Fred said.

He wasn't being himself. I could tell something was on his mind. It wasn't anything I could put a finger on. Maybe it was the tone of his voice.

"Okay," I said. "Something's up and I know it. Won't you please just tell me? I told you, didn't I?"

He nodded and motioned for me to hand him his Coke. I did and took a swig of malt. The little ice crystals tingled in my mouth.

"All right. That man you're pointing to . . ." he looked at me and nodded. "Now, like you said, he's standing in some cold water and, after a while, I'll bet both of you would be mighty happy to trade places, for a while anyhow."

While I puzzled over this, he reached beneath the seat and pulled out a pint of whiskey. He fumbled off the top, took a slug, and coughed. He put it back and motioned for his Coke. I handed it to him.

"What do you mean? What do you mean trade places?"

He cleared his throat and puffed on his stogie.

"That man out there, he's in cold water, drenched to his skin, I reckon."

"I imagine so, but what do you mean?"

Fred chuckled.

"Well, I bet that even now, that man, he's thinking about how nice it would be to be all warm and toasty in a hot bath, all steamy and hot, don't you imagine?"

"Yeah, I suppose so, but what's the point?"

"Son, I hate to say this, but you got so much hot water around you that you could fill up enough bathtubs for that man, his crewmates, his captain, and the owners of the coal mine they're hauling, and they'd all come clean if they didn't boil to death first."

"What?"

"Son, your daddy's plenty mad at you. You're in a lot of hot water."

He looked me right in the eye and nodded slow and steady. I looked right back at him. I wasn't scared of Fred. I cleared my throat, hoping that might take my mind off my stomach, which was poised to do a flip-flop.

"What do you mean? I didn't do anything, not really."

Fred surprised me with a smile. I shook my head and shrugged.

"Nice shiner you got there. You gonna tell your daddy about you, Bill, and the old dead cow?"

"How did you hear about that?"

"How you think?"

I shrugged.

"From Bill. Creekside is a small place. Your mamma was pretty upset this morning and she told me about the old car you rode up in last night around midnight, about how you smelled like a saloon, and how some old guy was cussing and acting ornery with your daddy. So I didn't say anything, but at lunchtime, I dropped in on Bill."

"You know Bill?"

"Of course I know Bill. Everybody knows Bill. Leastways most do. Lucky for you your mamma and daddy don't. Now you want some advice?"

I nodded vigorously. I was worried about the saloon part. I thought I had gotten by with that.

"You sure you want my advice?"

I nodded.

"All right, now listen. You know and I know that what you did down at Bill's wasn't all that bad. Getting caught in a storm could happen to anybody. The dead cow shiner . . ." He shook his head and chuckled. "Well now, that's something else, but we'll go into that later. Listen, they don't know you were driving the car, so you're okay there. And the beer, you could say that was all there was to drink and you only just had a couple of swallows, on account of being thirsty. But son, cussing your daddy, that just ain't right."

I started to defend myself, but Fred cut me short with a look that meant nothing but business. It was a look I had never seen him make before. It shut me right up.

"What kind of good can it do, if I tell you what's up and you don't listen?"

I shrugged.

"So you gonna listen or harden your mind and dig yourself in deeper? Can you listen?"

"Sure," I said.

"Say it out loud."

So I did. I said I could listen and he gave me that look again and my ears perked up.

"All right, now. Cussing your daddy is wrong. It ain't that cussing is so bad all by itself. In fact, sometimes it can do you some good, but you got to pick and choose your occasions real careful, elsewise it's most likely gonna backfire at you and cause you a heap more trouble than you started out with. Sure, it might feel good at the time, but the next thing you know, you ain't running from one mad dog, but the whole damn pack is on your tail and hopping mad to boot. Cussing your daddy is wrong, but worse than that, it's plain damn stupid. And it don't matter the right or wrong of it, nearly so much as the dumb or smart of it. You hear me?"

I nodded.

"Moment ago, you were just about to explain yourself and try to justify what you did. It won't work, even if you yell and cuss and argue until next week. There ain't no way to justify stupid. No matter how righteous you carry on, in the end, you come back to stupid. Dumb is not what you want. What you want in a situation is smart. Now look at you. What you got to show for your blowup? You got a bump on your head, a black eye, and a meeting coming up with a troubled, confused, and angry man. Don't even have to ask if that's what you set out to accomplish. Your face tells me that it wasn't. You've got to get smart. You can't just cuss a problem and make it go away. You got to think about it. Take it apart. Look at it. Size it up.

Look at it every which way and then figure out a way to deal with it. Only bang it with a hammer after you've tried everything there is. Sometimes that works, but like I say, it usually makes it worse."

While Fred was telling me this, we passed right by my road, but I didn't say anything. When he turned into the colored section, I still didn't say anything, and then he pointed to a house with red flowers on the porch. He tooted his horn and a woman with a basket of flowers gave us a wave. He waved back, but we kept on going until we came to a little church that had some ladders propped up against it. One guy was scraping off loose paint and the other guy was slapping on fresh. Fred pulled into the parking area and we crunched to a stop.

"Back there was Lucky, my wife, and this is our church."

I nodded, but didn't really know what to say. We sat there for a moment real quiet and listened to the birds. Then Fred looked at me and said, "I'll make you a deal. If I can help you get out of hot water with your daddy, will you come to church with Lucky and me next Sunday? There's gonna be a real good singing group up from Nashville, and then afterward, a fried chicken supper over at Miss Hays's. She lives right over there in that two-story house with the nice big yard. I think you'll like it and it might just be good for the both of us."

I couldn't figure out that last part, but fried chicken sounded good. The thing that clinched it was the part about my father. I just said yes. And it worked out pretty well, not perfectly, but that wasn't Fred's fault and it wasn't as fearsome as I thought it would be.

———

When Fred dropped me off, he winked at me and told me to get busy and not forget the cow. As he drove away, I waved. I wasn't sure yet whether I was going to church or not, but I sure hoped so.

Well, the first thing I did was change my clothes. I got out of my wrinkly ones and put on a clean white shirt, then I slipped on some nice pressed khakis. I cleaned my nails, brushed my teeth, remembered the socks part, and put on my dress-up socks and my good shoes. Then I remembered the shoe-shining part, so I shined them and somehow managed to keep clean. I combed my hair and used hair tonic so it would stay that way. I felt sort of stupid, like dressing up for a firing squad, but Fred had said that this part was important; it would throw him off. I looked in the mirror and it even threw me off, so Fred was right. I even thought about putting on a tie, but he had warned me not to overdo it.

Then I started my homework and essays, all the junk I had to write. Fred had told me that I had to have something to show my father—that words alone weren't going to cut it. He had suggested that the minute my father hit the door, I gather up whatever I was working on and walk right up to him and tell him that I wanted to have a word with him, just him and me, no mother, and that I should apologize to her, but tell her that I thought it was important that my father and I have a private talk. Now that part scared me to death, but Fred said it was the only way.

I sat right down and started my essay for old Hatchet Head about how manners are learned at home and how bad manners reflected blah, blah, blah, and how I personally could reflect honor as opposed to slovenly and disgusting blah, blah, blah. I quickly realized that this thing needed a positive tone or my father would smell a rat. I chewed on my pencil, then realized there wasn't too much time and a lot was at stake. I dove in: "School Spirit—A Product of Good Manners, Honor, Respect."

It really wasn't all that hard to write. About once a week, old Mr. Fenway stood up in front of the assembly and, with both eyes closed like he was listening to some real fine music only he could hear, rambled on and on about these very subjects.

"A fine young man of honor," he would say, "reflected the true guiding spirit of good old blah de blah, and was so much more than an instrument of the accrued wisdom of his masters and parents, but verily was the repository of the assembled wisdom of all of western civilization, yea, and even more, indeed of all civilization, its great thinkers, its religious traditions, its healers, its inventors, and blah, blah and blah, blah, blah . . ."

Of course, I had to tone it down a bit. My father never would have fallen for all that crap, but all I really had to do was fill in the blanks. The basic pattern was there. A blah of blah, blah became "A boy of manners . . ."

Well, anyway, I ripped it out pretty fast. I had just read *Tom Brown's School Days* and that helped. Also, I felt like Huck Finn and Tom Sawyer were kind of buddies of mine, so I let them have their says. When Tom started laying it on too thick, then I would let Huck step up and smooth it down a tad, then I would slip my two cents into the plate. Before too long, I had a pretty respectable offering. I checked my punctuation, and I even looked up a few words to check the spelling. I put my name on the top of each page and used a paper clip instead of crimping the top edge like I usually did. It looked neat as a pin to me.

My mother charged into the house first. I always admired how she could wheel that station wagon of hers into the garage without hitting the brakes, or anything else, for that matter. Roar. Screech! Blam! Clack. Clack, clack, clack, and then the sound of my name. I answered. Next thing, she was outside my door, and she said we need to talk. I told her I would be out in a few minutes, that I was working on a very important assignment. She seemed puzzled by that answer, but after a little banter about how we needed to talk before my father got home, she went away. A few minutes, later some friend called her up and I could hear her saying that she couldn't believe it, and you don't say. So I figured she'd be occupied for a while.

Talking to her first was not part of the plan. Fred had said that my father was the type who wanted to put the final stamp on things, so talking to her first would probably just make things worse, because whatever punishment she came up with wouldn't satisfy him.

He also said that talking to them both at the same time might be just about as bad, or maybe worse. They would both be concerned about different things and would get in each other's way and then rile each other up about what was most important for me to understand and feel terrible about. He figured my mother would be most concerned about the drinking and being out late, and he told me that she thought she had seen me get out from behind the wheel of the car, but that she wasn't sure. Fred said it would be best if none of that came up.

My father, he figured, would be most fired up about the cussing and lack of respect, and his curiosity would make him want to know about the man in the car. He said getting them going at once would be like staring at the business end of a double-barreled shotgun while the two of them fought over who was going to get to fire the thing.

Fred had also told me that he figured that my mother hadn't told my father that she had smelled beer on my breath or that she suspected I had been driving the car. He figured she hadn't told him, because she hadn't wanted all hell to break loose. He said the best thing to do was to try to settle up with him best I could and then maybe wait a day and tell her about the thirsty part and how the beer was all there was and about the driving. Just tell her I drove down the driveway and then stick to it. He said there would be hell to pay if they thought I was drinking and driving.

When he had told me this, he took a swig of whiskey and I passed him his Coke. He told me a man had to watch himself and take her slow and easy if he was going to take a drink and drive. He told me it weren't for hotheads, no way, no sir.

I was just about wrapping up my essay when my door opened. I jumped, thinking it must be my father, but it was my mother. She had taken off her heels and I hadn't heard her coming. She stood there, one hand on the doorknob and her head cocked, like she wasn't sure she quite believed what she saw.

"What?" I said. "I'm just doing my homework."

She shook her head and then just looked at me in the same

questioning way. I knew what she meant. When I had said it, the ring of it wasn't quite true, but hell, I couldn't let on, so I just stared back at her, and then she said, "You and I need to have a little talk."

I didn't want to say about what. That would open the whole thing up. I didn't know what to say, to tell you the truth. I held up my finger and scribbled out a few words: "respect, good manners and honor are all part of the . . ." She crossed the room, grabbed my wrist, and jerked.

"We need to talk right this minute," she hissed. "That, whatever it is, must wait."

Her tone and her look told me the game was up.

"I want to know one thing, young man. Do you hear me?" I nodded, she squeezed. "Last night . . . and I want the truth, do you understand?" She glared, gripped harder, while I nodded and squirmed. "Were you . . ." And then the phone rang and she clenched her teeth, twisted my wrist, took a quick breath, and blew it out like she was breathing fire. She let go and trotted off to answer the phone. She said we'd talk in just a minute, and I was thinking *not if I have my way, we won't.*

I was thinking about hightailing it out of there before the next storm hit, but then I heard her say, "Oh, Caroline, how on earth have you been? Oh really? Are you serious? How simply divine! Oh, Caroline, darling, you must tell me all about it . . . No, you simply must. But of course, I have a minute. It sounds just marvelous. Tell me all about it. You must be in heaven . . ."

I sat back down and continued writing. I decided to stick to the plan. Whatever it was that had befallen "Oh Caroline" was a godsend to me, and I winked at my lucky stars. If Fred was right about all this, I would be going to church soon enough to give thanks properly later. Meanwhile, there was work to be done.

I knocked out the rest of my essay and then wrote a couple of sentences about the stuff that had happened the night before. Fenway had told me to keep it simple, but I realized right off the bat that it wasn't going to be that easy to do. Everything that had happened was still wild in my mind, and it all swirled around like the clouds overhead had, and the lightning and the awful thunder and wind. I didn't want to write it like I was scared to death, and I didn't want to go into how I had gotten into that mess to begin with, so I just said that I got caught in a bad storm.

But before I had written too much on that one, my father got home. My mother looked in before she went downstairs to greet him. She told me we would talk later. She told me to keep working on my homework and gave me a look, which I read as "stay clear of your father." I nodded and she nodded back.

A few minutes later, I looked out my sister's window and I could see them chatting and having drinks out on the patio by the pool. My mouth was dry, so I had a drink of water, gathered up my essay and—the way it felt to me—marched off to meet the dragon with two heads that sometimes spoke as one.

———

I played it just like Fred had said. I walked right up to him and told him straight out that I needed to talk to him man to man. My mother looked kind of nervous and just shook her head, but I kept my gaze fixed on my father, who looked sort of stunned and taken off guard. He didn't say anything at first. He just looked me up and down. Before he spoke to me, he turned to my mother and asked her what was going on. Had she put me up to this? She told him she hadn't even had a chance to talk to me yet, that I had been doing homework and she had gotten caught on the phone. He looked back at me with sort of a worried look, then asked me what was going on. I told him that I wanted to talk with him in private, just the two of us. My mother blinked in surprise, but without any protest at all, excused herself.

Now this was the awkward part.

"Well, what do you have to say for yourself?"

I dove in.

First, I told him that I knew that just about everything I had done the night before was absolutely inexcusable, that it was wrongheaded, stupid, disrespectful, and dumb. He blinked at that. I told him that the storm had scared me to death and that somehow it had made me realize how good I had it. Then I told him I had resolved to make some changes. First, I was going to get tutored in math. (That part was true, but what I didn't tell him was that I hadn't thought of it. My teacher had demanded it.) My father nodded. I told him I was going to do my homework as soon as I got home from school, instead of waiting until after dinner. He cocked his head at that, but before he could say anything, I handed him my essay and he glanced at it like he was glad to be holding onto something solid, even if it was just a few sheets of paper.

He read the title aloud and gave me a questioning look. I told him I had written it since coming home from school. He nodded and started to read it. He found about a dozen words misspelled, but he said he thought if I cleaned it up a bit that it would make a pretty good essay. I told him I would clean it up and show it to him after dinner. I asked him if he would read it again after I fixed it up and then put his name on it to show that he had read it. He raised his eyebrows, but I told him that all the parents were going to do it to show that they had an interest in what the students were doing. I'm not sure that went over so well, but he said he wanted to see the finished product first. I told him that sounded fair to me.

He seemed about ready to speak, but before he could, I told him that the reason I had cussed was that I was so mad at myself for letting my schoolwork slide and for always being in hot water. I told him that the reason I ran was because I needed to be alone to think things out. I told him I'd had no idea what I was getting into or I probably would have just stayed home and not figured anything out. I told him how I had been scared to death and could have drowned if Bill hadn't saved me from the rising water. He wanted to know where the hell I had been, and I told him down in the bottomland by the creek. He wanted to know why, and I told him there was no reason to it, that I had just ended up there. Then he asked me about this man. Was he the one who brought me home? I told him he was and that the reason we were so late was because the storm was so bad and the car wouldn't start and that I would have called except that Bill didn't have a phone. (I didn't know if he did or not, but I hadn't seen one handy.)

"So you tell me this man, Bill, saved your life?"

"He might have, I guess. He got me out of the storm and took me into his boat and built a fire and warmed me up and gave me a pretty rough working over about how dumb I was to be out in such a mess."

My father nodded and looked at me hard. "What else happened?"

I told him that Bill had lectured me about responsibility and had told me it doesn't matter how smart you think you are, 'cause if you do dumb things, you're dumb. I told him that Bill was a marine just like him.

"That man, a marine?" My father looked amazed, and I wished I hadn't said it, because it seemed to fire him up. "If that SOB was a marine, he would have held his ground and stood up proudly. He wouldn't slink off like a polecat. He didn't put a hand on you, did he?"

When he said that, he looked like he would kill. It totally threw me off, and I almost lost it. I shook my head, but no words came.

"Did he hurt you in any way?" That same look dug in deeper, maybe worse. I found some spit and swallowed.

"No sir," I said. "He did not. He didn't lay a hand on me. He just told me to smarten up, that's all. Honest."

"Then what happened to your eye and that lump on your head. Where'd you get that?"

Fred had told me that the dead cow was my friend, but all of a sudden, I couldn't figure out how. Everything else I had said so far I had sort of rehearsed, but somehow I hadn't thought at all about the cow part. I couldn't really think how to tell him. That cow had gotten me in so damn much trouble already I couldn't see how in the hell it could help me now. Out of nervousness, I guess, I started laughing out loud. My father looked puzzled, then irritated, but I just couldn't stop laughing, and I tried. But it wouldn't do. I just had to laugh, and finally he laughed a little, too. And when he started laughing, that really cracked me up, and I started laughing so damn hard that tears came to my eyes. We both looked at each other and shook our heads in disbelief. Finally, we both wound down at the same time. I shook my head again and, when he raised his eyebrows, I thought it would make me laugh again, but it didn't. Suddenly, I was as calm as the water in the pool.

"Dad," I said, "I know you won't believe this, but I swear it's the truth." I nodded for emphasis. He nodded back.

"Try me," he said.

"All right," I said, "I will." I paused and looked him dead in the eye. "I got kicked in the head by a dead cow."

At first, he didn't react at all. He sat there and looked at me like he might have misunderstood, and then he cocked his head the way he did when he wanted to hear some more. But something inside told me to hold my tongue and let it lay where it was, which I did, until I felt like I would bust. He looked at me and I looked at him. Then he said it aloud and started chuckling and shaking his head. I shook mine and told him it was hard to believe and that I barely believed it myself, but that it was true, and that I had a witness and everything. Then he started laughing and saying "kicked by a dead cow" over and over, and I kept nodding. Then my mother came out and asked what was so funny, and when my father tried to tell her, he was laughing so hard he couldn't even talk.

She kept looking from one to the other of us until we were all three laughing, but her laugh was different. Finally, my father told her what I had said, and then she sat me down and asked me to please explain, and so I did and, to my relief, they believed me. My mother gave me a hug.

It ended up that my father signed my essay right then and there, and when my mother asked what had been decided and what else we had talked about, my father simply told her that everything was in order. She looked puzzled. My father asked me if I didn't have more homework to do. I told him I had quite a bit more. He nodded and suggested that I get right to it. He handed me the essay.

"Correct those words. Use your dictionary."

I told him I would and thanked him for his help. He gave me another brief nod. As I turned to go, my mother put her hands on her hips like she wasn't quite satisfied with the outcome. My father just chuckled. "Get busy."

I skedaddled. Good old Fred. Looked like I was going to church after all.

CHAPTER 5

BLUEBIRDS

F red and Lucky picked me up on Sunday morning, and not a moment too soon, as far as I was concerned. My mother had been driving me crazy. She wanted me to look perfect. She made me scrub my nails, and I did, but they didn't pass muster, so she did it too, until I thought she was going to take off my skin. She brushed my hair and then, just before Fred knocked, my father, who had been reading the paper, looked me over and suggested that she do it again. I stood there while the brush clawed across my scalp, and he told me to stand up straight and hold my head high.

"These people take their church seriously," he said. "Show some respect and don't forget who you are. Speak up bravely and look everyone in the eye."

All the fuss and bustle had riled me up, but I tried not to show it. I just nodded.

Man, it was good to see Fred, but boy, he sure was dressed up. He greeted us with a good morning and a slight bow, and I found myself bowing back without even thinking about it. Fred told them I would be back mid-afternoon, then he put his hand on my shoulder, and we walked to the car. Lucky was in the front seat and when I climbed into the back, she turned to me and told me how happy they were that I could join them this fine day. The way she said it made me feel special and safe. As Fred pulled off, he put his cigar in his mouth, but Lucky told him to put that thing away, that she didn't want to smell like some cheap old stogie. Fred raised his hand in protest, but she said she meant it, and so he winked at me in the mirror and put the cigar back in the ashtray.

She told me what a pleasure it was to finally meet me, that Fred had told her so much about me that she almost felt like I was her own young man. I remember thinking how it seemed peculiar that she knew so much about me and I didn't even know her, but the way she looked at me, soon I felt like I did somehow.

Hell, I had known Fred forever it seemed like. At least five or six years. "We go way back, don't we?" Fred said, nodding in the mirror.

"Way back," I said. "We sure do. Why heck, Mrs. Ruby . . ."

She raised her forefinger to her lips to stop me and smiled.

"Please, just call me Lucky. Lucky will do just fine."

"Okay, Lucky," I said. She winked at me and nodded approvingly.

"Well, anyway, Fred taught me how to ride a bike and . . ."

I was about to tell her some other stuff, but then I remembered that Fred had given me some of her chocolate chip cookies on my last birthday and that I had never thanked her. I figured better late than never, and so I did thank her and told her how delicious they were and how much I had appreciated them. She smiled graciously and asked me how I had liked the brownies at Christmas and the macaroons at Easter, and before I noticed Fred making funny faces in the mirror, I said, "Brownies? Macaroons?" Lucky gave me a penetrating look and I shrugged as I looked from her gathering frown to Fred shaking his head in the mirror, and I couldn't help laughing when she turned that look on Fred and I watched it deepen.

Fred sat stock-still and stared straight ahead like he hadn't heard a thing, and I was trying not to bust out and belly whoop. She pursed her lips and tried to look mean. I held my laughter by covering my mouth with my hand. I noticed her perfume, which smelled like lilacs, and when she slowly started shaking her head, I watched her eyes crinkle up and I noticed how pretty she was, but I was also glad she wasn't mad at me.

"Fred Ruby," she said.

He nodded, and I could almost hear him gulp.

"Fred Ruby! You didn't? You tell me you didn't?"

"Now, Lucky—"

"Don't you dare 'now Lucky' me, Fred Ruby!"

"Aw, Lucky."

"Okey dokey. We all know the truth here, whether you fess up or not. You've slipped up one time too many, Mr. Ruby. Now I guess I know the answer about that new washer and dryer, don't I? Don't I, Fred Ruby? You can bet your sweet tooth you do. Don't you, dear?"

"Well . . ."

"Well, yourself. Don't try to wiggle out of it. Speak up and remember you are under oath and you are being witnessed. Do you hear me, Mr. Ruby?"

Fred nodded and winked at me in the mirror.

"I see that wink, and winks don't count for nothing. Say yes or else."

"Yes."

"When? And I don't mean next week."

"Tomorrow evening?" Fred said quietly.

"Well, I suppose that might work, my dear husband," she said with a great big grin. It was her turn to wink at me and I winked back. "I'll make you some more brownies, but next time, I'm gonna make Mr. Sweet Tooth deliver you to the brownies, seeing as how Fred's delivery service ain't especially reliable." She winked again. "That wink counts," she said.

The gravel of the church parking lot clinked on the underside of the car. I nodded and winked back again, and then Lucky turned around and faced straight ahead. I looked at the church. It was glistening white. The paint still looked wet.

The parking lot was bustling with people of all ages and sizes. Little kids skipped around, holding hands, and old gray-headed folks leaned on walkers and canes. Groups of young men stood in clusters, and they seemed pretty serious until I noticed that they were studying the young women, who mostly seemed to be in smaller groups or in pairs and who seemed to be studying the ground. Every now and then, I would catch them sneaking a peek at the fellows. Young couples walked around arm-in-arm, and up and down the road, I could see people streaming in, all dressed to kill. Pinks, greens, oranges, yellows, and blues. Just a slow-motion swirl of color, except for the skipping girls and the little boys dashing around.

Fred and Lucky walked on either side of me, and they greeted people as we walked toward the steps. I saw a few kids my age, but I didn't recognize anybody. Then Lucky greeted a woman all dressed up in a shiny black dress with a big old flower on the front, and she was standing next to a kid I had seen at the gas station a couple of times. He and I were looking at each other, sort of sizing each other up, I guess, and I didn't even notice that I knew the woman. She said, "Well, Mister Eddie, ain't you even gonna speak to old Miss Pearl?"

I looked up and I barely recognized her. Her hair was all different, all shiny and piled up, with a big orange comb in it that matched the great big beads that stretched across her bosom. She looked so different, and then I noticed her eyes, and it was Pearl all right. She used to do our laundry. I had sat in the basement and talked to her for hours. She liked to talk about the old days, when her family had a place right under the big old maple tree on the edge of the woods in my backyard.

She gave me a great big hug and asked me if I was behaving myself. I nodded and said mostly I was. She laughed.

"Now, you go on, you scalawag. Tell me, did you ever find that Valentine ring I told you about?"

I told her I never had.

"Well, it's out there, and if you ever find it, I'll give you five dollars." She beamed at everyone. "My dear Thomas gave me that ring when I was just fifteen years old. I guess he knew something even then, God rest his soul."

All I had ever found was part of an old brick path and some broken plates and busted cups and rusted old things, hinges and such. There was an old cistern made of brick, but it was full of old cans so rusty that you couldn't even fish them out without them breaking. I told her I would keep right on looking.

She introduced me to the guy, her grandson, Johnny Tucker. We shook hands and he squeezed real hard, and so I squeezed back and I believe we would have started Indian wrestling on the spot if Pearl and Lucky hadn't gently put their arms around our shoulders. We both squeezed as hard as we could, and we were starting to make faces. Fred laughed and gently patted both our hands and called it a draw. We just stood there, grinning at each other.

Lucky said that it was time to go on in and so we started off. Through the crowd, I thought I saw Riverboat Bill go in the door, but I couldn't be sure. A few other white kids were there, but I recognized only one. It was Churchill. He was my preacher's son. I knew him from school, not church. I only went there about two or three times a year. Then I saw Paul. He was with Richard, a man who worked for his parents. I was starting to wonder what was up, but everyone seemed to flow toward the door, and there really wasn't any time to puzzle about anything except where to plant my feet without stepping on somebody's toes.

As we climbed the steps, Lucky said, "I sure hope you enjoy this as much as I think you will." I nodded. "Fred tells me you listen to music down in that basement of yours. Ray Charles and old Jimmy Reed and Elvis Presley."

"Yeah, I sure do," I said.

"Well, if you like them, I would be most surprised if you don't just love the Bluebirds." As she said this, I looked off into the corner of the lot, and in front of a bright blue school bus stood about ten people in shiny blue robes. They were all holding hands. Then we walked inside and Lucky led the way to our seats.

The whole way, Fred's hand was on my shoulder as light as a feather.

I sat between them. I folded my hands in my lap just like Fred. We were seated in about the middle, so by looking around a little, I could see almost everything, except for what was right behind me. At first, I mainly watched the people. I recognized some folks, such as Hays who, like Pearl, had done washing and ironing for my mother. Now Hays could sing, and sometimes I would sneak down the basement steps, and sit there and listen to her as she sang while she worked. She sang gospel songs. Not real loud or anything, so I figured she kind of wanted privacy, but one day she was singing and it almost sounded like two people, and then three, and I couldn't believe my ears. There was a back door out of the basement that led up to the garage, but I hadn't heard anyone come in, so I sat there kind of spooked and strained to hear with all my might. One voice was hers, the voice I was used to, which was rich and soft and full. Then all of a sudden, there was this deeper voice like a man's and then her voice again, sort of like an answer to the deep one, and then this high voice. Finally, I just couldn't take it any longer; I slipped up and tiptoed over to the laundry room door and peered in, and all I saw was a bunch of shirts, towels, and stuff hanging on hangers and no Hays at all. But then another blouse got hung up, and I saw her feet. She stepped out from behind the clothes and just kept right on singing, and damn if all those voices weren't hers after all.

She didn't see me at first, so I just stood there with my mouth open. It was some kind of song about Daniel and the lions' den. Just about when I had figured that out, she saw me, and I don't know who jumped highest, her or me. She threw back her hands and head and sucked the air out of the room, and I guess I did the same. I remember what she said.

"Lord, have mercy! Have mercy on my poor trembling soul!" She stared at me kind of funny, almost like she was mad at me or something.

"It's me, Hays," I had said. "I wasn't trying to scare you to death. I was just listening to you sing, that's all."

She shook her head and started to laugh. I couldn't figure out what was so funny. I asked her.

"Well, look at yourself, child. Just look at yourself. You standing there in that dark doorway wearing a darned top hat, and what's that, a black cape? Standing there as cool as Beelzebub himself, while I'm standing here dreaming of the angels. Lord, child, and I thought I was ready, too! Well, after the fright you give me, I reckon I must not be at that. Why you want to devil me so?"

I had to laugh. I hadn't thought about how I was dressed. I had been practicing my magic tricks. The disappearing egg and the one with the scarf that became five knotted ones that disappeared and then returned as one. I hadn't tried to scare her. It was just my magic suit. I had heard her singing and I wanted to hear. I told her so. Well, anyway we became pretty good friends after that, but she only worked for us a short while. She walked off one day and never came back. Didn't even want her pay. Hays sat down right in the front row.

I recognized Mr. Traylor. He sat down in the front row, too. My father had always told me that he was a remarkable man. For one thing, he had a chauffeur and a black Cadillac. He owned property and ran the garbage business and all kinds of other stuff.

Fred tapped me with his elbow and motioned with his head and nodded across the church and damn, if it wasn't Bill himself and he was all dressed up, too. He sat down and a whole colored family sat down with him, just like they did it every day of the world. I don't know how I knew they were a family, but I could tell they were, and somehow Bill seemed a part of it. He bent his old red face toward the colored woman and said something funny, I guess. She put her hand to her mouth and shook her head, and he laughed all gravelly like he did, and it was infectious and a lot of people chuckled, including Fred and me, until Lucky shushed us with a look.

After everyone was seated, it got quiet and then the preacher took his place and boomed out, "Good morning, brothers and sisters. Praise the Lord! Hallelujah, our Lord is raised up. Praise be to God on high."

The people responded with "Yes, Lords" and "Amens" and all kinds of other stuff. I didn't say anything and neither did Fred, but Lucky said, "Praise his name!" so loud that the preacher seconded her motion and off he flew.

It's kind of hard to say whether he spoke fast or not. I mean the impression I had was that he did, but looking back, maybe he didn't. I guess speed didn't have much to do with it. But soon he had everybody on the edge of their seats, and every now and then I would look at this old pine tree swaying outside the big arched window behind the altar, just to remind myself where I was. One minute, the preacher had me shuffling through the dust of Jerusalem and the next minute had me gliding down streets paved in gold. Then we sang a hymn that started out all soft and sweet, and then it stopped. Then this preacher sat down at the piano and hit that thing with such a lick that I thought that if his mother had been there, she would have scolded him, and man, that place started jumping. People were clapping, and even though I didn't know the words, I caught as many as I could and clapped and sang along. So did Fred and, I guess, everybody else did, too. It would have been hard not to, I can tell you that.

The prayers were sort of the same way. They would start out kind of slow and then all of a sudden, they would switch gears and then zoom! Off the preacher would go again, and then finally, this young girl stood up all by herself, right beside the piano. While the preacher man played real soft, she sang a song about how Jesus was her friend, and her voice was so clear and fine that my hair stood up like there was lightning overhead, but there wasn't. I could see that from the sunlight that poured through the colored glass windows on the side of the church and the way the pine needles lit up on the tree outside. She was like a sunbeam herself, all dressed in blue with a pink bow in her hair.

This was just the beginning, because as she was hitting the last note, there was some rustling and she was surrounded by blue. The preacher man stood, turned the piano over to a man in a blue robe, raised both of his hands, and bowed his head.

"The Bluebirds! Praise the Lord!"

Well, I'm here to tell you, they did more than that. They blew the roof off that place. I have no idea how long they sang or how many songs they sang. They weren't even halfway into the first song before everybody that could stand was moving with the music. Their voices blended, but still you could hear each one distinctly. It's hard to explain. Like I said, there were about ten of them, and it was like they would split up into three groups. Maybe one or two main voices, and then the others would all be singing different parts. Then they would come together and then come apart, and next another main voice would come out, and the others might just hum or something while this one would skip over the surface of the sound and then join it and disappear. Then another would come out and take over for a while.

Somehow it reminded me of fireworks, sky rockets—the kind that burst and shower down, all except that the sparks wouldn't burn out, but instead would all come back together again and just start all over and do something even better. It wasn't all loud either. Some of it was, but some songs were like a whisper almost, and when I thought about it later, I was glad I hadn't had to cough and, as I recall, nobody else did either.

I didn't know any of the songs, but a lot of them were like Bible stories, and that got me to take a peek at Hays, and she was smiling just as much as the singers were. Then I looked around and saw that *everyone* was, even me. Lucky put her arm around me and gave me a hug, and I looked up at Fred and he had tears on his face, but he didn't look sad.

The last song they did was called "Somebody's Calling My Name." One of the singers said something about Sister Sojourner Truth and some people said, "God rest her soul." And some others said, "Amen!" A lot of people nodded. It got a little quiet and then the young girl stood up on the piano bench and sang most of the first verse all by herself, and it was like the whole place was frozen solid. Nobody moved a whisker, and it was cool, like a breeze around your neck, and then one by one, the other voices joined in until the place was thumping. I could feel it in my feet and up through my knees, and pretty soon everybody was clapping along and some folks even started singing. There was a tambourine going on this one, and then there were two, and while the one might sound like water, the other might sound like a rattlesnake. After a while, I didn't care what they sounded like and all I knew was that they were dancing between my ears and my ears were dancing too, just like the whole rest of me was.

There wasn't any way to top that one, I guess, and they trooped out in single file singing, and it wasn't till they were outside that I noticed that the piano man had marched out with them. Somehow, I thought he was playing all along. They finished up on the steps with all of them singing, "Yes, Lord!" and about the most beautiful "Amen" anybody ever heard. I couldn't help but shake my head, and some folks were laughing and some folks were crying and some folks were doing both. I'm not sure, but I think I was grinning from ear to ear.

Afterward, everybody milled around outside the church for a while. All agreed that it was the finest singing they ever heard, but a lot of them didn't come out and say it just like that. Some of them would come up and look real serious and say to Fred or Lucky, "Wasn't God Almighty praised today?" Or like this one skinny pinched-up old woman, who took both Fred and Lucky's hands in hers and pronounced that heaven was deeply moved today by our glorious church. "Praise His Name." She gave me a look that was a little bit scary, to tell the truth. When the woman finally let go and walked away, Lucky said it was the little pretender's turn to crow, and Fred said something like she wouldn't give you an apple if her tree was full of them.

Lucky told me that we were going over to Miss Hays's for refreshments, and the way she said it made it seem real casual, but it soon became obvious that it was all planned out. People started drifting off in different directions, and a lot of folks told each other in passing that they would see them after a while.

Miss Hays greeted us at the door and she looked even more dignified than she had inside the church. Her smile and touch on my shoulder made me feel good and she told us to make ourselves right at home. I had cookies and lemonade. While I munched and sipped, I checked out the other guests. Johnny Tucker was there and Churchill was there, but it seemed like the adults kept us busy with talk so that we were kept apart.

Then Mr. Traylor walked in and the room seemed to get quiet. Bill walked in with some young colored guy all dressed up like an undertaker. His suit was so black and shiny that it reminded me of my sister's patent leather shoes, and his shirt was so white it hurt my eyes. The guy was pulling on Bill's arm and jabbering, while Bill just shook his head. Everybody was looking at them, but the guy didn't seem to notice, and kept right on tugging and yakking until he looked up and saw Mr. Traylor. Mr. Traylor didn't even look at him or say anything. The guy looked up, saw him, and shut up. I gave Fred a glance and he just smiled and said, "We better sit down."

It wasn't a very big room, but there were a bunch of folding chairs, so we unfolded a few and sat down. Soon everybody was sitting in a couple of rows shaped sort of like a horseshoe. Everybody was seated except for Hays. She told us that, first off, she wanted to give us a little history, and then at the end, she said we would talk about the park. I didn't know what she was talking about. There wasn't any park around there, but anyway, she started talking about the Underground Railroad and she told some stories that made me feel real good and some that made me want to throw up and hide. Everybody was real quiet, even Churchill and Paul, who had somehow managed to sit next to each other. Bill was quiet, too, and just stared at the floor. Mr. Traylor stared straight ahead without expression. He reminded me of an Indian chief. I tried to look like him.

There were stories about people getting double-crossed and stories about people getting hanged and shot and tortured. Not all of them who got hurt were colored people either, because stealing slaves was stealing property, and the way Hays said "property" made my skin crawl. I realized that I was making a face and I looked at Mr. Traylor, but he stared straight ahead like he was somewhere else, not even listening. There were other stories about heroes and glorious reunions and people crying with joy. She didn't point to me or anything, but she mentioned my grandfather's house. It was on the Underground Railroad. A tunnel out of the cellar led to a hillside that looked out over the bottomland, and that led to the river and freedom. Sometimes. Or murder or recapture. They had hidden Yankees in that cellar, too, and they never had been found out.

Then Bill got to talk. She didn't call him Riverboat Bill. She called him Mr. Maddox, with all the respect in the world, and even Mr. Traylor nodded when she asked him to speak. Bill stood up and motioned for Hays to take his seat. He took her hand like he was going to ask her to dance, and she put her hand on his arm like she was accepting his offer, and then she sat down.

"My name is Bill," he said in his rough old voice. "Some call me Riverboat Bill, I guess because I got the river in my blood, all its goodness and all its badness too, I suspect. The river ain't what it used to be. Now it mainly hauls coal and oil. Grant you, it will still haul just about anything that gets in it, so on occasion, it might carry about anything from an old paint can to a dead cow." With that, he winked at me. I was surprised because he hadn't even looked at me before. "As some of us here already know."

Fred gave my knee a nudge with his. "But in the old times that Miss Hays has been talking about, it carried everything imaginable. It was the main highway, and everything that moved through here depended on it. Good and bad alike.

"My grandpa was a ferryboat man and he owned a tavern at the mouth of the creek. He didn't take much to farming. He had some hogs and chickens and grew some vegetables and stuff, but mainly he ran the tavern and served the river men food and drink. He acted sort of like a message service and a post office, too. He ran a ferry across the river or sometimes just out to the boats that were passing through.

"He made his own whiskey and I heard it weren't half bad, and that even the locals could stomach it and did. He was a pretty respectable man. But he led a double life—one that all could see and one that almost nobody knew about. How he pulled it off, I do not really know. He must have had nerves of steel, because had anybody known who shouldn't have, he wouldn't have lasted a minute.

"My grandpa was part of the Underground Railroad. Why, I don't know. Some would have you think he was a good man and maybe he was. I don't know. My own father never knew him, and my grandmother never even knew about it, and I didn't find out about it myself until just a few years ago, and it weren't from diaries or anything that I found out about it.

"A personal tragedy," he said, "led me to this knowledge. Without that, I suppose I would have never known. He carried many a poor creature to freedom, and he didn't charge money. He never got caught or lost anybody over the side, which sometimes happened some places somehow.

"My point is to the young ones here. My point, if there is one, is this. White and colored have always worked together, and contrary to what you might think, more so in the past than in the present day. All this separate stuff that we have now wasn't always so, and people knew each other. And this good and bad stuff—it's all guesswork. You might say he was good, but I don't know about that. My guess is he wasn't all that good, and some tales that I did hear about him, I wouldn't want to mention in this kind of room. But good or bad, he helped carry some folks to a better life than what they had. He helped them to get free from slavery. Thank you."

He sat down.

Hays thanked Bill and told us to remember his words: "This separate stuff was not always so." A lot of people nodded. Then she went on to talk about the park that was planned down by the creek near Bill's. How it was to have ball fields, basketball courts and good things for everybody. She said there were still some details to be worked out with the owners of the land, but that she was certain in her heart that justice would prevail.

Mr. Traylor cocked his head a little and Hays motioned for him to speak. He remained in his chair and, in a soft voice, reported that, at this point, things looked pretty dim. The heirs of old Mrs. Green were claiming that the part of her will that gave the land over for the park was invalid because the old woman had not been in her right mind. Then he named off the law firm that these folks had hired. My ears perked up and then turned red, because it was my father's firm, and then he mentioned him by name.

He went on to say that a restaurant was being planned at the site of the old tavern and that the Greens wanted to sell the entire parcel of land to these folks and they had come out and said that they didn't want a "nigra" park to queer the deal. They got money, lots of it. That's what he said.

The next guy who spoke was in uniform and he was for naming the park after the Negro heroes who had served and died in every single war this country had ever fought in. He told about a black tank battalion that fought under General Patton in France in 1944, how they had fought with bravery and prevailed, and yet back home they were treated more like prisoners of war than the war heroes they were. He wanted the park named after that battalion.

Then the young guy in the shiny black suit launched into what sounded like it was going to be a pretty long sermon about freedom, and I saw Bill roll his eyes and Mr. Traylor shake his head a little. Hays raised her hand and the young man stopped.

"Five minutes, Mr. Foster," was all she said and he nodded, and when he started back up his tone was a lot quieter. He wanted the park to be in honor of the Underground Railroad. He wanted it to honor both black and white, and he wanted there to be ball fields and stuff, but in addition, he wanted there to be a small museum to tell the full story. That was the gist of it. Then he sat down.

Mr. Traylor shook his head and Bill said that it would never fly. Mr. Traylor nodded and said, "First things first. We don't have the land or the money to buy it. And a museum about the railroad won't happen for a hundred years, if ever."

The military man started to speak, but before he could, the young man in the shiny black suit jumped up and said that the truth must be told and that money must be found for the cause. Most of the people nodded in agreement, but Bill said that most people didn't give a rat's behind for the truth and that you couldn't ram it down their throats, because that would make things worse. Some folks grumbled at this, but then Mr. Traylor asked the young man where he planned to raise the money and he looked down at his shoes and that sort of shut everybody up.

The meeting got kind of sad for a while, because nobody seemed to have any solutions for anything. A lot of people spoke out, but nobody had much to say except that a park was needed. There was no agreement on what it should be named or why or how to deal with any of it.

I could feel the room getting a little close and angry and I wanted to do something, but all I did was squirm and look around. People talked about relatives who had been killed in the war, and others talked about their kin who had fled slavery and then saved money and bought family out of slavery. But all the talk was going nowhere. Finally, Mr. Traylor raised his hand and quietly said that everything was being done that could be done, and then he pointed his open palm to Hays, who announced that we should all bow our heads to pray.

Her prayer was real quiet, almost a whisper at first. She asked that we all would be filled up with God's love and that this day would be blessed with the peace of God and his divine understanding. She finished with her voice rising, saying that we knew the ways of God were mysterious and surpassed all understanding, but that she knew, though the time seemed dark now, in the end, righteousness would prevail. At the end, she just said, "Dear Lord, be with us in this and in all things for all our days."

———

After lunch that day, some of us guys had played softball, but it was real loose. To begin with, we didn't divide into teams and there were no bases, gloves, or anything. The ball was falling apart and finally one of the bigger guys clobbered the thing so hard, he knocked the cover almost off so that when it flew into the weeds, it looked more like a fat flying saucer than a ball. That ended the game, but then the arm wrestling began, and that led to Indian wrestling, which got me into a wrestling match with Johnny Tucker. I don't know who started it, but we almost got into a fight. At least everybody acted like we did and broke us up, pulling us apart with our elbows stretched back behind us, so that we were leaning toward each other as they pulled us free. But we were smiling all the time, and afterward we ate some more food together and joked around.

In the car, Lucky had said, "And don't you get all tangled up with that Tucker boy. That boy is wild. That boy is trouble."

"He seemed all right to me."

"Might be that he is. Miss Hays has taken him under her wing and they all say he has the Lord's touch when it comes to any stray or wounded creature, but I don't know, have mercy. I know I shouldn't say it, but . . ."

Lucky rolled her eyes, said she knew the patch that he was raised in. She warned me to be careful. I told her I would, but I was lying. I liked the guy. He seemed all right to me and he was about the only kid I talked to who seemed to have any thoughts at all about the park. He thought there should be one and I did too. Then he asked me what I was going to do about it and I said I didn't know, and he mocked me and repeated what I said. The way he said it made me mad, the way he sat there grinning and chewing and looking like he knew something I didn't know. I asked him what was he going to do about it, and he bunched up his lips and stopped chewing and looked away like he already knew, but he wouldn't tell me for anything. I asked him again and he closed his eyes real hard and said, "Something. I'm gonna do something. It just ain't right." He shook his head.

"You're right about that," I said. "It ain't right. Your people have got a bad deal forever. I mean they've done everything, died and stuff in wars."

"In wars, yeah, and worse. How about the backyard, white boy?"

"I told you it ain't right, I said. It ain't and I know it. And you don't have to look at me like that."

He just kept staring and then he started chewing again real slow and shook his head, and he looked at me like he didn't believe it.

"What? What?" I said.

"Why you saying 'ain't'? You know you don't talk like that, white boy."

"I talk the way I want to. Why do you talk that way?" He stared off. "Well, why?" I asked again.

"Who knows?" he said. "I just do, that's all."

"Well, me too," I said. "I just talk the way I talk."

We were sort of staring at one another with our foreheads almost knocking together, when I felt a hand on my shoulder and saw another settle on Tucker's. We looked up. It was Lucky and she was shaking her head and smiling at us like she knew what was up and she wasn't going to have any of it.

"No more tussling or rough stuff or I'll skin you both."

She was smiling and Fred was right beside her, smiling too, but I knew she meant it and we both nodded and told her we understood. So Tucker and I went back to eating chicken like it was going out of style. We went back to talking about the park and how we wanted to do something about it. Trouble was, we didn't have a clue what we could do to help. Tucker was mad at everybody— the people who owned the land mainly, but also all the grownups who just sat around and yapped and didn't do nothing but talk about whether it should be named this or that. He said all they would do is talk and talk and pray forever and nothing would ever get done.

He was also mad at the "lawman" who was causing all the trouble. I hoped he didn't know that the "lawman" was my father, but he did, and he came out and said it and stared at me pretty hard. I told him I didn't know anything about it and that I would find out what I could.

"So which side are you on anyway?" he asked like he already knew. And I suddenly felt sort of sick, almost dizzy, like some big space was opening beneath me and there was nothing visible holding me up. I looked back at him as strong as I could, but all I could think to say was something like I would try to come up with something, and then I suggested we meet up at Creekside Auto after school one day soon and talk about it again. He rolled his eyes and shook his head.

"One day soon, we'll talk again," he said mockingly. "Maybe you're just like the rest. Talk, talk, talk."

"Wednesday at 4:30?"

"All right, but bring a friend you think you can trust, because I think we might need some recruits."

"What do you mean?"

Tucker looked at me like he was thinking. "Just bring a guy or two, whoever you can trust. I have an idea this thing might be just a little more of a job than you might think."

"What you saying?"

"Just do it. Couple of guys. Three or four, if you can. I got a feeling."

"Well, what about you?" I asked.

"Don't you worry. I'll do my part."

About that time, Churchill and Paul had come up and asked what we were hatching. Actually, it was Paul. He said, "What kind of trouble you two cooking up?" His big sleepy eyes twinkled with dark friendly mischief. Churchill stood behind him, about half a head taller, arms crossed, head tilted, big ears poking out and taking it all in.

"Nothing," we said.

"Look at them, Church, and tell me they ain't thick as thieves."

Churchill nodded. "Think you might be right, Paul. They're up to something."

We really weren't, yet, but somehow, I felt something happening, like sand sliding between your toes when a wave sucks back off a beach. I shook my head and winked at Tucker. He rolled his eyes and shook his head, but then he winked back.

"Maybe we are and maybe we're not," I said. "Tell you what. When I know, how about I give you a holler?"

Before they could answer, Fred, Lucky, and Mr. Traylor were standing there, and we were introduced. There was something about Mr. Traylor. I can't say what it was. It wasn't his size. He was small and skinny. And it wasn't his eyes. They looked sort of cloudy and dim, like he might have been blind almost. I don't know what it was, but something you couldn't put a finger on. It wasn't his voice. He almost whispered. But I tell you this, when he did, you listened somehow. All he said was that it was a great pleasure to meet me and that he had a great deal of respect for my father and that both my mother and father were fine people. The way he said that seemed to pull me toward him and up, so that when I shook his hand, careful not to hurt it, I felt like I might have been standing on my tiptoes. Part of me was riveted to his dark brown face and the little reddish-brown flecks and blotches that surrounded the shiny blacks of his eyes. There was a part of me that wanted to nod at Tucker and say, "See I'm okay. I'm from good people," but I couldn't take my eyes off Mr. Traylor. I don't know why.

———————

Lucky made a big fuss over me when we dropped her off. She teased me about eating so much fried chicken and said she feared for me if I ever got a chance to sample any of hers, which she said was ten times better, and that her potato salad was beyond compare. When she looked at Fred for confirmation, he agreed that it was plum out of this world. I grinned and nodded, but I was so stuffed I could barely sit up.

Fred and Lucky lived a stone's throw from the church. We dropped off Lucky so that she could pull something out of the oven. She made Fred promise to bring me back for cookies and brownies. Fred nodded much in the way I had seen him nod at my mother.

"Don't you forget that washer and dryer, Fred Ruby," Lucky said as she shut the door of the passenger seat I had just slid into. She patted my cheek. "You come back," she said.

I nodded and told her I would. She smiled with sparkling eyes.

When Fred started to drive away, Lucky walked beside the car and warned me some more to be careful with that Tucker boy, and then she told Fred not to be too long and he smiled and told her he would be back directly. She made him promise and he did, but he winked at me right afterward, and I suppose he figured that that promise was canceled out by something a little more important, and I guess it kind of was.

We hadn't gone ten feet before Fred had his cigar chomped in his mouth and the thick heavy smoke was curling around his head. When we got out to River Road, he turned the wrong way.

"You liked that music, didn't you?"

"You'd have to be dead and buried if you didn't," I replied.

"Well, there's all different kinds of music. What say we hear us some more?"

And that's what we did. We went to a joint, as Fred called it, that was sort of out of the way of any houses and kind of stashed up against a stand of old trees and scrub. Part of it was made of concrete block painted yellow and green, and part of it was wood that looked old and rotted. The roof was rusty tin.

As we walked across the gravel and approached the open door, Fred put his hand on my shoulder and told me to stick close to him. It was bright and sunny where we were walking, but inside that door, it looked like dusk. It smelled damp and sour and the smoky air choked me up like smoldering dirty straw. I could hardly see a thing, but I didn't have to, because Fred guided me by the shoulder right up to the bar. He ordered a Falls City beer, a Coke, and some peanuts, and a big old shape reached down behind the bar and when he stood up again, he had a face full of gold teeth and a real big voice.

"Two bits," was all he said.

"Hawk here?" Fred asked.

"He's here. He play in a minute. Done broke a string."

The man looked at me, squinted up his eyes, and tilted his head. Fred introduced me to Pole Cat—Mr. Ebenezer "Pole Cat" Green, who shook my hand real soft, and I was glad of that because his hand felt big enough to wrap around a beer keg. Fred told him everything would be all right. Pole Cat nodded and said he didn't want no trouble.

We sat down at a table that had a candle burning on it. It was stuck into a big mound of wax drippings of all different colors. There weren't many other people, a group here and there; people talking quietly mostly and every now and then somebody calling out for a beer. Over in the corner, a man was messing with a guitar. Fred told me that was Hawk. He said he was Tucker's daddy. I looked at him hard. He had long silver hair and a big broad face. I looked back at Fred and gave him a look. Fred chuckled and said, "He's most nearly white, is what you're thinking, but you're wrong. He's colored just like me, except he's about three parts Cherokee."

"Indian?" I whispered.

"Father, pureblood, mother about half and half, I reckon. He's colored all right, just like me."

When he started playing, at first I didn't really like it. Or maybe it was more that I just couldn't figure out what he was trying to do. He was playing electric guitar and he was playing bottleneck style, and I hadn't ever heard that before. At first, it sounded all screechy and scratchy, but then he started singing and his voice wrapped itself around his playing and before I knew it, I was humming along and singing out: "Now how long, how long, how long that train been gone?"

After a while, I could see almost plain as day. The strings on that guitar flickered like streaks of fire, and Hawk's fingers thrummed and picked so fast sometimes I could barely see them, and then sometimes moved so slow it seemed amazing that so much sound came out. Finger-picking style was what Fred called it. I found myself nodding my head whether I wanted to or not. And in between songs, people called out and clapped and some of them yelled out names like Muddy Waters, Texas Red, Lightning Hopkins, Howlin' Wolf, Elmore James, Lonnie Johnson. I had never heard of any of those guys, but finally somebody called out Jimmy Reed, and I knew of him and so I yelled it out, too.

Hawk played a song called "Baby I Was So Wrong." I knew some of the words, but Hawk kind of threw me off, because he changed them around to suit himself, but it still sounded pretty good. Mainly, he played songs he had made up himself, and he had some wild crazy stories that he told about how he had come to write them. Some were dirty and one was about a jail in Alabama that made me sick to my stomach just to hear it. That song was called "Alabama White Woman Blues." It made me feel ashamed to hear it, and mad, too. After it was over, I was shaking my head and Fred told me to hold my head up, that I had nothing to do with it.

We didn't stay there too long. Some people came in that Fred didn't like much. Said they were common. They were loud and falling-down drunk, that's for sure.

As we were bouncing out of the parking area, I was thinking about all the terrible stuff I had heard about all day. I was still thinking about that Alabama woman, and how she had put old Hawk in the jail. Then I was thinking about lynchers and double-crossers and just plain old nasty people that had been killing and hurting the colored folks all along the way. It made me feel dirty and sick inside. It made me feel ashamed to be white. I said something like that to Fred. He shook his head and said it wasn't right for me to feel that way. He said I hadn't done nothing to be ashamed of. There's good and bad alike, both colored and white.

"Take Bill's grandpa," Fred said. "Some would say he's good because he carried slaves across the river, but then even some of those would say he was bad because he was a bootlegger, a moonshiner, and that's what he was. But like Bill said, who really knows? Who can judge a man? What else did he do good or bad? It ain't possible for us to say."

"If nobody knew about him, not even his own wife, how did Bill find out, I want to know? What was he talking about, a personal tragedy made him know?"

Fred shook his head like he didn't want to talk about it.

"Bill's had it hard," was all he said.

That didn't satisfy me and I kept after it until finally he told me, and what he told me made my stomach crawl. He drove over to an empty spot that overlooked the river, stopped the car, and made me promise not to tell my mother and father about this part of the day. After church, everything was strictly between me and him. He gave me a look and I nodded.

I'll make it quick. This is what he told me. Right after the war, Bill had moved back into his family's old house. His folks were dead. His mother had died right before he got back. Bill got into the trucking business and did pretty well. Before long, he had three trucks. Then he got married to a pretty woman and everybody loved her. They lived right next to the colored section, but she didn't run the colored kids off when they played in her yard, and she treated everybody like they were special. Bill was devoted to her and he quit his drinking and hard living.

One of Bill's trucks was brand new and about as big as a semi. Shiny as all get out with great big old wheels. He was so proud of it that he washed it off every evening. It shined like a fire truck. Well, one morning it was gone. But it hadn't gone far. This kid from the colored section had stolen it and taken it for a ride and then had parked right in front of his own family's house. Bill had called the cops, but he didn't press charges when he found out who did it. He got his truck back and some money for gas and that was that.

The kid wasn't right in the head. He had done that sort of thing before. He had actually stolen a semi rig once and parked it just like with Bill's, right in front of his house. His family didn't know what to do with him. They said that the boy didn't drink or anything like that. He just liked trucks, and they said he was like a sleepwalker. They caught him once when he brought one home and they said he acted like somebody walking around in a dream.

Bill demanded that the boy apologize, and after he did, Bill gave the boy a job. First just cleaning the trucks and then sometimes he let him drive. Bill and his wife took this boy in. His family was poor. They gave him a uniform and clothes and treated him like a son. Everything seemed to be going fine, but it wasn't.

At this point, Fred reached under his seat, pulled out his pint, and took a swig. He lit his cigar and looked out over the water and shook his head.

"Some say he might as well have killed Bill, too—such a pretty woman."

"What happened, Fred?"

"You know what rape is?"

"Sure," I said. I think I was grinning, but I felt weird and tingly.

Fred looked at me and shook his head. "Nothing to grin about."

"I know," I said.

"Bill was out on the road overnight. He was in the big rig and I don't remember who for, but it was a big deal and everybody said later that it was sort of like a celebration when Bill pulled out. Sarah, that was his wife, had passed out Cokes to a lot of the kids. It was something to do with the highway department, I believe. Anyway, Bill took off and that was that. The boy, a colored boy, that they had treated like a son, raped and murdered Bill's wife, set the house on fire, and burnt it to the ground. I was there when it was burning and there was nothing to do but let it burn. Somebody got out a table and some chairs and junk like that, but that was all. Couldn't find the wife, and when they did find her, they could tell she was stabbed to death and her neck was broken.

"The boy admitted everything. They say he didn't bat an eye. Nodded yes to everything. Rape. Murder. Setting the house afire.

Reason? The boy just grinned and shrugged his shoulders. The boy was insane.

"There was a trial and everybody knew that that boy was going to the chair and everybody, including me, thought he should. But Bill stood up at the trial right before the sentencing and said he was sick of killing. They say he was drunk and others say he just looked horrible, but all of them agree that if he hadn't said what everybody knew, but didn't want to say, that boy would have been electrocuted. They say he turned to the family and to the boy and said there's been too much killing already. They say that he asked the judge to put the boy in the state hospital for the family's sake and for his sake, too, and then they say he sat down and let out a moan that sounded like it poured out from hell."

Fred didn't say anything for a minute or two, and neither did I. We just watched the river run. I didn't know what to say. Fred relit his cigar and blew out a big puff of smoke.

"The boy was declared insane and put in the hospital. And Bill just stayed drunk. Moved onto his boat. The boy's mother took him food, and then he took sick and wouldn't eat or talk to anybody. He nearly died. He wanted to. I don't know how she did it, but one cold winter night, the boy's family somehow got Bill off that boat and into their home and they brought him back to health and into his right mind. They even got him to go to church with them and that was a first for everybody. They're the ones who told Bill his grandpa had carried some of their people across this river to freedom."

"God, I don't know what to say," I said.

"Don't have to say anything."

Fred started the car and eased back on to the road. We didn't say much all the way home.

CHAPTER 6

PARK

After school the next day, I took off to see Riverboat Bill. I don't really know why, except my head was swimming with so many thoughts that maybe I felt like a walk and a talk might calm me down. Everything was turning green. Little green shoots popping up at my feet everywhere. When I got to the creek, there were some baby ducks zipping along behind their mother. When they saw me, they took off skipping across the water, and the mother looked at me and nodded her head. I called out for Bill.

No answer. I called again. His car was there, but still no answer. I had to laugh when I looked at that car. It was about the worst looking thing that ever saw a road, and I had driven it. I took a certain pride in that. In the daylight, it was hard to say what color it was. Red basically, but it had swatches of white where it had clipped things, and brown holes where the metal was rusted out, and one rim was blue and one was black and it just went on from there. I called out again and finally I heard something that sounded like Bill. Sort of a growl. I called again and it was Bill all right. He stuck his head out the door, but he was looking the wrong way.

"Over here, Bill. I'm over here."

He turned his head and stared at me. He kept looking at me like I wasn't even there, and then he shook his head and went back in.

I almost walked away, but then I called out again, almost like something made me do it.

"What you want now? It ain't storming."

"Just want to talk, that's all."

He made some kind of low-down sound, but then he did come out. He shook his head and scratched his chin, all the while looking at me. After about a minute, he asked me what about. I said I wasn't really sure, and he nodded like he was letting that digest, then he took a swig of beer and climbed into his skiff. He almost fell overboard, but then caught himself by grabbing the motor. He cussed a bit, but then he started laughing. Right before pulling on the starter cord, he looked at me hard and squinted up his eyes.

"What you up to, boy?" was all he said. Then he yanked on the cord and cussed each time it didn't start until it did, and then said, "Oh, praise the Lord!" as the white smoke clouded up all around him. "Holy smokes!" he cried out as he puttered across. Even from where I stood, his eyes looked fire engine red.

Bill was a little bit drunk, but he was all the way upset. Some "hired gun" of the Green family had showed up that morning and asked to see his lease. At first, Bill thought the guy was kidding him. But he wasn't, and Bill had never really had a lease. It had been a handshake agreement with old Mrs. Green. She had told Bill he could stay there as long as he wanted. But this whippersnapper had said that, without a signed lease, Bill would have to move within thirty days. Bill said he had har-harred at that. Where was he to go and how was he gonna get there?

"This tub ain't never had a motor. I could rig up an outboard, but moving her off this creek would sink her for sure. The river would be licking her chops, and besides, what about the car? Where would I go?" He looked at me hard and shook his head. "It ain't much, but this is my home. It's all I got left, and I don't want no other."

He polished off his beer and pointed to the cooler. I got him another. He said the guy told him the lawyers were drawing up papers, and the way he said "lawyers" made me wish I hadn't come.

"Sit down," he said. "It ain't your damn fault and hell, for that matter, it ain't your daddy's either. He's just another Green hired gun. He does what the family wants; that's what they pay him for. I'm only a small potato that's in the way of their big plans to be rid of the place so they can pay off death taxes, I reckon. And you know how them lawyers are. They hate taxes worse than anything. They'd rather children starve and old folks go hungry than see one of their own have to pay taxes. That's just the way they are."

I nodded, not knowing much about taxes, but I was remembering the night before at dinner when I was telling them about my hopes for a park, my father had said calmly that he didn't think that was in the cards. I had asked him what he meant, and he had said that he understood why some people wanted a park, but that the Green family members were against that, because they wanted to sell. I asked if they needed the money. I had always heard they were as rich as pharaohs. My father had chuckled and said for tax purposes. He said they still had plenty of money, but they were selling that little piece and the main house and grounds and a bunch of other things too involved to get into. Then he went off on how the taxes in this country were ruining everything and that people couldn't afford to live like they used to live.

Bill said, "Old man Green would be spinning in his grave if he knew about this. He would have told all those snotty-assed kids to shove off. Hell, we served together, and many is the time he lowered his big backside right where you're sitting and knocked down some of that good whiskey they made and smoked cigars until you couldn't even see him for all the smoke. He would have said the hell with g.d. taxes, make more whiskey. He didn't much care for lawyers, said all they knew how to do was tell him what he couldn't."

Bill started laughing, and he laughed until coughing made him give it up. When he got hold of himself, he asked me if I had heard stories about the old man. I told him I hadn't really, except for something about a tractor.

"Yeah, well that one's tame enough, I guess. The old man was wild.

I call him old man, but he wasn't much older than me. We were both pretty old for the service, and he looked like an old man, the way he carried himself as big as he was and all. Anyway, everyone called him old man Green.

"He loved his whiskey and he could probably drink a whole gallon, but not a drop more. I mean hellfire and head for the hills. There was just no stopping him. Even those ones who liked to drink with him learned to recognize when he was getting close, and sometimes he was a real gentleman, if you very politely suggested that perhaps, just maybe, it was time to slow down a bit. He might say, 'Say, Bill, I do believe you might be right. I did have a rather small lunch today. Empty stomach, you know?' But you had to say it just right or else he would squint his eyes like an old boar and charge the bar like she was a sow in heat. God help you if he did. He was a big man, and even if all he did was bump something or fall down, he could do a world of damage.

"Funny thing was, he was mostly meek as a mouse around Mrs. Green, and eventually she got him a driver to haul him around. He agreed to it, but he most likely wouldn't have if it hadn't have been for that tractor."

"So what did he do? I heard something, but I don't remember."

"Well, he had been duck hunting and dropped his favorite shotgun into the river. He went in after it and found it, too, but then back in the blind, he got so cold, hell, it was December, that he started pouring down the sauce, trying to fire himself up, and Lord knows he succeeded. He got drunk as a skunk. Somehow, he set the blind on fire, but they got that out. Then on the way back, he about broadsided a barge, and that's hard to do in daylight. Then he was plenty mad and chased after the thing and nobody could stop him. Hell, it was his boat and he was big, like I say, and besides, all those folks that were with him kissed his rich ass anyway. So then, he almost swamped in the wake and everybody was wet. But anyway, when he got home cussing and drunk and soaked, old Mrs. Green just held out her hand and he put the car keys into it.

"Now, I was there because I had helped pull the boat. They were all drunk and frozen, so I helped and the old man was going to take me to Old Pine Tavern for a steak dinner to pay me back. He told Mrs. Green that, and she just shook her head no. Didn't say a thing. Just walked away and left the room. I told the old man that I'd hoof it down the hill, but he got that look about him and grabbed my arm and said, 'Bill, goddamn it, a deal's a deal. I'm buying.' And out the door we went and he was still soaked. The whole way over to the barn he clenched my arm, and I didn't know what he had made up his mind to do or I most likely would have wiggled free and tried to talk him out of it.

"We go into the barn and before you could say Jack Robinson, he's up on this big old John Deere and cussing about where the lights were, and how the hell do you start the bloody thing, and on and on, till I figured he was kidding. Hell, it had a big old slat-sided wagon hooked onto it. Then he fired it up, and before I could even think, he was rolling out, screaming, 'All aboard, all aboard.' I jumped in the wagon and I was trying to yell at him to stop and he just laughed and ground the gears, and the next thing I know we're flying down the hill for the creek. He yelled out, 'For the love of Mary, where are the bloody lights!' And then he cackled and we rattled on down the hill and made it through all the curves and barely swiped up against anything, until we got to the Pine Tavern. Then he lost it somehow and he zigzagged back and forth across the road and then veered into the parking lot and right through the front door. It was an awful crash. He got most of the way in but then the tires stopped him when they crashed into the building. He shut down the engine and yelled back was I all right, which I was somehow, even though I felt like I had been wrestling a Brahma bull. Nobody was hurt, but nobody was real happy. We ended up eating tuna fish down here. After that, the old man paid a little more attention to Mrs. Green."

"Did he get arrested? Did they sue him?"

Bill laughed. "Arrest a Green? Hell no. He had it fixed up as good as new. He was a man of his word. Everybody knew that. He was just a little drunk. Hell, the whole time we were eating our tuna fish, he kept apologizing about it not being steak, and the next night his driver brought him down and we went up to The Point and had steak in the joint up there. No, he was a good man, and his missus was a good woman, too. Honorable people, unlike those hornets they hatched who're trying to put me out. They're a different breed, that's all."

Bill just couldn't believe it. How could they do such a thing to him? He cussed them all. He cussed the schools they went to. The fancy-ass clothes they wore. He cussed the way they talked, their poodles, cocker spaniels, and their questionable ancestry.

"They didn't come over on the Mayflower, I'll tell you that much," he said. "There's some that live over that way"—he pointed toward the colored section—"that refers to them folks as cousins, if you know what I mean. But damn it all, boy, what am I gonna do?"

I shrugged, not knowing what to say. I shook my head.

"Mrs. Green, if she were alive, would set those people straight. She wanted this here creek and the land here to be for everybody, even Bill. She knew where she came from. She held her head high. She treated everybody right, but buddy, you never wanted to cross her, I'll tell you that. Why, she could cut your throat with the tip of her tongue. Old man Green, he tiptoed around her generally, but she knew what was going on and she knew about the times I pulled his fat out of the fire and his ass out of the creek and how sometimes he'd lay up here drunk, until he figured it was okay to go back home. She knew about that, and even though we weren't close or anything, not like me and him, she treated me with respect and you know what? She sent me a case of bourbon and a basket of fruit every Christmas. Always with a note. Thanks for everything and happy holidays. She knew the old man needed a friend like me to keep him honest and out of trouble somehow. She knew I tried to anyhow."

It got quiet for a while and Bill sat there staring at the table. I listened to the water slosh and slide past the hull. I wanted to ask Bill about the park. What he thought about it. What could be done and all that, but it didn't seem like a good time, so I kept quiet.

"So what brings you this way? I've been rambling on about nothing. What brings you here?"

"I hardly know what to say now," I said. "I guess I came here to talk to you about the park, but that might not be so important right now. I mean with this talk of them trying to move you out and all."

"Well, boy, you're wrong about that for several reasons. For one, the park is a good idea all by itself, plus Mrs. Green, she wanted a park, and that's a fact. Hays wouldn't lie for anything, and she saw the lady write her wishes into her will, and for another thing, purely selfish, the park is about the best hope I got."

"Well, do you think there's a chance it'll work out?"

"Afraid to say, but I'd say slim, if I had to. See, most folks around here don't give a damn one way or the other. The ones you saw yesterday, as nutty as some of them might seem, are about the best of the lot. Most folks, white or colored, just look out for their own ass, and they don't figure that stuff like this is important until they got trouble on their hands. They're a lot of kids out here now, and it ain't like before where you could play ball out on the road if you felt like it. People can't just roam around with everybody knowing everybody. It ain't like that anymore and hasn't been for some time."

I said that I thought it should be a park to honor the Underground Railroad, and when Bill rolled his eyes, I said, "Or maybe for the veterans who fought in WWII." Bill shook his head.

"Should be, maybe, but what about Korea? What about the Civil War? There were coloreds there, too. Trouble is, just like with your Underground Railroad idea, most people just don't want to think about it. It pains 'em. Colored folks mostly don't want to think about slavery, and whites sure don't, except for those ones that think it was a good idea. I hate to say it but most white vets don't give a damn about colored soldiers and what they did and what they went through. It's an awful thing to say, but a lot of prisoners of war were treated better than the colored soldiers were, and nobody wants to bring that up, and if you do, they'll call you a nigger lover. They'll tell you Negroes didn't see action, or not like the whites did, and they'll say they were lazy or cowards. I don't care what facts you bring up to prove 'em wrong, they just shake their heads and turn away. Believe me, I've seen it. And a lot of folks don't know, and most folks don't care."

"If nobody cares, what's the chance? I mean, how can you make them care?"

"Hell, I don't know, but maybe enough do that we can make a difference. Take Mr. Traylor. He cares and he's smart. He knows how to work the angles and he knows how to work behind the scenes, and believe me, there's white folks that understand. It's just that most of them are not the types to raise up their voices real loud. And so that's why Traylor and me and some others that have talked this thing out, hoped to keep it quiet and not fire up everybody. Just as soon as you bring up the railroad or anything honoring colored soldiers, you'll rouse up all kinds of jackasses that want to send the niggers back to Africa and every other kind of nonsense, and then you'll get colored folks stirred up, and that will scare off the good ones, both colored and white."

I told Bill that it didn't seem fair. People needed to know these things. He agreed, but then he asked me if I thought a plain old park was a good idea. I told him I did. He said, then you had to work it right. He asked me how many statues I'd seen of colored people. I told him I hadn't seen any.

Bill stood up and stretched, so I stood up too, but he motioned for me to sit down. He said he wanted to tell me another story about old man Green. He asked me if I had heard about how he died. I shook my head no. Bill sort of chuckled and got himself a beer.

"It ain't funny, but something like it was bound to happen one day anyway. Green got drunk, no surprise there. He had a driver, a good fella by the name of Marcus. Marcus had just the touch that old Green needed. He was so calm he could talk a cat down out of a tree. He knew just how long to let the old man pour it down and then somehow, he was able to talk him into putting down his glass and getting on home. He would sit out in the car listening to the radio, and when he figured the boss was close to danger, he would walk to the door of the joint, open it and stand there, hat in hand. Green would turn on his barstool and almost always follow him out.

"All except that night. He was ornery and he wanted to stay at The Point, because he was all fired up at some guy about politics or something, and this guy wanted to fight him, but said that Green was so out of shape that he was afraid he would kill his ass. So anyway, Marcus had his work cut out for him. How to get his drunk, pissed-off boss out of a bar fight when he, Marcus, wasn't even welcome in the bar. Marcus went to the phone booth out front, called the bar, asked for his boss. He told Green that if he didn't walk out the back door of that bar in two minutes flat he was leaving, going back to Mrs. Green, and turning in his resignation, and she could come pick him up. Then he hung up without waiting for a reply. He pulled around back, and old Green, who had excused himself to pee, rolled out the door and off they went.

"Marcus told me later that Green had been red as a beet and mad as a bull. But he said he calmed down quick like he always did and started teasing him, saying stuff like you wouldn't really sic the missus on me, would you? Marcus said the old man then started grumbling that he needed to get in shape. That if he ever ran into that hayseed again, he was gonna knock the bastard's block off. He was gonna build himself up, and if that SOB called him a flabby old fart again, he was gonna mop the floor with him.

"Well, the next day, it was all over the creek and then it was in the evening paper. Green was dead. Seems he decided to start getting in shape that very night. Got home. Put on his trunks and dove into the pool to do some laps. Trouble was the pool was in the process of being repaired. There weren't no water in it. Splat! He broke his damn neck. They found him the next morning, dead as a mackerel. It was sad, but it was funny how the papers carried on about it. 'Tragic accident claims head of prominent family.' They listed all the clubs he belonged to and his military record, and they had this twenty-year-old picture of him that made him look damn good, and they went on and on about him. And not to take away, after all, he was my friend, but can you imagine what they would have said if it had been Marcus? I mean, can you?"

"No," I said.

"Well, I'll tell you what. If they said anything at all, it would have been because he was found dead in the Green's pool. That would have been news. But if he had dived head first dead drunk into his own empty pool, they wouldn't have said nothing, and if he had done it in the Green's, they would have said a crazy drunk Negro, meaning drunken nigger trespasser, died doing something stupid and wrongheaded.

"As it was, there were folks who claimed it was Marcus's fault for letting him get so drunk, and there were those who tried to blame it on the other colored man who had drained the pool, but of course, nothing came of it. There was nothing to it. But a lot of colored folk were worried. But Mrs. Green put a stop to that. She kept Marcus on and the other man, too."

Bill said that the deal was to keep race out of the thing, and that's why they had tried to get all the churches, both white and colored, involved. Mr. Traylor and Hays and some others were working on it with the church groups and felt pretty good about that part, but the problem was the Green heirs. They wouldn't budge.

I asked Bill who the buyer was and he didn't know. He said nobody did and that nobody was sure there was one. But he said that wasn't the point really. The main thing was the will. The old lady wanted a park.

Well, we were sitting there and a car pulled up. The door slammed with a heavy thud. Bill said it was Mr. Traylor, and it was. Mr. Traylor knocked on the door, which was open, and waited out on the deck until Bill walked over and invited him in. He was all dressed up, just like he was at church the day before. He sat down and nodded to me. He looked glum, but when he spoke, his words were clear and bright.

He said that the Green family doctor would testify, if it came to that, that the old lady was on medications of a sufficient dosage to make it highly questionable that she was in her right mind when she added on to her will. He looked at me dead-on across the table. He asked me if I thought there should be a park. I said yes. He nodded. He drew himself up, leaned across the table, and looked me over for about a whole minute. Nobody said anything. When he started talking, it sort of startled me. He looked at me the whole time.

"Young man, I am the same age your grandfather would have been if he was still alive. I am seventy-eight years of age." I nodded. "And I have known your father since he was a boy. I hauled the garbage. My boy's first bicycle was one that they threw out." He chuckled and settled back in his chair. "I have always respected your people."

I nodded, sort of worried about what might be coming next. He raised his hand.

"Can you keep a secret?" he asked. I nodded. He asked me to say it out loud and I did. "The secret is your daddy wants there to be a park as well."

That surprised me. "So what's the problem?" I asked.

"That's off the record, you understand. You tell somebody I said that and I'll deny it with a straight face, you understand? I just want you to know, so that you don't think I've got bad feelings towards you or your family. Now, as for the problem . . . The Green family and their company are major clients of your daddy's law firm, and the Greens do not want this land encumbered in any way, shape, or form. He represents their interests, and he claims there is legitimate doubt about the last addition to Mrs. Green's will, but he told me, off the record, that he would do what he could."

That made me feel a little better, sort of like a cool drink. For a minute there, I felt like I was on the hot seat. Then I thought I could tell Tucker, if he razzed me again about my dad, and then I remembered the promise. That made me feel sort of confused.

"What's he going to do?" I asked.

"Bill, you remember how we said we thought it was about taxes more than anything? Well, you were right."

"So there's a tax angle he can work on, is there?" Bill asked.

"Yes, sir. Something to do with donating the land and a bond issue through the county. But the trouble is, there might not be much time, and like the boy's father told me, those kinds of things don't happen overnight. Besides, the Greens apparently do have a buyer, although I don't know whom. But one thing I did find out, there is at least one Green who seems to be leaning our way, and maybe two."

"What you mean?" Bill asked. "They sent somebody down here today to tell me I had to clear out. Said I had thirty days. Said they were gonna block the road, tow my car, and send me packing."

Mr. Traylor waited a bit until Bill settled back in his chair, and then he spoke quietly. "Bill, I don't know what's going to happen there. As far as I could ascertain, nothing's been signed yet, and I would guess that guy was from the realty company that is handling the sale. I bet it's mostly smoke. I can't say for certain, but that would be my guess.

"But I do know this from Hays, and you know she raised those Green kids. She says the older daughter is secretly on our side and the boy is wavering. See, they're getting all this advice from accountants and lawyers, and those children are not trained to that and their heads are spinning. The other girl is a go-along. She's never had to think about money. The real estate agents and accountants speak and she says 'Okay, whatever you say.'

"Hays is working on them in her own quiet way. They're proud people and used to getting their own way, so you can't push too hard. You have to nudge a little here and there. She's doing just that."

Afterward I got a ride home from Mr. Traylor. He had a big black Cadillac and a chauffeur, too. Mr. Traylor was full of surprises. When his driver opened the door for us, Mr. Traylor slid in first so he could tidy up his office, he said. I looked in and, sure enough, he had a fold-down writing table, a small bookshelf, and a rack for newspapers. He had an adding machine and a pencil sharpener, too, and a wastebasket full of crumpled paper. He said that was the most important part of his office.

On the way home, he chuckled and asked me if I had liked his magic trick as much as I had let on that I had. I told him I had liked it a lot, and I had, because it was good, but the main thing was I had been totally surprised that he knew magic tricks. He just didn't seem the type. And it wasn't your ordinary simple card trick either. He was passing cards and everything, and I never could catch him doing it. Once I thought I had, and I'm still sure he had palmed a card, but when he opened his hand for me, there was nothing there but skin.

He had pulled the pack of cards out just before we left. He did it while he was talking about the park and I figured he was reaching for a smoke. Then he started shuffling the cards and cut them into two piles. He stopped talking and winked at me. He asked me if I knew a trick called, "Raiding the Castle." Well, anyway, in his quiet voice he told this story about four brothers who were kings. Somehow, four knaves had captured their queens and their castle, which was the ace of spades, and as he told this story, cards that were supposed to be one place were all of a sudden in another. I would swear to the lights above that I saw him put a queen in one place and a king in another and a jack here and another queen there. Well, anyway, Bill and I were laughing and saying "show us your hands" and he would, but we couldn't catch him. Finally, he shuffled the cards: first, he turned up the ace of spades (the castle), then the king of hearts and queen of hearts, and then the rest of the kings and queens together again, too. He handed me the deck and asked me to find the knaves. I found the four jacks buried on the bottom of the deck.

As we rolled along toward home, he asked me how I liked school, and I told him it was okay. He asked me if I liked to read and I told him I did and that seemed to please him. He said that was the main thing a man needed if he wanted to get ahead. He said he would still be doing odd jobs if he hadn't learned to read. The school he went to only went to the eighth grade, and he had only made it through the seventh, because he'd had to go to work.

He didn't take me all the way back to my house. He let me off at the end of the driveway and apologized for not taking me all the way.

I thanked him for the ride and he shook my hand. His eyes were cloudy, but somehow twinkling.

"I would take you all the way back, but everything is a little delicate right now, you understand?"

I told him I did and thanked him once more for the lift. He nodded and shook my hand again through the window of the car. Just before easing away, he winked, and when I looked in my hand, I was holding the ace of spades.

———

It all started out pretty innocently, I guess. Tucker and I both felt like we had to do something. We didn't know what that was, but on the afternoon that we met up down at the gas station, first off we both agreed that we had to do something. Hell, we both were supposed to have brought somebody. I had tried to talk some guys at school into coming with me to meet up with Tucker, but nobody was interested. They asked me what we were going to do and it didn't much help to convince them when I said that I honestly didn't know. I had talked to Ben and Andy, because they were hell-raisers, ready for adventure, but they lived in town. Churchill and Paul, who lived pretty close, close enough to ride their bikes, just laughed and asked me what I thought we were going to do about anything anyway. I was going to ask Albert, but he left school early and didn't come back that day, so I showed up alone. Tucker brought a colored girl.

When I rode up on my bike, he was leaning against the soda machine talking to her and I figured she was just a friend of his or maybe his sister. Her name was Laura and I thought she was real pretty. She had eyes that flashed and sparkled and she shook hands firmly like a boy. She was taller than we were and, as it turned out, just as strong, but I didn't know that yet. All I knew was that she was a girl, and me and Tucker were on a mission. When she didn't leave, I wondered what she was doing there.

They were splitting a Coke and the three of us stood around, first on one foot and then the other. I guess we didn't know what came next. I *know* we didn't, or else we most likely would have gone our separate ways. Well, anyway, I was thirsty, so I reached in my pocket for change, but I didn't have any. Both of them saw this and Laura took the Coke from Tucker and passed it to me. He gave her a look like "what are you doing?" She said that I was thirsty, as simple as pie, and gave me a smile. I acted like I didn't want it. No thanks and waved it away. She gave me a funny look, but not quite like Tucker's, who tilted his head and squinted his eyes.

"What's the matter, white boy? Can't bring yourself to drink after a neeegrooo?"

He wasn't smiling. I reached for the Coke, took a big swig, swallowed it down, and burped. Then I took another and passed it back.

"What's wrong with you, Tuck?" Laura asked. "Maybe he just has manners."

"Maybe," was all he said. I was glad he turned away and motioned for us to follow, because my ears were burning and I'm sure they were turning red. He had been right, and I felt like I had been caught someplace I didn't belong. It made me feel weird. It hadn't been bad. It still tasted like Coke, but when she had offered me the drink, all I could think of at first was dirt and spit. When I took the drink, it was like looking the other way and doing something grubby. It made me feel weird, that's all I can say. But I guess the strangest part was that it was only Coke. It was sort of like cussing for the first time and you realize that shit, damn, and fuck are only words, and you figure out that the ground ain't gonna shake and swallow you up. I felt stupid. Laura smiled at me, took my hand, and pulled me along. Tucker was twenty feet ahead of us on his way to the creek.

"He knows a place where we can wade across. He says it comes just a little bit past your knees."

I nodded and followed. She didn't seem to pick up on my mixed-up feelings, which were getting more mixed up all the time. There was something about her that stirred me up, the way she had leaned into me when she'd said that, her smile, or something in her voice. Maybe it was the caramel color of her legs or the way her hand felt strong as she pulled me. I don't know what it was, but I was busting my pants and my stomach felt queasy, but not from the Coke. I had a hard-on that wouldn't quit. I was glad I was wearing jeans.

Fortunately, when we reached the creek, we had a little powwow. Why were we going over to "the park"? Tucker just thought it was important. Well, anyway, we jabbered about how we had to do something and going there seemed like a good place to start. Laura, who was crouched down beside the creek testing the temperature of the water, wanted to know why we couldn't go in by the road. The water was cold. Why did we have to wade across? Tucker said this was the best way and that was that.

All the jabber kind of calmed me down, but then Tucker sat down on a log and started taking off his shoes and socks. He stripped down to his underwear. He said the water came up to about here and he pointed to his crotch with a grin. Laura and I both laughed, and she said she wouldn't do it. No way. But she did, and I started to have the problem all over again. The water was so damn cold, though, that by the time we were halfway across, there was no problem.

On the other side, we sat on a log in the sun and warmed up for a couple of minutes, and then we got dressed and started wandering around. Hell, there was nothing there really: a field that had a low spot with some water in it and a couple of ducks. We jumped a rabbit. We threw some big chunks of gravel at an old cottonwood tree. Laura was the best shot. We had about five contests and she won all of them. That drove Tucker nuts, but I acted like it didn't bother me.

We had a footrace down the road toward Bill's. His boat was supposed to be the finish line, but since Laura, who we had given a head start to, was still winning, Tucker and I decided that the old tavern should be the finish. So while she complained, we caught up with her and Tucker passed her and I might have, too, if she hadn't grabbed me and knocked me off balance.

At the tavern, we squabbled about what was fair and what wasn't. We were all out of breath and laughing and shoving. We went inside, but that is sort of misleading, because the place had no doors or windows or floors and no roof—there were only stone walls and an old fireplace with a tumbledown chimney. High water had carried in a bunch of trash, bottles, cans, and driftwood. Some of the stones had places that looked like they had been smashed with a hammer, but Tucker said they were bullet holes. Laura found a nickel in the fireplace, but it wasn't all that old. I guess we were hoping to find something that was real historic—something from the old days when it was part of the Underground Railroad. I don't know what we expected to find, but we didn't find anything like that. A crow feather. A dead cat skeleton. Just junk mainly.

Outside we watched the river flow. Tucker couldn't believe anybody would want the place. I said I thought the place maybe could be fixed up and turned into a museum about the railroad, and Tucker said I was crazy, that it was smaller than a classroom and that there wasn't nothing there, just a bunch of falling-down rocks. What kind of history lesson would that be? Laura said there could be pictures that would tell the story, and I agreed.

Tucker wanted to know where we planned to get the pictures. He bet nobody stood around taking snapshots. Laura laughed at him. She said somebody would have to make the pictures. She started describing some of the ones she would make—a mother with a baby and a little child, half naked and barefoot, and the moon real little and a boat lit up by a white man with a big beard holding a lantern, or a picture of a man and his wife praying as the boat got close to Indiana. Tucker told her she was dreaming, that she had to throw in some dogs and white people chasing with torches and guns and ropes and chains.

As we were walking back toward Bill's, I pointed at the field and said that at least there could be some baseball diamonds, basketball courts, picnic tables, and stuff. We all agreed to that, but Tucker thought there ought to be something about the railroad, and he kicked the gravel hard and cussed.

"But there's nothing there," he said, "just old rocks and some bullet holes."

When we got to Bill's, he was standing on the deck drinking a beer. We walked over.

"Now what you up to?" he asked with a grin.

I shrugged and Laura and Tucker both greeted him. They called him Mr. Bill. He knew them both by name. We didn't talk too long, but Bill was pissed off, because the real estate people had come back, and he called them all kinds of names until Laura just had to laugh out loud. Bill acted like he was going to jump off the boat and come after her. He said he was going to string her up and skin her alive, and she laughed all the louder. Bill said the bastards were up to something. He said he had watched 'em driving stakes with little red flags on 'em all up and down the road. I hadn't noticed them before, but there they were; it looked like they stretched out all the way to River Road. When we left Bill, he was still cussing "the bastards." We decided to walk back by the road. Tucker said that since we all knew where the wading spot was, that it would be all right.

We figured they were planning to widen the road. That was pretty easy to figure, but when we got to River Road, there were two stakes that were bigger than any of the others. We puzzled over that. Finally, Laura said that she thought they were planning to put a gate there. And we all agreed that that was probably the case. Laura's eyes lit up. She started to laugh. Tucker asked her what was so damn funny. I pointed out that Bill wouldn't be able to get in or out if they put up a gate. She kept laughing. Tucker and I looked at each other and shook our heads with disgust.

"Let's move the gate," she said with a giggle and a wink.

"What gate you talking 'bout, girl?"

"Yeah, what gate?" I said.

She shook her head at us and put her hands on her hips.

"Just move the stake," she said. "Trust me."

She paced off the distance between the stakes as they were, and then kept walking until she had paced off the same distance on the other side of one stake. Then she turned to us and said, "Put that one, here." She pointed to her feet.

Tucker started laughing. "Girl, there's a ditch there. That's a low spot. Nobody would be that stupid. They'd have to move the road over. They don't want to do that."

She pointed her finger at one of the little stakes back in the grass. "Move that one there over to about there. That would be about right."

Tucker and I looked at each other and shrugged.

"Well, at least it'll screw 'em up for a while."

It sure did.

CHAPTER 7

THE LOFT

The next morning on the way to school, we drove right past a work crew standing around a dump truck. They were drinking coffee and smoking, but they had been digging. There was a guy, probably the foreman, looking at a clipboard and scratching his chin. That's all I saw, but I figured our little plan had been found out. I asked my father what he thought those guys were doing there. He didn't know.

Like I say, I figured they were on to us, but I was wrong. The day seemed to unravel from there. I screwed up a pop quiz. Almost got caught smoking in the parking lot, and then in the game, I went without a hit and overthrew third base and let a run score. We lost the game. Coach chewed me out and Albert hadn't showed up. I really had wanted to talk to him about the park. He always asked good questions, not like most guys, who started out already knowing the answers they wanted to hear. And besides, if he had been there, I bet we would have won. There was just something about Albert. In his quiet way, he wanted to win.

Fred and I were cruising home, not talking too much. It was clouding up and the air felt heavy. Fred teased me about getting him in trouble with Lucky. Turned out those sweets had cost him a washer and dryer. I teased him about holding out on me.

But mainly we just rolled along and smoked, Fred on his cigar and me on a Kool non-filter, which was about the only thing I didn't like about Fred. I hated those things, but a smoke's a smoke, and I was out. I wasn't even thinking about the stupid gate when we drove by. I was spitting tobacco flakes out the window when I saw it.

"Holy smokes! They did it!" I cried out without thinking.

"Did what?" Fred said.

I realized that maybe Fred wouldn't think Laura's joke was funny, so I tried to tone down, but it was hard to do because they had built the gate just like we'd planned. And what a gate! Two brick columns as tall as a man and a heavy black gate that opened out into a ditch. The gravel road lay there just as open as before. I held in my laughter.

"Well, they built a gate," I said, trying to sound cool about it. Fred gave me a look like he was trying to read me.

"What?" I said.

"What you know about that gate? If'n you knows anything about that gate, you might want to keep it close to your chest."

"What do you mean?" I asked. "Is something wrong?"

Fred didn't say anything right off. First, he pulled into the post office parking lot and turned around. When we got back to the gate, he eased onto Bill's road and stopped.

"Somebody's done stirred up a hornets' nest here. See how she's built?"

I nodded, barely able to swallow my grin.

"You better get your sunglasses out."

"What?" I asked, but Fred was onto me.

"Your eyes are talking. Don't give me this 'what?' I don't want to know nothing about it, you hear me? Not now anyway," he added with a smile.

So we drove on back to Bill's. He was out on his deck drinking his beer and he seemed glad to see us. When we walked up, he started pointing out toward the gate and bent over laughing. Fred put his hand on my shoulder and gave me a squeeze and a look. I just stood there, and Bill got himself together and offered us both a beer. Fred asked me if I had any mints, and I nodded that I did. Fred accepted for both of us.

Bill thought it was the funniest damn thing.

"The stupid jerks built the damn thing in the wrong place, and they built it like a brick shit house too. Hell, it might be steel reinforced. How could anybody be that dumb? I mean they're all mad as hell. The real estate guys want the contractor's head and the contractor wants theirs. And the Greens are mad as hell at both of them, and you can bet their lawyers are sharpening their knives. The cops have been here scratching their heads and poking around, and everybody's mad at them, because they thought it was funny at first. I mean, how the hell could anybody be so dumb as to build a gate that opens on a drainage ditch?"

We all shook our heads at this and took a swig. Bill went on about how the cops had asked him if he knew anything about it. He told them no, but that he thought it looked well built. They hadn't thought that was too funny. They asked him straight out if he had moved the stakes. He told them that even though he thought the road would look a little nicer with a curve there, that he was just as puzzled as anyone about the whole thing. They asked him if he had seen anything suspicious. Any strangers? He had said, "No sir." When he told us that, he looked directly at me. Fred tightened his grip. I just stood there.

"Fred, is our scholar going into engineering, road building, and such?"

"If he is, he's awful quiet about it."

"Good," Bill said. "If I wanted to be an engineer, I sure wouldn't claim that project."

Fred had to get me home. We didn't stay long, but before we left, Bill told us to watch the news. A film crew had been out. They had interviewed Bill about the gate. Bill figured they had found out about it from the cops. The reporter said it made good copy: a funny way to end the news. They had asked Bill how he liked his new entrance. Bill had told them it suited him just fine.

Fred seemed pretty jolly as we rolled on home. He was chuckling and shaking his head, teeth clamped down on his cigar stub, grinning. But as we were driving past the gas station, I saw Tuck and waved, but he didn't see me, so I asked Fred if we could go back so I could say hi to him. Fred took his stogie out of his mouth and gave me a hard look. He shook his head no.

"You better be watching yourself." He paused. "I can add two and two, and there's plenty other folks can, too. You hear me? You let on you think it's funny, and it sure as snuff won't be for you. In fact, you let on that it's not funny or any damn way, you'll start 'em thinking. There's lots of folks would like to cozy up to this and know something. You just lie low and don't let on to nothing. Hear?"

I promised I wouldn't, and before I went in the house, I popped a mint to hide the beer. I wanted to tell somebody. I wanted to stand on the roof and crow and howl and laugh. But I couldn't tell my brother and sister. Hell, they'd have something on me. My mother was on the phone, so I waved to her and motioned that I was going to ride my bike. She nodded. Off I went. I had to talk to Tucker. I rode back to the station, but he wasn't there. I bought a Coke and listened to some guys talking.

This one guy, Mickey, a couple of years older than me, couldn't say three words without cussing. He pumped gas after school and he was telling these two men about the new gate, and it was about all I could do to stand there and not bust out, because he was laughing his head off and cussing like a drunken pirate.

"Sons o' bitches, goddamn butt holes crapped their stinky-ass, mother-humping gateposts right in front of that shit hole ditch and then hung the gate right over the goddamn bastard!"

His eyes got real big and he pushed his greasy hands down the front of his jeans. "Goddamn, they was white boys. Not a nigger in the whole dumb-ass crew! Can you believe that stupid shit?"

I finished my Coke and took off. They were all laughing. As I was peddling off, I heard something like "Dumb cock-sucking coppers couldn't find their ass with both stinking hands says niggers done . . ."

That's all I heard him say. A car going past and then the wind in my ears drowned him out. I had to get hold of Tucker, and Laura too, I guessed.

Trouble was I didn't know where they lived. I wanted to warn them to keep quiet. I raced home, got a phone book, and took it to my room. I couldn't find anything that looked like it might be Tucker's number. I remembered Laura's last name was Green. I remembered that because it had struck me as odd that she would have the same name as the enemy. I tried looking up her number, but there were a million of them, or at least it seemed that way. Finally, I narrowed it down to about ten that I thought might be it, and as it turned out, I got her on the second try.

I tried to sound Negro, so nobody would be suspicious. I practiced a couple of times and then dove right in.

"Hello, is Lawraah thaah?"

"What? No! Nobody by that name lives here." Click.

"Halooo, is Lawraah thaah?"

"Yes, she is. May I please ask who's calling?"

"Yes'm, this is Jacob," I said.

"Laura's studying. This ain't a joke, is it?"

"Nome."

"What?"

"No, ma'am, I mean."

"Where'd you learn to talk, Jacob? You wait just a minute."

She clapped her hand over the phone, but I could hear her call anyway.

"Little Laura. Oh, little Laura."

Then some stuff that sounded like a cavalry charge and ricocheting bullets. Then Laura saying "Jacob who?"

"Hello?"

"Laura? Laura, this is Ed. Can you talk?"

"Of course I can talk. What's wrong with you?"

I could imagine her mother standing right beside her with her head cocked, listening. *Who is this Jacob that talks funny?*

"I mean, are you alone in the room. I mean, keep cool, don't let on, okay?"

"What you talking about?"

"Okay, Laura, don't say anything. Please, just trust me. They did it. They built the gate just like you figured they would. I saw it on the way home from school. Did you know?"

"No."

"Listen, we stirred up a mess of trouble. Everybody's talking about it. A lot of folks are mad as hell . . ."

"They really did it?"

"Shhhh! Yeah, just like you said, but we can't let on. Don't tell anybody, okay?"

She started laughing and saying she couldn't believe it. They really had done it? Ha, ha, ha. It was too funny. I told her it was going to be on the news, and then I asked her what Tucker's number was. She told me they didn't have a phone. I asked her if she could get the word to him about how important it was that we keep quiet. She laughed and said that he wasn't stupid, that he didn't want his backside burned. Then she laughed again when I told her to tell him that it was going to be on the news. I asked her what was so funny. No TV either.

"Mamma says you talk funny. Why did you tell her your name was Jacob?"

I stuttered out something stupid like I was just trying to cover my tracks, and she laughed at me and told me I was being silly. She said that she would see Tuck the next day on the bus, and then she decided we should have a powwow after school. But where? She asked me if I knew the old falling-down barn up on the hill that looked down on the creek. I did, but I was surprised that she did. It was on my grandfather's property. I asked her how she knew about it. She just chuckled and asked me if I thought she lived on Mars. I laughed and said no to that, but it struck me that I didn't know where she lived, so I asked her. She told me she lived almost right across from me. Across River Road, in the house painted white with the green roof.

Somehow, I felt like I should have known that, but I didn't. I had no idea where Tucker lived, and I was thinking how strange that was and, like she had read my mind, she told me that he lived up in Happy Hollow across the creek. We left off that we would meet around four thirty the next day. She was giggling when we hung up. I felt like an idiot.

For some damn reason, my ears were red and burning. I told myself I didn't care what she thought. I wasn't being silly. I wasn't afraid. I was just trying to warn them to be careful.

I almost never watched the news, so I was going to say that it was an assignment if anybody asked why I was watching. But both my mother and father thought it was good that I was taking an interest in the world and never said anything. There was all sorts of gobbledygook. Some senator from up east said something my father didn't like one bit, and he said he thought he was terrible. A dangerous man, is what he called him. I must have looked inquisitive. My father looked at me and said the man was a liberal, and the way he said it made me swallow hard. I knew that wasn't as bad as a communist, but it sounded pretty damn close. My mother sipped on her drink and said that he was a Democrat, and my father looked at her sternly and said "of the very worst ilk—a liberal Democrat." My mother nodded, and I did too.

At the tail end of everything, the newsman smiled and said something like, "Have you ever had one of those days?" Then he grinned. "Well . . ." Then there was a picture of the gateposts and gate and the ditch bigger than hell with the road off to the other side. "A day when you asked yourself how can you get there from here?" Then a picture of a man looking at a clipboard, scratching his head. "How could this happen?" Then a picture of the man with the clipboard waving *go away* and a voice says, "No comment." Then a picture of another man in a suit. "No comment." Then a picture of Bill. "Looks right well built, I would have to say." Then a picture of the gate and the road beside it leading back to Bill's, then back to newsman. "Just one of those days, folks. Keep smiling. Good night."

"Well, that wasn't so bad," my father said.

My mother asked him what he meant. He told her that that gate was on the Green property and that the damn fool farm manager and the real estate person had decided to put a gate up to secure the property, and that either they screwed up or the contractor did. But it turned out the thing he was relieved about was that some reporter had called him, since he was the Green family attorney, and wanted him to talk about the park and the will and all of that stuff. My father had refused, and the reporter had said there was going to be a segment about it on the six o'clock news. My father had expected all kinds of comment.

"They never get it right," he said.

The next morning, my father was reading the paper at the breakfast table when he suddenly burst out, "What in the world! I never said any such thing! The man's put words in my mouth."

The reporter, according to my father, was just trying to stir up trouble. My father was quoted as saying that there was absolutely no reason to discuss the possibility of a park, because there was no possibility. Most of the rest of it was rot, too. People saying what they'd heard about the will and the park. At the end of the article, some passerby was reported to have seen four Negro males moving the stakes. The reporter closed out by saying that although the police had no leads about the vandalism, that speculation was running high that it was the work of an angry Negro gang.

"Are the battle lines being drawn?" was how he ended it.

My father was disgusted. He said they were trying to make a federal case out of nothing, somebody's dumb mistake, or an act of petty hooliganism.

"They're just out to cause trouble," he said.

I was thinking to myself that at least people were thinking about the park, but of course, I kept it to myself. At school, Paul tried to tease me into admitting that I'd had something to do with the gate, but I didn't let on. I don't know whether he believed me or not. Nobody else said anything at all about it. I might have trusted Albert enough to tell him, but he was home sick again.

───────

When I got to the barn, Laura was already there. She was in the hayloft. Tucker wasn't. She explained that he was being punished. I felt a chill, but it was just that he had been in a fight at school. Some guy had called him a redskin nigger, and Tucker had cracked him. His mother had him home doing chores. I told her I thought it was terrible somebody called him that. She laughed and said, "What? A redskin? Or a nigger?" I think I said they shouldn't have called him either one, and she said they say "redskin" every night on TV. She brushed it off. She said he should have let it pass. The guy was just poor white trash anyway.

"The whole thing is silly," she said. "Indians ain't red. I'm not black, and that boy he hit is black and blue, all because of a bump in a hallway at school and no mind to say something simple like 'excuse me.'"

Then we started off on the gate, and we were laughing with our eyes all crinkled up and watery. I asked her how she knew they would do it, and she laughed and shook her head and smiled. Man, the light caught her face somehow and, for a second, I thought I saw a rainbow around it, and then I didn't. I must have been staring though, because she looked over her shoulder and then back at me in a way that asked me what I was looking at. I shrugged. She kept staring at me with a questioning look. I said nothing, but I wanted to tell her how beautiful she was. I didn't though. I just reached out and took her hand. She smiled and pointed at the other end of the loft. She said we could see everything from there: the whole park.

From the outside, the old barn looked like a big old gray thing with a rusty brownish-red roof. It looked like it had been there forever and like it would probably remain there forever. But it hadn't been kept up for years, and since my grandfather had died, it hadn't been kept up at all. Some farmers used it to store hay, but that was about it. On the side of the loft we were on, the boards were pretty good, but you had to watch where you stepped, because there were holes here and there. Well, anyway, she almost stepped into one and then I did. She got a scratch on her ankle, but I got one that ripped up my whole shin. It was sort of funny, but mine burned like hell. We plopped down on a hay bale and I was rocking back and forth, gritting my teeth and sort of laughing. She pulled up my pants leg and whistled. It was raw with little drops of blood popping up like beads.

I started to pull my pants leg down, but she stopped me and said that I would ruin my pants and then she counted the drops. There were ten. She said it wasn't fair, and she pointed to her ankle. She only had one. I told her she was lucky.

She was looking at me funny. I asked her what, but she just smiled. She asked me to hold her hand again. She told me she had liked it when I had held it before. Did I think she was being dumb? I told her no and couldn't take my eyes off her, her eyes, her lips, the little line that was raised and sort of lighter that surrounded them. She looked away. I put my hand on hers, and she turned her hand over, and our fingers slid together. She looked at me quickly and then away.

"You keep looking at me funny," she said.

"So do you," I said and squeezed her hand.

She squeezed back. I felt like clearing my throat, but I didn't. I just sat there and listened to somebody hammering something way off in the distance and some voices so far away they might have been whispers.

"I like you," she said.

"I like you, too," I said.

I was thinking about kissing her, and it was a crazy mixed-up feeling that made me feel all tight down on my wrists and up in my shoulder, and I noticed some place behind my ears that I had never taken into account before. There were other things too, but before I got around to figuring them all out, I snuck a peek at her (I had been staring straight ahead out into the branches of a gnarly old locust outside the loft door) and she was looking at me.

"You thinking what I am?" she asked, real quietly.

"Maybe," I said and then I cleared my throat, trying to make my voice sound right. "I mean, I think I am."

She blinked and looked down a little and we turned just a fraction closer.

"Is it wrong? It isn't, is it?" she whispered.

I swallowed and the corners of her lips turned up slightly, and she touched the bottom of her upper lip with the tip of her tongue, and her eyes looked like they were laughing and something else that I wasn't so sure I had seen before. Not really scary, but it made me feel my own eyes, which felt like they were stuck and held in place by some kind of pressure pushing in a circle from the inside out. It made my forehead tingle. My earlobes burned and my ears were jangling.

"No, you don't want to?" She looked down.

"No. No," I whispered. She started loosening her fingers. I gripped her fingers and felt the slick moistness between us. "No, shhhh, shhhh," I said. "I mean, I don't think it's wrong, if we want to. Do you?"

We moved a little nearer.

"I want to," she said.

We both moved at once, and at first, we kind of bumped our lips together, so that we both pulled back and our eyes were laughing, but I don't think we said anything. We just kissed and slipped our arms around each other. Our tongues touched and I thought that maybe she didn't like that. It had been a mistake, or an accident, I should say. I had never French kissed before. But it felt good and I wanted to do it again, and in a minute or so, I got my courage up and parted my lips and touched hers with my tongue, and they parted. It was wonderful. As if a hand had gently clasped us and pushed us over, we reclined into the straw. We kissed and kissed, but then my hands got a little carried away, and she stopped me.

"We better stop," she whispered. I tried to kiss her again and she let me, but she sat up and started brushing the straw out of her hair. She wasn't mad.

"You're not mad at me?" she asked.

I shook my head.

"Mamma would kill me if anything happened."

I shook my head. "What's going to happen? We were just kissing."

She looked at me sort of sideways and down. She smiled and puckered her lips and blew out some air. I breathed in, shrugged, and exhaled.

"Oh, it's not that bad," she said.

"What's not?" I asked.

She laughed. "You know? We got to be careful. At least I do. Don't you try to tell me you were so stirred up you didn't know where your hands were?" She smiled. She didn't seem upset.

"Do you think that would be wrong?"

"I don't know. They all say so." She laced her fingers together and rocked forward. She turned and looked at me. "You look like a scarecrow." I gave her a look. She laughed. "Your hair. At least one side of you does. You even have straw sticking out of your collar."

I brushed at my hair and she fussed over me a bit. I tried to kiss her again, but the mood was broken. We sat there. There were some pigeons scratching and cooing on the tin roof overhead. A crow cawed to his mates and a chorus of caws answered him. I felt like I should say something, but I didn't know what. You could still hear hammering off in the distance, but it didn't sound like anybody was building something. Thump, thump, thump, and then thump.

"What's that hammering sound?" I asked her.

She looked at me and shrugged. I shrugged too. The crows started going crazy. She touched my hand, more of a tap than a touch.

"You don't think it was . . ." I started to say.

She raised her fingers to her lips. "Shhhh. Someone's here," she whispered.

"Hey! Anybody home?"

It was Tucker. Laura stood up quickly and started brushing off.

"Nobody here, but us chickens," Laura called out with a musical giggle.

He scrambled up the ladder and his head popped up through the floor. He looked around like he expected to see something strange.

"What you looking for? Ghosts?" Laura asked. "Come on up."

"What you all doing up here?"

"Tending to the wounded," Laura said, pointing to me. "What're you doing here? Thought you was locked up this afternoon?"

"Well, I was," he said, "but I busted out."

"Tucker," Laura said with her hands on her hips, "your mamma is gonna whup you good now." He climbed the rest of the way up and started toward us, and before he had taken two steps, his foot went into a hole, but he caught himself.

"Damn, this place is a booby trap," he said, sitting down and massaging his ankle.

"Your mamma's going to tan your hide," Laura said.

He shook his head. "Naw, she's not. She had to go downtown with Miss Hays and do some business with Daddy. She'll be a while yet."

"Again?" Laura said quietly.

Tucker just nodded. "Damn that smarts!"

"Now, Tucker, hush your mouth. You know you wasn't raised to cuss."

He rolled his eyes and smiled at me. "You hush, girl! Come tend to the wounded."

Laura shook her head and let out a deep sigh. "Men," she said, and she shook her head again. Then she gave me a wink.

CHAPTER 8

ACE OF SPADES

Hawk was in jail. Fred told me while we were waiting for my brother and sister to come out to the car. I had asked him what business Hawk had besides music. Fred squinted up, looked at me, and chewed his cigar.

"What was he doing downtown with Miss Hays?" I asked.

He continued to look at me like something was darkening behind his eyes.

"Where'd you get that information?" Fred asked.

"Where did I get that?" I shrugged and said, "From Johnny Tucker."

He breathed out some smoke and his eyes got big, then small.

"Hawk's got himself locked up again," he said. "What you know about it?"

"Nothing."

"It ain't right, no way, no matter how dumb he can be."

I asked what happened and Fred said Hawk had bumped some white lady with his guitar case on his way from the bus stop and he had been drinking. The lady made some kind of big deal, and a policeman saw it and hauled him in for being drunk and a public nuisance. Trouble was, it wasn't the first time.

"Man just can't learn to keep his mouth shut," Fred said. "Must be the Indian in him." Fred shook his head and said that the woman who made all the ruckus was no damn good. Fred never cussed. I looked at him hard.

"She's a bad woman. White's got bad, too, you know?" I nodded. "She ain't nothin' but a downtown whore. I'm sorry, but that is the truth."

"So what's it mean?" I asked.

"Thirty days, most likely. It ain't right. Man going to work. Shee-it."

"So the business about Miss Hays and him, that Tucker was talking about was . . .?"

"To try to get him out," Fred said, "but it didn't work."

They held him over for trial, and Fred said he'd have to serve if something special didn't happen. They'd fine him and most likely, he wouldn't be able to pay, so he'd have to serve.

I asked Fred what kind of a job Hawk had been going to, and he shook his head and said he just played the joints and that some of 'em paid a few bucks and gave him food and drinks, and some of 'em just gave him drinks and let him pass the hat.

"The man don't like to hear that," Fred said. "The bail man don't either. He'll do time most likely."

"You mean, if he had a different job or just had the money, he probably wouldn't have to?"

Fred nodded.

"That's not right," I said.

"Naw, it ain't right, but that's how it is. He knowed it. He shoulda kept his trap shut."

"Well, what exactly did he say?" I asked.

Fred grinned around his cigar and winked. He looked like he was chuckling in spite of himself.

"Now, you keep this to yourself, 'cause it ain't that nice. He called the white woman out loud for what she is. He called her 'a stinky-ass ten-cent skunk slut.'" I started laughing "That ain't all. That ain't all." He was laughing, too.

"Well, what?" I asked.

"He called the copper 'a cracker skunk, Dudley Do-right, bot-tom-licking motherfucker.'"

"Jesus Christ! He didn't! To a cop?"

Fred nodded and his belly jiggled trying to hold in his joy.

I burst out with a war hoop of laughter. "Oh, my God! He's screwed."

Fred nodded. "Most likely."

I was wondering why Tucker hadn't gone into it. All he had said was something about business downtown. I asked Fred. He looked at me, shook his head, and said he reckoned Tucker was ashamed. Fred shook his head again. My brother and sister climbed into the back seat. Fred said it just wasn't right. My brother and sister wanted to know what wasn't right. Fred gave me a look. I made up some nonsense that didn't fool anybody, and they both complained that nobody ever told them anything.

They were still complaining when we rolled past the gate. There was a big "No Trespassing" sign driven into the ground beside Bill's road. Fred motioned at it with his head. I nodded. Turns out the hammering I'd heard from the hayloft the day before was a couple of guys nailing up "Keep Out" signs all up and down the creek. From the loft, we watched them. They must have nailed up about thirty. Of course, we couldn't read the signs from that distance, so out of curiosity, we walked down across the bottom land and read them from across the creek.

"We'll see about that!" Tucker said. Then one of the guys who was putting the signs up stopped hammering, looked up, and saw us. My first inclination was to run, but I fought it.

"Just act like nothing," I said.

Tucker flipped a beer bottle into the creek and Laura fired a rock at it and almost hit it. The man leaned against the tree he had been posting the sign on and watched us. We acted like we didn't even know he was there. We pretended to be interested in the bottle bobbing and lazing downstream. The man started walking toward us. He got right in line with the bottle. There was no way to act like we didn't see him. He stood there and grinned. I waved at him and said howdy do. He shook his head and just grinned.

"You all kids, get your butts out of here. This is posted land."

He didn't say it real loud, but the way he said it sounded like he damn well meant it. He reminded me of old Hatchet Head. There was something about his voice that was dry and nasty.

"This land here ain't no posted land," Tucker said.

"What you know 'bout posted land, cotton top? I said haul your asses out of here."

My ears were burning. "This ain't your land," I yelled.

The man grinned bigger, lifted up his hammer, and put it in his other hand. He reached into his pocket and pulled out a pistol real slow. He pointed it right about at our feet. We were looking from one to the other like our feet were frozen to the ground. He kept grinning and lowered the pistol, closed one eye, and took aim on the bottle. He fired. It sounded like a cannon. I never knew a pistol could be that loud. There was a splash of torn-up water where the bottle had been.

"Let's get out of here," Laura said.

We looked at each other and slowly started to walk off. I expected him to say something at our backs, but he didn't say a word. We were madder than hell, but we didn't show it until we were pretty far off.

"That sucker is crazy," Tucker said. "Did you see his eyes?"

"He had no right to do that. This used to be my grandparents' land. This isn't those people's land."

Tucker was furious. He said if he'd had a gun, he would have dropped the bastard, and Laura told him to hush up. But Tucker had had it. He vowed he was going to get the guy somehow. Laura said the best way to deal with folks like that was to stay away from them.

Tucker kicked at the grass like it was the guy's head and yelled out, "You can't run forever, girl." She shook her head. "We got to do something!" he said quietly.

We didn't walk straight back the way we came, in case he was watching us. We hopped a broken-down barbed wire fence and traipsed along it until we came to the wooded hillside below my house and my grandfather's house, and we doubled back there and ended up at the barn.

We went back up into the loft and the light was pouring through the big loft opening. We walked to it and managed to avoid all of the holes. We looked down on the park and could see our man swinging a sledge as his partner held the stake. Thump. Thump. Thump. Thump. Our man dropped the sledge to the ground and leaned on it, as "thump," the last blow of the sledge reached our ears.

I think we all felt helpless. I know I did. Tucker kicked the side of the barn. Laura poked me in the ribs and said that Tuck wanted to break his own foot just to spite the man. I didn't know what to say. I felt sort of in the middle. I was mad, but I didn't really feel like the man was the problem, not really. Just a small part of it somehow.

Then I got an idea. I asked them if they ever snuck out at night. Laura said no and Tucker gave me a funny look. Well, anyway, to get to the point, I asked them if they could meet me at midnight the next night. They wanted to know why and I told them I wasn't sure, but could they each bring a hammer? A hammer? I nodded. Laura told me I was crazy.

Tucker laughed. "What you think you gonna do, build the museum all by yourself?"

"No," I told him. "We're gonna drive somebody crazy."

"Who?" Tucker asked. I winked.

"Him?"

I nodded again. "Why not? It'll mess 'em up for a while."

He grinned. Laura looked puzzled.

"What are we gonna do?" she asked.

I told her I wasn't 100 percent sure, but I reminded her that we had done what she wanted. "Well, it worked, didn't it?" She nodded. "Trust me. Bring a hammer."

Laura asked how we were gonna see where we were going.

"The moon. It's a half-moon," I said.

"I can see in the dark," Tucker said.

"Then it's done."

We all nodded.

As we walked toward the ladder, Tucker led the way. Laura grabbed my hand and squeezed it. I leaned toward her and tried to sneak a kiss. She smiled at me, but pulled away, shaking her head, pointing with her free hand at Tucker.

"Careful, lovebirds. The shadow knows, and he don't lie," Tucker said as he pointed at our shapes splashed on the far wall. He laughed and shrugged, shook his head.

Laura put her free hand over her mouth and looked down. Then she looked at me and winked. As he was climbing down the ladder, Tucker looked at us and rolled his eyes. He shook his head and slowly closed them. He didn't wait for us at the bottom. He just took off running. Over his shoulder he yelled, "Midnight."

We stood at the foot of the ladder and watched him zigzag up the road. Laura said that she felt silly. I told her she shouldn't. She lowered her head a little, smiled, and said, "But I do anyway, straw man." Then she plucked a straw out of my hair and put it in the pocket of her blouse. "Do you really have a plan? Or are you just kidding?"

"I think so," I said.

We walked through the shadow of the barn and into the sunlight. When Tucker turned the corner up ahead, she turned to me and we kissed again quickly. Then she laughed and playfully pushed me away and told me that was enough for one day. I shook my head and kicked up some dust, but I felt pretty good. So did our shadows. They were holding hands.

———

Fred was puffing on his stogie, my brother and sister were talking about something in the back, and I guess I was thinking about Laura. Fred asked me if the cat had got my tongue. I shook my head no and told him I was just thinking. Truth is, what I was thinking about, I couldn't tell him. In fact, it didn't seem like there was anybody I could tell. Didn't seem like anybody would understand. I could barely understand it myself. *A colored girlfriend?* My friends would think I was crazy. Some of them would think it was disgusting. *Kissing a colored girl?* I could hear 'em. *Yuck!* They would give me a load of shit, and Fred—I looked at him—I just didn't think he would think it was right. Then I wasn't really sure what I felt about it. I imagined the feel of her lips and I saw her face like I saw it in the barn, and her smile and the way her hand felt, strong and smooth, and I must have let out a sigh, and then I caught Fred looking at me kind of funny.

"It's nothing," I said.

"Sounds to me like you've got some kind of spring fever," he said. "You just watch yourself."

I nodded, trying to look serious, but we were already at school so I didn't have to say anything. When I got out of the car, Fred seemed like he was thinking about something, too. I wondered if he knew somehow. I wanted to tell somebody, but who? The way Tucker had acted, I wasn't even sure how *he* would feel about it.

Finally, at midmorning, I bumped into Albert by the soda machine. I told him I needed to talk to him about something. We decided to skip study hall and meet in the locker room, which we figured would be empty. But it wasn't. Old Hatchet Head was down there measuring with a tape measure, but he didn't see us, so we snuck out the back of the gym and cut out to this place behind some bushes where we couldn't be seen.

I didn't tell him about Laura all at once. I was going to tell him about the park and all the stuff that had happened first and then sort of ease into the Laura stuff, but as soon as we sat down, I noticed that Albert was even paler than usual. I don't know, kind of almost hollow, and something about his eyes, not glassy really, but sort of shiny, just different. I asked him if he'd been sick. He said, "Yeah— sort of achy and tired." I asked him if he was all right. He nodded and said that he guessed so, but he had to have some tests. I asked him what kind. He shrugged and said he didn't know. He asked me what

I wanted to talk about, so I told him about the park, which he knew a little about. Then I told him how I felt about it, that it really ought to be in honor of the Underground Railroad and the Negro soldiers who had fought in all the wars.

Albert heard me out and then asked me what chance I really thought that idea had. I told him I didn't know. He shook his head and said he couldn't see it. I protested that it was only fair, and he agreed, but then he pointed out that the NCAA tournament couldn't be held here or anywhere in the state of Kentucky, because some of the teams had colored players and some teams wouldn't play 'em, and no hotels would put them up. I didn't know about that. I told him that was awful. He nodded, but by the time he said the rest of the stuff he said, I felt like it was hopeless. I hadn't thought about a lot of the stuff before. Segregation was a word I hadn't heard very often, and when I did hear it, I hadn't thought too much about what it really meant.

I never did get around to telling him about Laura and kissing and all that. I did tell him about the gate and the guy with the gun, but I think he figured out that something was going on between Laura and me, because he told me to be careful, but then he grinned. I asked him what he meant. Did he think I was crazy to get all involved in this stuff? He shook his head and said, "Nah, not crazy," then he shook his head again. "You just got to do what feels right to you."

As we were walking back to the gym, he asked me if this Laura was pretty, and I felt like a chicken when I told him that I guess she was, in her own way. He slapped me on the back and told me to get off it. I'm pretty sure he saw straight through me. I asked, "What?" He laughed and pointed to his eyes. "What?" I pointed to *my* eyes.

He nodded and smiled. "You can't fool me." He bumped me with his shoulder.

"Who's trying to fool anybody?" I said.

"You," he said and smiled.

The rest of the day went so smoothly it was almost spooky. I didn't get close to any trouble, and that was unusual. Mr. Fenway walked over to me after lunch and told me that he had finally had a chance to read my report about the dead cow, and he told me that he thought it was pretty well written, but he said he still couldn't figure out what I was doing out there, wandering around in the dark. Then he sort of smiled and closed his eyes and turned away. Math tutoring went okay, except that I was told we would have to go all the way back to the beginning, but I knew that anyway. Practice was all right, except Albert got dizzy and had to quit, and that wasn't good, with a game coming up and all.

Like I said, everything was smooth. It stayed that way until just about dinnertime when I was up in my room, pretending to do homework. I was actually preparing for the midnight adventure. I got this idea to make a stencil of the ace of spades that Mr. Traylor had given me. At first, I didn't really know why.

I was going to make a few replicas out of laundry shirt cardboard. I had India ink and an X-acto knife. I went to work and got carried away and made twenty or thirty of them. I was just scrubbing off the ink when I heard my father come in, but what was funny was that he came in through the front door. Then I heard him talking to somebody, and then I heard two or three other voices besides his. Something told me to listen, and I did. I went to the top of the stairs and could hear pretty well, because they were right beneath me in the living room.

My father was saying that first, nobody was going to sue anybody. "Get that straight?"

Somebody else said something about hundreds of dollars, and this other voice said something about principles, and then another voice—one that sort of made me feel funny inside—said something about being a laughingstock. I could hear my father saying "Gentlemen, gentlemen." The voice that rubbed me wrong said it was niggers sure as hell, and he was damned certain he weren't going to be the butt end of some ornery dumb-ass nigger joke, a laughingstock.

"Gentlemen, gentlemen," my father said again. "Please hear me out. They have already agreed that the gate must be moved."

"Not on my dollar! I mean it, and I ain't taking blame. It was niggers that done it."

Something told me to hightail it, and something else got me itching to have a look at these characters. I almost started downstairs right then, but my brother stuck his head out of his room and asked me what was going on. I told him I didn't know, but that brought me to my senses a bit. I went back to my room, got my reading glasses out of the drawer, put them on and also put on an old baseball cap. I grabbed my math book for good measure and stole a peek in the mirror. Looked just like a bookworm. Something told me to play it safe. I slipped downstairs and crossed over to a part of the hall where I could see the room reflected in the mirror. There was my dad standing by the fireplace, scratching his brow and shaking his head. He said, "We don't want to make a mountain out of a mole hill, do we?" And then that voice that rubbed me wrong said something like "How would you like to be called a jackass?"

I watched my father stiffen and his eyes got big.

"Now wait just a minute," my father said.

All of a sudden, my mother was right beside me, holding a tray with some beers on it. She told me to put the book down and take the tray into the next room. I tried to shake her off, but she wouldn't have it. So the next thing I know I'm serving beer, and I just about drop the tray, 'cause it was him, Hatchet Head's twin, the guy with the gun. I swallowed hard, walked right up to him, and served him first, and when I turned away, I felt like he had his damn beady eyes poking the back of my neck. My father introduced me. Turns out they were all there—the contractor, the real estate agent, and the farm manager, Mr. Damon Hoyt.

When I was introduced to him, he wasn't looking at me. He was sort of looking down, so I figured it was just my imagination playing tricks, but then he looked up—right at me—and sort of tilted his head. He didn't say anything, though. I was walking out of the room and my mother was walking in with potato chips and pretzels, and I figured I was in the clear when he just comes out and says, "Say, son, haven't I seen you someplace before?"

Thank God for old Hatchet Head, or I might not have been able to pull it off. That was just the kind of stunt he would have pulled. Let you get about halfway out of his clutches and then spring his blindside trap. I stopped and walked back into the room and looked him over and said, "Maybe. Maybe down at Creekside Auto or maybe the post office." I told him he did look sort of familiar. Then I shook my head and shrugged. He shook his head, too, and then he said something about a couple of nigger kids with some white boy snooping around. My father said something like, "Surely you don't think my boy would . . ."

That's all I heard. I stashed the tray, went down in the basement, and got my hammer and a box of nails. I stashed them out in the garage. Albert was right. Maybe I was dreaming. There were a whole lot of people like Damon Hoyt. Nigger this and nigger that. Here a nigger, there a nigger, come here, boy, jungle bunny, cotton top. How would you like it if someone called you a jackass? Ha, ha, ha!

A lightbulb went off. I dashed back up to my room. I tore the last shirt cardboard out of my drawer, took down my Golden Bible Stories picture book, flipped through it until I found the picture of Jesus riding on an ass, and sat down at my desk. I exaggerated the donkey's ears, and I made the eyes mean. I put a rough-looking cigarette hanging out of his buck-toothed mouth. I made his butt rude, and beneath it signed "by order of J. Ass, farm manager." I was cackling with glee when I heard my mother call that dinner was ready. I hadn't even heard the idiots leave.

At dinner, my little brother asked why those people were so loud. He was only seven and very shy. He thought they sounded bad. My sister, who was eleven, told him that they were cussing. My mother looked up from carving her meat and asked her what she had heard. My sister shook her curly head and said it wasn't nice.

"They said 'nigger,'" she said.

My father said, "We don't use that word in this house, ever, do you understand?" He looked around sternly and then nodded. We all nodded back. He said, "We say 'colored people' and 'Negro,' if we want to be correct, because that is what they like to be called."

My mother asked if we knew what a colored woman liked to be called. My brother and sister shrugged and shook their heads. I kept chewing. I felt my father looking at me funny, like he was thinking about something.

"A Negress," my mother said.

"A Negress?" my sister said, laughing. "That sounds funny."

My brother shrugged.

"That's what they like to be called. The toney ones, anyway," my mother said.

"Well, anyway," my father said, "we don't talk like those folks. It is an unfortunate state of affairs. There are a lot of ignorant people in the world."

I should have kept chewing, but in my mind, I saw that bottle blow up, and then I thought about that stupid catcher insulting Fred. I opened my big mouth and said, "You can say that again."

My father asked me what I meant. I said, "The same as you. The guy was obviously dumb as a post and mean by the look of him."

My father looked at me hard and said, "What guy?"

I looked down and said, "The skinny one. The guy with all the teeth."

My father said, "The manager, Mr. Hoyt?" I nodded. He looked me over and cut off a bite. "What do you know about him?"

"Nothing. I don't know nothing about him."

"*Anything*," my father said.

"I mean *anything*," I said.

"You're not involved in this in any way, are you? You're not running with the coloreds, are you?"

Before I could answer, my sister said, "Don't you mean Negroes, Daddy?"

But one look silenced her and she looked down at her plate.

"Answer me," he said.

"No way," I said. "What do you think I am?"

He looked me over good and forked the bite into his mouth, shook his head. "I don't like that man either. Negroes," he said, "must be kept in their place, but men like that do no good at all. All they want to do is stir up trouble."

We all nodded. I looked down the table at my mother who was smiling, nodding, and looking side to side at all of us.

"They are just not like us at all," she said.

My father nodded quickly. "That's right," he said.

The grass felt mushy. The breeze was soft and smooth against my cheeks. My light was the moon, and it was unsteady. The clouds collided and overwhelmed it every few seconds. Pale outlines, then black as pitch. It was no problem here. I knew the way. Step by step, practicing silence, I avoided branches and roots tossed in my way. I could have taken the road, and would have, if the dog had not barked and pinned me down. I scratched behind her ears, whispering that everything was going to be all right. The shortcut was quicker. I had no choice.

I wasn't wearing black. I wore a dark blue sweater and blue jeans. I carried my tools in a pouch my father had used in the war. It had been for maps. USMC was inked on the cover. The rough canvas strap dug into my neck and rubbed, but it felt right somehow.

We were to meet at the dead locust tree on the curve before the road headed back to the barn. From there, I figured we would go to Tucker's crossing spot and then get to work. They had it easy. All they had to do was walk down the lane and duck if any cars came by, which they wouldn't this time of night. When the moon went out, I was stuck with my memory. I clambered over things and bumped into a few. But the clouds were moving fast and weren't too dense, so I was moving along right on time. I could feel it in my bones.

I cut through some old overgrown boxwoods and my toes scratched gravel, and as soon as they did, Tucker said, "Shut up, keep it down."

"What?" I said to his shape that was crouching down in the road. He motioned me over. From where we were, we could see down on the park. Not the whole thing, but the part by the road and the main sign. He pointed. There were lights there. Taillights.

"Who do you think it is?"

"How would I know?" he answered like he was mad.

I listened but I couldn't hear anything. Some crickets, some leaves rustling. No voices.

"Where's Laura?" I asked. I figured she would have come with him.

He looked at me funny with small eyes.

"Well, where is she? Is she coming?"

"How the hell would I know? She's your girlfriend, isn't she?"

What to say? I didn't know what to say, I said, "Maybe, but where is she? Is she coming?"

We both heard the gravel scrape at the same time and there she was.

"Where you been, girl? You're late," Tucker said. "Your boyfriend here has been worried about you."

"Don't you mess with me, Tuck. You got no cause to mess with me and you know it."

My ears were sort of burning. Tucker squirmed and said he was just kidding. Laura told him he better keep his kidding to himself, there was work to be done. So we discussed my plan. Inside the barn, I took out my flashlight and showed them the cards I had made. I saved the jackass for last. They laughed when I told them what had happened with old Damon Hoyt.

"You had to look that devil right in the face?" Laura asked.

"Yep," I said. "I had no choice."

She shook her head and drew in her breath. Tucker said he would have kicked the guy's ass. I told him we were going to do worse than that. We were going to drive him nuts. *How?*

"Well, we're going to nail these cards up right over the top of their 'Keep Out' signs, and then, for a grand finale, nail the jackass right out front on the 'No Trespassing' sign." I told them old Hoyt would run around telling everybody that some gang was involved and just make a total ass of himself. They liked that part, but we had a problem. The truck was still parked at the entrance. I couldn't see that it was a truck, but Tucker could. He asked me if jackass drove a truck, and I didn't know. So we sat around in the barn, and Tucker and I smoked, but Laura wouldn't do it. She said it was stinky.

We didn't have to wait too long before the truck left. Then we had to get Laura across the creek and that was a bitch. Hell, getting there was a bitch. The moon decided to play tricks and hid most of the way to Tucker's crossing place. Neither Laura nor I could see where we were going, and Tucker slipped off ahead of us. We banged into stuff and got whipped by branches until finally, in a loud whisper, Laura had insisted that he come back and lead us. We ended up holding hands, with me at the rear. Tucker acted put out and I felt dumb being pulled this way and that, stumbling along, but not wanting to complain.

Then we got to the creek and it was the strangest thing. Laura wouldn't take her clothes off. Hell, it was dark as pitch. The moon was just a faint glow through a dark cloud. But she drew the line, nope, and that was that.

Anyway, we got her across the creek. She carried our clothes and we carried her. Turns out we didn't need the hammers. Laura was worried we would wake up Bill. Tucker said the old fool was dead drunk asleep anyhow by now, and Laura had said that that was no way to talk, and Tucker had said, "Girl, if that man wasn't a white man, if that man was a neegrow, he would be arrested and in the joint seven days a week."

But we didn't need the hammers, because the nails weren't driven in all the way. Tucker wanted to pry the no-trespassing signs off, but I didn't like that idea and neither did Laura. We just ended up hanging our aces of spades on the nails, and then we did have to nail in our jackass sign, but it took only one or two whacks.

It was funny, like Tucker could see in the dark. I mean, this was my idea and my plan, but once we got there, he was totally in charge. The moon didn't really come clear until we were starting back across the creek, and then Tucker and I were joking about carrying the river queen across the water, when she started peeling down. The two of us looked at each other with disbelief. He said, "What is with you, girl? The moon is like a spotlight now." Laura just laughed. Her eyes reflected some of that spotlight, which poured a clear path across the muddy old creek. She stood up, stripped down to her underwear, and was the first one into the creek.

"It ain't you all that scares me. It's the dark," she said.

CHAPTER 9

KEEP IT SIMPLE

I snuck back in the house without a hitch. I was chuckling inside even as I tiptoed up the back stairs. I could hardly wait to hear the buzz around the creek. I think I fell asleep wanting to bust out laughing. I was proud of my jackass sign that was going to drive old Hoyt nuts and our ace of spades calling cards were going to make him come up with all kind of craziness. I could hardly wait to hear the rumors fly.

Next morning on the way to school, I looked for my sign, but it was gone, so I figured he had already found it. I felt like chirping like a spring bird. I couldn't wait till after school. We were going to meet up at Creekside Auto and listen in on the gossip. Also, Tucker said it was his turn to come up with something. I was wondering what that might be. The next step. First, piss 'em off. Second step, make 'em madder, confuse 'em and drive 'em crazy. Third step was up to Tucker.

I must have been kind of laughing under my breath, because the next thing I know, Fred is asking me what's up. Instinctively, I said, "Nothing," just like Fred was any other grown-up. He sort of wrinkled up his forehead and chewed on his stogie. His eyes got little.

"Just thinking," I said.

He nodded, but didn't say anything. Something didn't feel right, and I didn't quite know what it was. I stared out the window at the new green leaves. I felt the wind in my hair. I stared straight out over my shoulder and watched the leaves turn into a smear of solid green. I couldn't tell him what we'd done. That bugged me, but I just couldn't. I wanted to see how it played out first. But I needed to say something. We always talked. Hell, I told Fred everything. If I didn't talk, he would know something was up.

"Any news on Hawk?" I asked.

"He's out."

"Out! How?"

"Hays talked to the Green girl, and she agreed to put up the bond, and I think maybe your daddy might have something to do with it. Anyway, he was supposed to be out this morning first thing."

"My father had something to do with it?"

Fred nodded. "That's what the word is. Your father is good people and he works things in his own way, and a lot of it is unseen and unknown. There's things happening now. This is a small thing, but it's connected up to bigger things, if you know what I mean."

I didn't know what he meant, but I took a guess. "You mean the park?"

Fred shrugged. My sister asked what park we were talking about and Fred said he wasn't exactly talking about a park. Besides, he mumbled, "Parks is just a small part of a picture that's a whole lot bigger." My sister wanted to know what picture. I did too, I guess, but I didn't want to sound dumb, so I kept my mouth shut. Fred puffed on his stogie and blew out a cloud that whirled across my face and out the window. He winked and nodded.

———

School dragged along. The clocks moved slowly. Lunch was grubby. Classes were ordinary and practice was dull. Albert was sick again.

At the end of practice, Haghead called me aside. He put his arm on my shoulder, which was weird, and walked me down the third base line away from the others. He didn't say anything. When we got to third base, he stopped and we faced each other. He told me to be quick in the shower and meet him in the headmaster's office. Pronto. He said it would just take a couple of minutes. I must have given him a funny look. *What did I do?* He read me. He told me to be there. He said I hadn't done anything. There was nothing for me to worry about. Just be there. Pronto! Then I swear he turned his head away, but I could still see that his eye was full of tears. Hurry up! Pronto! He turned all the way away from me, and I don't know why, but I ran like hell all the way back to the gym.

You know what it's like when you're in a Superman hurry? Seems like mostly everything decides to tangle you up and get in your way. Doors. The gym door was stuck. I got it open, but if I had been stronger, I would have pulled it all the way off its hinges and thrown it aside. The locker room was full of bodies and horseplay. Rat tails in the shower and the place packed and everybody poking and whistling different tunes. I decided to skip the shower. I peeled off the uniform okay, but when I tried to jump into my pants, I somehow managed to step into them backwards. Well, as I was hopping around, everybody was laughing and shoving. Then, red as a beet, probably with shame and anger, I cussed at them all and, of course, that just made it worse.

"What's the rush? Where do you think you're going in such a hurry?"

I tried to ignore them. But then my shoes were missing, and if Andy hadn't clued me in with a motion of his head, I wouldn't have known they were on top of the lockers. Well, anyway, I charged out of there as fast as I had charged in.

"What's *his* problem?"

I didn't know what the problem was, but I knew there was one. Never before had I hurried to the headman's office without someone by my side encouraging me. When I got there, Hagman was standing in the doorway. I was breathing hard, and he put his hand on my shoulder and guided me into the office. Mr. Fenway sat behind his desk puffing on his pipe, and the smoke floated across the room like a layer of clouds. His eyes were closed as usual, and nothing about him gave off any clues. Hagman guided me to a chair. I sat down and he stood beside me with his hand still on my shoulder. Nobody said anything.

After forever, Hagman cleared his throat and Fenway sort of twitched and cleared his as well. Then his eyes opened to sparkling slits, fluttered, and then shut again. He took a puff on his pipe and carefully laid it in the ashtray.

"Son, it befalls to every man the time of being the recipient of sobering and altogether unwelcome news."

I guess he wanted this to sink in, because he didn't say anything for at least a minute. I felt like screaming, and when he finally did speak, I couldn't even make a sound.

"Your friend, Albert, is gravely ill. He will live no more than a few days. There is nothing to be done about it. We can pray, of course, and we should, but he has leukemia of the most pernicious kind. There is no earthly hope for him. I'm sorry to have to be the one to tell you this."

Hagman's hand was still on my shoulder. He squeezed it pretty hard and I looked up at him and he poked out his chin like he was standing at attention. I felt like I was dreaming. I took a deep breath after I realized I had been holding it. I looked around this way and that. I don't know what I expected to see. I saw the smoke swirling. I shook my head. I think I laughed. I know I laughed, and then I looked right at Fenway.

"You're kidding? You made this up?" Even as I said it, I knew he wasn't joking, but I said it anyway. "You're just kidding?"

He shook his head, but said nothing. Nobody did. I took some more deep breaths, but this time I wasn't trying. They just came one after the other, all by themselves.

Mr. Fenway started talking, but I could barely hear him. I heard him say "hospital" and then he said that Albert wanted me to do something for him.

"He has chosen you to be the one to break the news to his classmates and teammates. And he wants to talk to you before you do it."

I was just sitting there, shaking my head. I couldn't believe any of this was happening.

"I believe you will be surprised at how well he is taking this. He has accepted it. I have a number that you can call."

I stood up and took the scrap of paper that he held out to me.

"When should I call?"

"Now. Use the phone in the next room. Close the door if you want to."

"Right now?"

He nodded. His eyes flickered open. "Just be yourself. Go on."

I walked out of the room. Hagman had his back to me and was staring out the window. There was a big fly on the dusty pane just sitting there. It's funny how you notice things sometimes. There was some lipstick on the mouthpiece of the telephone. I started to dial the number, but I couldn't see it. It was all bleary. I wiped my eyes and dialed.

I don't know what I expected, but I was surprised when he answered on the first ring. I hadn't even got my breath yet. He sounded all right. He knew who I was as soon as I said, "Hey." I don't know why that surprised me, but it did somehow.

"How you doing?" I asked and felt dumb as soon as I said it.

He laughed. He actually laughed. That threw me. I didn't know what to say then. He cleared his throat and told me that he really didn't feel all that bad, sort of like the flu. He ached all over, but not too bad. I asked him did he need anything. He laughed again. He sounded sort of like he had a cold.

"Yeah," he said. He needed a new lease on life. And then he said he was kidding. He didn't sound all that sick really, but he did sound a little husky and tired, but the spark was still there. *At least he could laugh.*

He asked me if I would do him a favor. I told him sure, anything.

I expected him to laugh, but he didn't. Then I heard voices in the background and the sound when you put your hand over the mouthpiece. It sounded like things grinding together.

"Hello, I'm back. Listen, just tell everybody that I will miss them and that I'm okay. Everybody is treating me real well. And that everything is okay. Somehow it really is. All right?"

I said that I would tell them. His voice got that hard edge, which was strange, because Albert seemed so soft somehow, not weak, but gentle. Now he had the edge.

"Do it. Tell them. It's all right. And listen, if they want to give money or something, tell them I want them to give it to that park we were talking about. That would be a good thing. I would be proud of that. Sports mean a lot to me."

Then there was the noise again. Voices muffled and the grinding sound. I couldn't believe this. If the clock had sprouted arms and legs and started singing "Ain't Nothing but a Hound Dog," it couldn't have been more peculiar. The fly buzzed into the room and busied himself bashing into the glass. When Albert came back, he coughed a couple of times and then he spoke up and said he had to go.

"Keep it simple," he said. "Just tell them it's okay. Believe it, okay?"

I said something, I guess. He said good-bye and the phone rattled and the dial tone came on. I sat there and studied the fly. Buzz. Buzz. Buzz. I hung up. I walked back into Fenway's office. Hagman was sitting in my chair. Mr. Fenway said that I should deliver Albert's message in homeroom the next day, just before assembly. Could I do it?

"Yes," I said. "I can do it."

He nodded. Hagman nodded.

"Hang tough, son," he said. "Hang tough."

I nodded and left. I walked past all the other kids and climbed into the car. Fred gave me a look, but didn't say anything. Neither did I. My brother and sister were in the back playing tick-tack-toe. I don't know what I was thinking or if I *was* thinking. I do remember staring at some purple bird doo on the windshield. We eased off.

It was a sunny day. The pink and white dogwood blossoms fluttered and swayed. I couldn't believe it. The sky was blue with some puffy white clouds tinged with yellow and orange. The ride was smooth.

"What's troublin' you?"

"Albert."

"What you mean by Albert?"

"He's dying. I just talked to him at the hospital. He said he was all right, but he's real, real sick with leukemia. He's gonna die . . . soon. Any day."

Even after I'd said it, I couldn't believe it. I kept expecting things to turn inside out or upside down. The lights to come on. Somebody to shake my shoulder and tell me to wake up. But the breeze in my hair was real, and the cigar smoke and the hand that patted my hand was Fred's. My sister reached over the seat and gave my head a hug. I pulled away like I didn't like it, and I don't know if I did or not, but she hugged me again and I didn't move. My little brother wanted to know what was going on, but my sister shushed him or tried to.

Just could not, could not believe it. It didn't make any sense. He was the nicest guy maybe in the whole stinking school. You could talk to Albert about anything. Anything. If he didn't like what you were saying, he would just laugh and say, "Naw, not me" or "You don't think that really, do you?" He made you think, and he knew so much about sports; I never even talked to him about them. It made no sense to. You could ask him a question, though, and he never made you feel stupid. Maybe I wasn't his best friend, but there was something about him that made you feel like he might just be yours. I don't know. None of this stupid stuff made sense. I hit the dash with my fist. *Why? Why?*

I looked at Fred, feeling dumb for lashing out. He gave me a look that was about three sets of words in one. "No one knows" was the first part. "Calm yourself down" was the second. "It will be all right somehow" was the third.

"I don't believe it," I said.

"Things is hard to believe some times. It's just a dern shame."

I didn't really much feel like heading down to Creekside to meet up with Tuck and Laura, but I didn't feel like sitting around either, so I went. The motion somehow did me some good. That was the weird thing about it. I pedaled my bike until the breeze whistled in my ears, and it felt fresh and clear. It was a beautiful day, in spite of everything. It didn't seem right that everything looked so damn rich and golden and green. But it did.

In spite of myself, I started chuckling about what the yakety-yak was going to be. I pictured old Hoyt finding the jackass sign and the ace of spades calling cards, and I deftly dodged a startled squirrel and laughed aloud. I figured he was plenty pissed off and probably had told everybody that a gang of crazy coloreds had done it. Of course, he probably would say it a little rougher than that. "Crazy, uppity niggers" is what he would have said. Then I wondered if Tuck knew that my father had helped to get Hawk sprung out of jail. I kind of hoped he knew, but then I figured I better keep that to myself. I didn't want to embarrass anybody.

As far as us learning what Hoyt had said, all we had to do was get ourselves some Cokes and hang around the gas pumps, and sure enough, Mickey would sound off all the local news to just about anybody who would listen.

Tuck and Laura were already there, so I figured I wouldn't have to wait long to hear what happened. I got a Coke. Tuck asked why I was so late. I told him I was held up at school because a friend of mine was pretty sick. He gave me a funny look. So did Laura.

"Well, he's real sick," I said. They kept looking at me like they didn't get the connection. I blurted out, "He's going to die and I had to talk to him." Then I just turned away and said, "I can't talk about it right now. I got here as fast as I could, okay?"

We walked around the side of the station, and I kept my eyes busy watching my toes bother the gravel and cinders.

"So what happened?" I asked. "What's the word around here?"

"Nothing," Tucker said.

"Mickey hasn't said anything about it at all?"

"Not that we've heard," Laura said.

Well, that was disappointing. We walked back out front and Mickey was sounding off, but it had nothing to do with us. I figured he had to come to something about it. I couldn't believe Hoyt would just keep it to himself, so we stood around and listened for a while. Mickey was funny to listen to anyway.

He was going on and on to some guy in an old pickup, slapping his thighs with every other cuss word, which means he must have had cherry-red thighs by the time he punched out. He was telling about the paperboy, Tommy, a skinny neighborhood kid who drove a VW bug. Seems he had come in to get gas that morning and when he was about to leave, Mickey and his buddy Carl had decided to have some fun with him, so they lifted up the rear end of his car. Try as he might, he couldn't get away.

Mickey did a pretty good imitation of Tommy's voice, which is sort of high and squeaky, and told how the engine would squeal and Tommy would squeal right along with it. "Put me down, you motherfuckers!"

The more he yelled and revved, the more Carl and Mickey laughed. And then Mickey said, "Next thing I know, I'm straining my damn ass, holding up the son of a bitch, laughing to bust a gut, eyes closed tight as a pair of assholes, when I hear this voice right beside me. It's the motherfucker himself; he says, 'All right, smart-ass. Put the sorry little foreign bastard down now.' I don't believe my ears, so I sneak a peek, and goddamn son of a bitch, if that sawed-off little squirt hasn't climbed out of the son of gun and planted his sorry self right beside me! I look down and, God almighty, them wheels is still spinning and that engine is still squealing and there he stands, arms folded on his chest just grinning. He says, 'Why don't you put the motherfucker down now, Mickey boy?' And Carl says, 'How'd he do that?' I said, 'We'll cover that son of a bitch in a minute, but right now, hold the mother up or our ass is grass.' Then Tommy grins and he says, 'You know what a choke is, don't you?' Carl nodded. 'It's in reverse, fellas.' Well, that sorry little bastard just stood there and grinned until—and I hate to admit it—we was both near shitting bricks. Then just casual as a Broadway queer, he strolls his skinny butt back to the door, climbs in, slammed the door, and damn, we lost the son of a bitch. Hellfire, the little fart had got it into first and tore his ass out of here, screeching like a hell-born banshee. I'll get the motherfucker, though. I don't know how. But it ain't over yet."

I guess that's how we felt about Hoyt. We hung around for a while, but Mickey never said anything about it and nobody else did either. Laura was tired and Tucker was hungry. It was like none of us felt right. Tuck said he would come up with something, that we would get the son of a bitch. Laura just shook her head and told me she was sorry about my friend. She gave me a hug. We left it that Laura would call me when Tuck had the next step figured out.

I was just as confused as hell. I hung around the station for a few minutes. I bought some peanuts out of the machine. I was sure I was going to hear something, but didn't. I didn't want to go home, I didn't know where to go. Then I thought about Bill.

———————

In some ways, I didn't feel all that good, but then in others, I felt better than I thought I should. Just pedaling again got me feeling better. The old locust trees on the lane caught the light in their rugged bark, the golden places and the darker places too looked like little spots where mysteries might have been hidden. I ditched my bike at the barn and walked down the hill and across the field to the creek. The sun was right in my eyes, but when I looked down, the colors were like rainbows on the edges of things. I mean the grasses—whether left over from winter or just brand-new spring— flickered, not just tan or green, but every color I knew, and you could see right through them like the wings of a moth quivering. I felt like I could stomp into all this color and it would splash like a puddle. I looked down at my khaki pants and they were purple, orange, blue, green, tan. All I know is they weren't just khaki, that's for sure. The creek was orange, and there was a buzzard swooping, and when he crossed the sun you couldn't see him at all and when he floated clear, he sure wasn't black.

Bill was sitting on his deck drinking a City. I waved to him. He raised his beer. I hollered could I come on over. He shrugged, asked me could I walk on water, little cool for swimming. I didn't know how to answer that, so I just stood there and kicked at a root. He struggled to his feet, looked at me, and shook his head. Next thing, I'm surrounded by purple oily smoke and looking at rainbows floating on the water sloshing in the bottom of the boat. We made her fast, and Bill sent me in for a couple of beers.

Everything looked about the same. That surprised me, because somehow it seemed like a million years since I had been there last. Bill yelled in for me to bring him his smokes. They were on the table sitting on top of a magazine called *Leatherneck* from the USMC. On the cover, there was this sharp-looking dude, clear sky all around him, looking off into the wide blue yonder, all starched and shiny in his dress blues. Beside that was a framed photograph of a man and a woman drinking beer and sitting on the running board of a truck. They were holding hands. I figured it must have been Bill and his wife a long time ago.

Anyway, I plopped down on the deck and took a swig. Bill lit a smoke, cleared his throat, and we just sat there. Suddenly I had nothing in my mind at all. I mean blanko. I looked around thinking *here I am, after asking this man to get up off his ass and cross the creek to come get me, and I got nothing to say.* I thought about bringing up the stuff we'd done the night before, but then thought better of that. So I just sat there and he did, too. A woodpecker swooped over the creek and knocked on a tree. A duck quacked. The boat swayed a little bit in the current, but there was really nothing to hang a thought on. All of a sudden, I noticed that Bill was barefoot and had the ugliest old twisted toes, plus the dirtiest, worst-looking toenails I had ever seen. I mean, they were yellow and brown, like he smoked cigars with them all night. That thought got me to snort down a laugh, and I looked up at him and he kind of looked me up and down himself.

"What's eating you?"

"What do you mean?" I said, looking away straight into the sun.

"Horse shit."

He was looking straight at me with his cigarette hanging off his lower lip. His eyes didn't look mad really, but I felt sort of boxed in. I asked him if I could have a smoke and he nodded. I fired one up and took a swig.

I didn't know how to say what I wanted to say, 'cause I didn't know yet what I wanted to say. Where do you begin when you don't know where you're going and you ain't particularly sure why you're where you are?

Bill burped and blew some smoke out of his ugly old nose.

"Beg your pardon," he growled, "but you're begging my patience, scholar. What brings you here?"

"Just wanted to talk, I guess," I said. He raised his eyebrows and squinted. "Well, I mean, things are happening all in a hurry, but then, like now, they seem to come to a screeching halt and it's like being spun around a bunch of times and then stopped all of a sudden. Know what I mean?"

He dropped his chin onto his chest and took the cigarette out of his mouth. He started to flip it into the creek and then thought better of it and put it back. He shook his head.

"Is that you on the table in there?"

"What are you talking about, boy?" He did look sort of mad now. "Me on the table?" He gave me a look. He shook his head. "You mean that old photo? I know you ain't referring to that pretty boy marine. Ha!"

I nodded yes. He looked at me hard and long, and he nodded yes. "Long time ago," he said quietly and then roughly said, "So what's your point?"

I shrugged. I really didn't know.

He flipped his smoke into the creek and after he gulped his beer, lit another one. He watched me over the tip of his bottle. I gulped one down, too. I thought of the story Fred had told me, and all of a sudden, I realized it wasn't just a story for Bill, and I wished I hadn't said anything at all about the picture. He shrugged and blew out a big cloud of smoke.

"This is my anniversary. May you blessed be." He raised what was left of his beer, held it out toward me, and held it there, moving the bottle slowly from side to side. I held mine out and we clinked the bottles together. He winked at me. "That's better. You ain't just a bump on a log. You do respond after all. So now, let me ask once again." He paused and when he spoke next his voice sounded scratchy and dry. "What brings you my way?" Then he gave me a look that wasn't mean, but it was so damn sharp that it killed the cat that had got my tongue.

"I think a friend of mine is gonna die."

Bill tilted his head, but he didn't say anything. Neither did I. I wanted to say something, but I just looked away toward the sun. I didn't know what to say. Finally, Bill said something like, everybody's gonna die sometime.

"Yeah, I know that, but…" Then I went blank again. My mind saying, *but what*? *But what*? Over and over, and no answer coming back.

"You got a friend who's bad sick?"

"Yeah, the principal told me after school, and I talked to him, my friend that is, and he sounded just like himself, but he's got leukemia real bad and he's okay, he says, but he's gonna die soon, and he wants me to tell the class and stuff good-bye, I guess, and I got to tell them tomorrow that he's okay, but that he's gonna die."

I think I said this in a hurry, because when I got through, I had to take a breath like I had been running or something. Bill held up his hand like he was signaling me to stop. "Now hold on just a minute. You say your school principal and your buddy and you had a chat after school where your buddy tells you he's okay, but he's going to die right soon, so he wants you to tell your all's classmates all about it tomorrow?"

I nodded. He scratched his head, closed his eyes, and seemed to let something sink in. He squinted at me like he was asking me a question, and then he said, "That's the god-dangdest thing, queer as a cow wearing pantaloons." I laughed at that, in spite of trying to be serious.

"No, seriously, that is one strange request, and I have heard a few in my time. I heard some in the war, believe you me. But dang, if this one don't come near close to taking the pantaloons off the cow and running 'em up a flagpole!" He looked fierce when he said that and he flipped his smoke into the drink for emphasis. He grinned, though, and I laughed in spite of myself.

I caught myself and said, "What do you mean?"

"What I mean is, to tell all your friends that you're okay when you're just about dead is pretty doggone unusual, but to sit around casually and shoot the bull about it in the principal's office after school is out is about the weirdest two cents worth anybody ever threw in my pot." He paused and took a swig, and before I could say anything, he coughed real hard and growled, "For Christ's sake, why in the bloody blazes didn't he just tell everybody himself? He could walk up to 'em one at a time and say, 'Howdy, sorry to trouble you, but I'll be dying right soon and I wanted you to be aware of the fact that I'm okay, okay?' Or he could've, if he felt like time was short, stood up on a soapbox and made a speech. And a speech like that would more than likely draw a fair-size crowd, so it most likely would be a decent way of spreading the news. Point is, why you? Why didn't he just tell them his own self? That puzzles me."

"You don't understand," I said. "He wasn't there . . ."

But before I could explain, Bill said, "Now looky here, scholar, don't you go getting spooky on old Bill. I got a belly full of ghosts as it is. Just keep it simple, you hear me?"

Somebody was coming up the road. We could hear the gravel crackling and pinging. Bill told me to go inside, get us another beer, and keep out of sight until we knew what was what. I ducked in.

I looked out the window, and through the smudge, I saw a black pickup stop right next to Bill's car. It was Hoyt. As he walked toward the boat, I backed away from the window. It was a small window about the size of a library dictionary and so dirty nobody could probably see in anyway, but I didn't want to take any chances. I could still sort of see him, but I mainly listened. He was cool at first. Said it was a nice day, wasn't it? Bill said it was a fine day. Hoyt asked him if everything had been quiet and peaceful. Bill said he hadn't heard anything louder than a duck. About then the woodpecker cut loose and hammered away and Bill said that the woodpeckers were a little too frisky to suit him personally. Hoyt just rocked on his heels and nodded.

Bill asked him the purpose of his visit. Hoyt asked him if he had seen any niggers or any kids looking suspicious hanging around. Bill said he hadn't seen anybody to speak of. He said that Hoyt was the first man to come down the road all day. Hoyt rocked on his heels again and spat down next to his boot.

"What about last night?" he asked with a slow grin. "You hear anything last night?"

Bill said that, as a matter of fact, he had. My ears perked up at that. My heart started thumping. Hoyt raised his eyebrows and nodded, but Bill didn't say anything. He made Hoyt ask him what he had heard. Bill started in saying how generally he was a pretty good sleeper and how it took a right smart noise to rouse him up from his beauty rest, but last night . . . He paused and I heard him light a cigarette and I watched Hoyt shake his head side to side 'cause he thought no one was looking. He gave Bill a hard glare that would have blown him off the deck, and then he started grinning quick, I guess when Bill started looking at him again.

"Yes, you were saying . . .?"

"Excuse me," Bill said. "A man needs refreshment from time to time, you understand?"

Hoyt nodded and continued his phony ass smile.

"Well, the carp were spawning all night long."

Hoyt's smile disappeared and my face muscles twitched up.

"Carp spawning?"

"Yep, and the bastards must have thought this here old boat was the Taj Mahal because they were going at it the whole night through, banging on the bottom, smashing against the sides, thrashing up the water, and then thump, thump, thumping again and again until I like to go crazy. Put me in the mind of a young man, sure enough. Know what I mean?"

Hoyt looked sort of stunned.

"I mean to tell you, if there had been a cold shower handy, I would have taken it, for sure. Those damn fish got me all stirred up. And on the eve of my anniversary, too. I heard plenty, but a lot of good that does an old widower man like me. I couldn't wait till daybreak, I tell you, but do you think that stopped 'em? No sir!"

Hoyt was shaking his head, not so much to say no, but to say stop.

"No sir! Those perverted sex maniacs kept right on until shortly after lunch. I'll hear plenty more tonight, you can bet on it. But hell, it's just old nature, ain't it? You were young once weren't you, Hoyt? Course you were. Har, har, har!"

Hoyt grinned and nodded. "But you didn't hear any *people* messing around?"

"All I heard was fucking fish."

Hoyt held up one of my cards. You couldn't tell what it was. It just looked like a black blob on a white card.

"What about this? This mean anything to you?" he asked, with his nasty little grin hanging over the card.

"What's this baloney?" Bill growled. "I thought you was a farm manager. You taking up head shrinking as sort of a sideline?"

The grin disappeared and the card got closer as he thrust it out to arm's length. "What does this mean to you? Tell me what you know about it."

Bill cleared his throat and chuckled. "All right, I'll play. But on one condition."

I swallowed hard and watched Hoyt nod. His grin reappeared.

He asked what that condition might be. My ears perked up.

"The condition is," Bill drew out his words slowly. "The condition . . . that you must promise to adhere to utterly is . . . that no matter what I say, you will quit practicing your medicine here and go back to being a farm manager so that this citizen can enjoy what's left of this fine afternoon in peace and untroubled solitude. You savvy?" He growled the last part pretty rough. Hoyt nodded and said he agreed.

"All right then," Bill continued. "You asked for it, and I'm holding you to your word. Here goes. Now, what I see is a cave. A dark, damp place, but wait! There is a candle flickering in the cave, and the shadows are jumping up the walls, and the candle won't hold still and so the shadows can't either, and sometimes they get real big and sometimes real skinny . . ."

"You drunken old fool!" Hoyt yelled. He threw down the card, stomped on it, turned away, and strode back to his truck. He left in a cloud of gravel and dust.

I poked my head out and Bill winked at me. I handed him his beer.

"I think I must have hit a nerve," he said.

"Wonder what the hell that was all about?" I said.

"Damned if I know. That son of a bitch is crazy. Stretched tight as a new barbed wire fence."

When I'd finally made Bill understand that Albert was in the hospital, he changed his tone and talked real quiet. As I was riding home, I thought about what he said. He apologized for making a joke about it. When I told him about how Albert wanted any kind of gifts to go to the park so that the kids out this way would have a place to play sports, he shook his head and said Albert sounded like a fine young man. He said the church was collecting, but that he didn't think that it made a hell of a lot of difference.

"But what the hell, who knows?" he said.

About the speech I had to give, he told me to keep it short and not to worry about the words, because they would come out natural, if I just let 'em.

And that's what I did. On the blackboard, which was green, the word for the day was "guile"—crafty, deceitful, cunning. Once again, it was a sunny day and I stood in front of the blackboard and let the words fall out. Everybody was quiet. Only one of them knew anything about it and that was Andy. He had talked to Albert, too, and Albert had told him to keep it to himself. Andy told me that Albert was in and out of a coma. That he was going fast. Turned out Andy was right. Albert died over the weekend.

CHAPTER 10

SHADOW

The limo was shiny and black. The seats were soft and clean. The glass sparkled. Not a speck of dirt anywhere, except on the shoulder of the black suit coat the driver wore. One flake of dandruff. That was hard to figure since his hair was so slicked down with grease it was hard to imagine anything falling out of it. I caught his eye in the mirror and then looked away. His eye looked like wet glass set in a face that was glossy, sort of like Albert's had been at the funeral home the night before. The rest of the pallbearers settled into their seats. The door thudded shut, and ever so slowly, we purred toward the church.

I expected Andy to say something, or Ben, or at least Jerry. But nobody said anything. Once again, it was a beautiful day. We led the procession from school to the church. They didn't close the school down, but I don't know how they kept it going. Everybody liked Albert, and a lot of the students and teachers were rolling along behind us. Hatchet Head had a carload, so did Hag Face. I stared out the window and felt my stomach twist and turn.

Mostly, I guess, I felt weird about Albert, the funeral, the whole thing. But other strange stuff had been happening, too. Like getting caught by Mickey when Tuck, Laura, and I were sneaking back from the park and coming up from the creek behind Creekside Auto.

It was dark and it was late so we didn't think anybody was around. We were talking about the cop who had been parked on Bill's road about fifty yards back from the entrance. He didn't see us. Tucker snuck up real close and said that the guy was asleep. Laura and I had been all set to run for it, but Tuck pulled it off. He hadn't told us what he had done until we got across the creek. That's what we were snickering and talking about when Mickey started laughing from the shadow of a tree. It scared the shit out of us. I hate to admit it, but I jumped about ten feet. So did Tucker. Laura was the only one who stood her ground. When I asked her why later, she said she had been too scared to move.

At first, we didn't know who or what it was. Laughter in the shadows without a face is a damned disturbing thing. I was starting to cut out, when Mickey flashed a flashlight on his face and told us to cool it, that he wasn't gonna do nothing. I was still about halfway ready to run, but he cussed about twenty blue streaks and somehow got it across that he hated pencil-dicked, broomstick-up-the-butt Hoyt worse than any living son of a mother-humping bitch, except for that asshole of a drunken, radar-gunned, slippery fart known as Lieutenant Roscoe Sneed, who he, by God above, hated worse. He said he was gonna tear the ass right out from under the license-snatching cocksucker.

Mickey had a way of getting your attention, that's for sure, but when he said something about snatching the ass right off the son of a gun, Tucker and I walked back about a step or two and stood beside Laura, whose mouth was stuck on wide open. The entire situation was sort of unusual, I guess. Tucker wanted to know what Mickey had in mind. We had a powwow in the back room of Creekside Auto.

Turns out that Sneed had caught Mickey speeding a couple of times, but what drove Mickey up the wall was that the guy had this souped-up Interceptor, and Mickey's souped-up rod hadn't been able to beat it, although, according to Mickey, he almost had. But he didn't think it was fair that the county would give this drunken bum of a cop what amounted to the hottest car on the road. It wasn't fair.

We nodded. So how did he know that's who was on the park road, Tucker wanted to know. Mickey asked him if it wasn't a gray Dodge. Of course, he didn't say it quite that clean. He smeared his question with cuss words so strong that I expected Laura to look away, but she laughed, which surprised me. Well, it was him, all right. It was a gray Dodge. Tucker asked Mickey what he was doing here anyway. What was his deal? So he told us.

Mickey was guarding the station. Somebody had busted in and stolen some tools. Easy way to make money. Sit around, drink Cokes, watch TV. Watch us sneak back behind the building and disappear. He winked. He told us he knew what was going on. He could add up two and two. All these bastards talk down here at the station. All strutting around like God almighty, forgetting that Mickey's got ears. He hated Hoyt. Hoyt had stolen his father's job. Right before Mrs. Green died, he convinced the kids that Mickey's father was stealing them blind, which was a lie, but anyway, somehow he got him fired. Mickey's dad had had a heart attack and Mickey blamed it on Hoyt.

"But there's more to this mother," he said. We nodded. "They're in this together."

"In what together?" both Laura and I asked.

"Listen, little buggers, they don't call me the shadow for nothing. Did you know they was cousins? Well, they are. They don't look like it. One a fat bag of lard and the other like a wire with a shit-eating grin, but they are. They're both about as sneaky as copperheads, and they blend in, so mostly nobody knows. I heard 'em, the dumb bastards, drunk as shit, whispering over the jukebox up at The Point."

Mickey said he had been drinking a Coke and playing pinball. Apparently, they didn't realize that anybody could hear them. Mickey said they were bleary-eyed drunk. Talking about the bass boat they were gonna buy and about the fishing camp they were gonna put up down at the lake. He said they had all kinds of plans. They said they were going to get rid of Bill. Send him downriver to Davy Jones's locker. Mickey said that's when his ears really perked up. He said Sneed sort of snorted into his beer and said something like was Hoyt sure those folks would really pay up. And Mickey said Hoyt banged his bony fist on the jukebox so hard it made it skip and everybody turned on their barstools. He said a minute or so later, Hoyt whispered loudly that the agent had as much as guaranteed it. They want the man gone, period, goddamn it, period. 'Nuff said. They'll pay, he said. Mickey said that Sneed wanted to know what the plan was. When Mickey told us what Hoyt had come up with, my jaw dropped open and my blood ran cold.

———————

The door clicked open. I blinked and stepped onto the pea gravel. A whispering man opened his black-suited arms, crunched along beside us, led us to the rear of the hearse. Andy nodded at me and then looked away.

The damn thing was heavy until we got it on rollers, and then it was almost like Albert was laughing, lying there up on one elbow with his goofy grin and his eyes looking right through you. "Come on, I ain't that heavy. Put some muscle into it!"

The music dripped from the ceiling and the room turned as we rolled down the aisle. I saw no one. I saw lots of fingers at the corners of eyes. We sat to one side. We stood up. We sat down. We kneeled. Some people knew the words when we sang. Some couldn't even find the right page.

The last song was "Amazing Grace" and it sounded pretty damn good, mainly because of this one voice in the back that seemed to enclose all the rest and lift them up and smooth them out. When we were rolling the casket back down the aisle, I looked up into the balcony and there were six or seven colored people up there. One of them was Hays. She was the voice. I guess it really hit me at the grave. There were flowers everywhere. The trees were flowering. Shrubs were blooming. There were flowers all around the hole.

When we got back to the school, I just skipped out. I walked to Cherokee Park and hid out in the woods overlooking Beargrass Creek. In the limo, we had talked about raising money for the park, but nobody's heart was really in it. Andy summed it up when he said, "Well, what can I say?" and shrugged, holding out his empty upturned palms. That's pretty much the way I felt about it. I didn't want to hear anything at all, but a gurgling creek sure as hell beat a whole lot of talk. I smoked and tried to think about other stuff.

Like what we were laughing about when Mickey surprised us. See, Tucker had snuck up to the car and then snuck down to the creek again, then he snuck back and crawled right up to the rear wheel of the cop car. That's all we knew until we crossed the creek and he told us that he had pried one of the "Keep Out" signs off a tree and had stuck it, nail side up, right in front of the rear tire.

Mickey had a plan that made Tucker's trick look pretty simple, but after he told us what Sneed and Hoyt were planning to do, it really didn't seem all that terrible, just sort of challenging and exciting. We were going to drive the bastards crazy.

What Mickey told us was this: They were planning to cut Bill's lines so that his boat would drift out into the open river. They weren't going to cut through with a clean slice. They were going to do it in such a way that the lines would look all frayed and worn out. *Hell, I thought to myself, not much challenge there. They are all frayed and worn out already.* He said they figured the boat would sink or get run down by a barge or go over the falls, but one way or the other, they swore they were going to get Bill out of there and then get some kind of reward from the real estate agent.

We couldn't believe it at first. But Mickey swore it was true, and when he convinced us, swearing up and down on everything, Laura looked real worried. When were they planning to do it? What if they did it tonight, while we sat around jawing about it? Mickey just laughed and said the mother-humpers weren't going anywhere. What did he mean? If they cut the lines, Bill could be killed! Mickey just laughed. Bill weren't going anywhere. He done fixed it, is what he said. How?

"First off, they aiming for Friday night."

Laura said, "But what if they change their mind? What if they do it tonight?"

"Second off," Mickey said, "I done told you I fixed it. See, the slimy shit brains figure Bill will be passed out drunk, dead to the rotten world on a Friday night, and the dumb bastards are right, sure thing. But they done fucked up by waiting, because what they plum overlooked was that Bill is a church-going man of a Sunday morning, at which point the shadow already done gone to work." He paused and lit a cigarette, like he was firing up a fancy stogie.

"Well, what?"

"There is now at the waterline an eyebolt with a thirty-foot towing cable attached, and on the bank right next to Bill's boat's ass end is a sturdy cottonwood root with this very same cable securely attached. Bill ain't going nowhere."

We were all nodding and grinning. Mickey blew out a big cloud of smoke and punctuated it with three intersecting smoke rings.

Does Bill know about all this?

"Shhh," says Mickey. "Don't even think about that. Listen, if he knew what they was planning, it would spoil the whole mother-fucker. Think about it. He would raise holy hell, and Sneed and Hoyt would just call him a crazy son of a bitch and me a stink-ass liar. Naw, the best damn thing about it is this—we let the sons of bitches get away with it, but then we fuck the mother-humpers up so fine and dandy that they get caught with their britches down around their ankles. Can't you just see it?"

"How we gonna do that?" Tucker asked.

"Leave it to the shadow. We will need explosives . . ."

"*Explosives!*" We all three said at once.

"Cherry bombs. M-80s. Nothing bigger than that. I have the logging chain and the cable, stakes, and sledge hammer. Tell you what; we need an old can of paint. No wait. That smells too much. Oil. Never mind. I got lots of old oil. That smells natural around the water. Ever notice that? Seems like the two just go together.

Oil and water. They'll never know what hit 'em till their asses are in the shadow's sling and I fires the mothers off their high and mighty and sets 'em down someplace they won't believe."

I sat there and dazed away the afternoon. Mickey seemed about half crazy and about half fox. We were supposed to have our next meeting with him at midnight tonight. I was hoping he was going to come up with something good, but I had a funny feeling deep down inside that was all churned up and tangled. I was trying to figure out if I felt this way because of what had already happened, Albert's dying and all, or what I felt might be about ready to happen. Seemed like everything was getting all mixed up—the park, the Greens, the legal angle, then Hoyt and Sneed. I tried to see my way through the tangle, but even though I was sitting still, inside I felt like I did that night when I first met Bill and I was running along the creek bank in the thunderstorms. One minute I would think I had the lay of the land all figured out and lit up bright, then bam! All dark and stumbling and crashing into contradictions and confusion, sort of like branches that poked you out of some dark place that you would have sworn was clear.

I picked up a chunk of rock and chucked it into the creek. We had to do something—that was all I knew. I felt like I was being tugged along by some kind of current or pushed by some kind of thing that I couldn't see but could feel right behind me, clawing at my back and neck. I tried to shrug off the feeling, but it wouldn't go away. I was caught up in something. I knew that much, but what it was and whether it was good or bad, I could not say. It felt wrong and right all at the same time. "We'll see," I think I said. *Who knows? Let's see what Mickey comes up with. We'll see.*

———

When the sun looked about right, I headed back to school. When I got there, school was just letting out. I grabbed up my books and climbed into Fred's car. It was like I was invisible. Nobody said anything to me, until Fred pointed out that I had dirt all over the elbow of my suit coat and some leaves in my hair.

"Don't look like you've been fighting," he said.

I smiled back and told him I had just been thinking. There was no way out that I could see. There was no backing up and no backing out. Fred slipped into traffic as easy as always, and I was thinking that I wished everything could roll along that smoothly. Inside I was churning, and outside was the soft afternoon air.

"You ain't fixing to get in trouble, are you?"

"What you mean?"

Fred looked me over slowly, like he was studying me. He took his stogie out of his mouth and scratched his ear, but he didn't say anything.

"Well, what?"

He winked at me.

"You been out tomcat prowling after the folks have gone to bed?"

"Huh?" I said with a shrug.

"What you know about a certain Officer Sneed? Hmm?"

"Well, nothing really. What do you mean?"

He squinted up and nodded.

"Sneed is one bad SOB. I run into him down at Creekside the other morning. He was having a tire patched. He was cussing like a son of a gun. Said he picked up some kind of 'Keep Out' sign nail back on Bill's road the other night. Said he started up to leave after parking there for a while, and he hadn't gone a foot when he done knowed something's wrong. It was his theory that somebody planted it there just for him. He said spooks done it. Same spooks who made the entrance all whopper-jawed, is what he said."

"No kidding?" I said, trying my best to look neutral, like it didn't matter too much to me, but when Fred started chuckling, the laugh I was holding in burst out like a wild thing. It was the best thing I had heard all day, except for Hays singing at the funeral. That was damn good, but damn that Tuck! He got him! Those bastards! Those no goods. Those shifty-eyed, squinty, rat-brained pricks. This was war, and it felt good to be winning. I laughed and laughed, and realized I was looking forward to our powwow with Mickey. I wondered what he would come up with.

All of a sudden, I realized that Fred wasn't laughing. I looked at him sideways. He was shaking his head and sort of nodding at the same time. Like he was saying yes and no all at once. I think I shrugged.

"Sneed is a bad son of a bitch. Do you hear what I'm telling you?" I nodded.

"Do you know what that means?" I nodded. Fred looked almost scary, like he was mad and then some. "It means he is crazy enough to shoot you dead and find a good reason for it later. He is crooked and as dangerous as a mad dog. He's drunk about most of the time. The only people he won't mess with is the Greens and Bill, and that's because Bill's got something on him. But anybody else . . . I ain't kidding. He is a killer! The man ain't right. Just watch yourself."

I got there first. Mickey was watching the news on a little black-and-white TV. The room was gray with years of dust, ashes, and grease. Smoke drifted around the room. I sat down in a busted old chair and I told him the others would be along shortly. He nodded but just sat there with his feet propped up on the desk. His boots were so soaked with oil they looked black, but I could see they once were brown. I felt uneasy, and even though the room was so thick with smoke you could hardly see across it, I lit up a cigarette to calm my nerves. Mickey just watched the screen and didn't say one thing, until the newsman said something about more advisors were being sent over. He turned off the TV.

"God damn! I sure don't like that shit. My big brother's over there." He looked at me hard.

"Over where, Korea?" I asked him.

"Fuck your Korea. Brother is in Vietnam. Vietnam! You ever heard of it? Advisors, my ass. It ain't no stinking basketball game. It's fucking war! Act like it's a whoopsie-doo, do-si-do motherfucker. They're shooting at my brother. He's fighting for his fucking ass, and they're talking about giving good advice. Blow up the motherfuckers! That's your advice!"

"He's in combat?"

"Bet your ass. Advisors, my butt. The news makes me sick. Nothing but bullshit artists and crapola heads that can't find their ass with both hands. Tell you what. This country is asleep at the wheel. I'm telling you. Dead asleep."

He shook his head and flipped on the set again. He kept the sound off.

"Look at here. Now here we have a real cute sight, a nigger preacher marching around. I bet it's Mississippi. Stirring up a bunch of shit, and look over there; bunch of crazy bastards in white robes burning a fucking cross. I mean they're all fucking nuts. I can't watch it. Advisors! Shit! My brother's getting shot at. Why don't the sons of bitches fight their own stinking . . .?"

Tap, tap, tap. The door opened and in stepped Tucker and Laura. Mickey clicked off the set and leaned back in his chair. I was worried about what he might say next. Part of me wanted to grab the two of 'em and run out the door, but I just sat there and felt the current pulling at me. We were in this together.

"Okay, here's the plan."

Laura sat down on a case of oil. She looked about as nervous as I was. She smiled at me, but then she looked down and I could see that her hands were clenched in the hem of her shorts. Tucker leaned against the wall. He looked like he was ready for anything. Cool as a cucumber. I wondered how I looked.

Mickey reached down on the floor and put a brown paper sack up on the desk. He called it Exhibit A. He pulled out a handful of cherry bombs and M-80s. He pulled out a battery and a spool of wire. He smiled at Laura. Asked her if she liked fireworks. She shook her head. Tucker laughed and I guess I did, too. Mickey took a piece of wire and touched it to one end of the battery. He asked her could she do that. She nodded at him and gave him a look. Okay then. He pointed to a duffel bag in the corner. He motioned for Tucker to open it up. Tucker looked down into the dingy green bag like it might hold a cobra. But it didn't. There were two mauls and two stakes about three feet long. There was some heavy wire cable attached to them. He nodded to Tucker and me. Could we drive a stake? We nodded. But then the three of us kind of looked at each other. What was going on?

"Listen. I can see you all are sort of wondering. That is called confusion. But if you think you are confused right now, just wait till those low-down mothers find themselves in the middle of what looks and sounds like World War III, and Bill's boat just drifts off a ways and stops, and they figure out that the front door is locked and they ain't going nowhere. That, my friends, will add up to some confusion."

The picture was starting to gel.

"See this here oil?" he said, holding up a Mason jar as black as tar. "A little of this on the ground around the pilings and a little smeared up and down the lines. The slimy cocksuckers will be greased up good."

Mickey pointed at another bag even dirtier than the first one.

He asked me to bring it over and put it on the desk. I grabbed it, yanked up, and practically tore my arm out of its socket. I could lift it, but I bet it weighed seventy-five pounds. Mickey just laughed and told me to leave it be. It clankety clanked when I set it down.

"That there is my job. That there is a logging chain. Roscoe Sneed is staying put."

"How? What's it for?"

"I got a canoe," Mickey said, nodding and lighting up a smoke, like that explained everything. We looked from one to the other. "I fish the creek quite a bit. Everybody knows that. There's some nice little holes down that way. So, in the next day or so, I plans to take my sorry butt fishing. I plan to be out at least an hour or so before dawn. The shadow most likely will never be seen, but if, by chance, I am, then I'll just busy myself with my tackle. Tangled line. Lure caught up on a cottonwood root. They won't suspect shit. Before I fish my fill, that bank will be strung up like Christmas and the Fourth of July. The bag with the stakes will be stashed right close to the entrance. There's a brush pile right handy, and in that very same mother-humper, there will be a battery with one wire attached and another just begging to be. Hellfire! For fun, we might just torch that operation, if there's time. But we don't want to overdo it 'cause we got to get back to the canoe, which is right around the bend."

He nodded at us, like the whole thing was a done deal that he was looking back on, instead of one of the craziest, looniest things any of us had ever heard of.

"Canoe?" Laura said.

"Sure. They ain't going nowhere, but if anybody does happen to be looking for anybody, namely us, the mother-humpers sure as hell ain't gonna think to look for a canoe slipping along close to the bank heading up the creek. By the time anybody thinks of that, we'll be snug as bugs. They'll never know what hit 'em. Believe me, the shadow knows."

"I don't know," Laura said. "Don't you think we should just tell somebody?"

We all looked at her. I was thinking she might be right. Tucker nodded at me and said he was in. I started to say that the whole thing sounded a little risky, but Mickey cut me off.

"Who you gonna tell?" He raised his voice. "Who is gonna believe you?"

"Come on, come on," Tucker said. "All you gotta do is touch a wire and run like hell, if you want to."

I guess I was too chicken to chicken out. I didn't say much of anything. Like I say, part of me said yes and part said no. Finally, I said, what the hell, I was in. After a couple of minutes, Laura signed on, but she said the whole thing sounded crazy. What if something went wrong?

"Oh, Laura," Tucker said with disgust, "nothing's gonna go wrong."

"All we gotta do is lay low and be cool," Mickey said. "Slip in, lay low, move quick, move quiet, and slip out like motherfuckers. They'll cook in their own juice. Believe me, the shadow is talking."

"What about that logging chain?" I wanted to know. Mickey just winked and said that was his job.

That night I slept like a log. I didn't even dream. Everything had become so strange, maybe I didn't need to. Before I fell off, I listened to the night sounds a house makes, the creaks and pops. I tried to sort the whole thing out. I felt like I was standing on the tip end of a diving board in the pitch-black dark. I wasn't sure what was down below.

But in the morning, with all the familiar sounds—the showers, the running around, everybody getting ready—I saw it all differently. For one thing, we weren't the bad guys. Hoyt and Sneed were. Even Fred said that Sneed was a killer, and Mickey was right: *who would believe us?* I knew my parents wouldn't. Fred might. No, probably he would, but who would believe *him*, a colored man accusing a cop of something he hadn't even done yet. Anyway, the way I figured it, we had to act. It was up to us, and besides, all we were going to do was set off some fireworks and temporarily block off an entrance. Hell, if we did it right and everything worked out, since Bill's boat was about two football fields from where we were gonna be, we ought to have one hell of a good start on 'em. Like Mickey said, they wouldn't even know what hit 'em.

But something was bothering me about the plan, and it wasn't until I munched down my last piece of toast and was heading out to the car to go to school that it hit me. Who was gonna catch them? What if they just took down the cable and drove away? Sure, the noise of the cherry bombs was gonna attract some kind of attention, but what if it didn't? I was thinking that maybe after we got back to Creekside, maybe we should call the cops. Tell them there was bad trouble down on the creek. Or the FBI. Or the Coast Guard. I needed to talk to Mickey about that. My mother kissed me on the cheek and told me to have a good day. I told her I would. She told me not to talk with my mouth full. I nodded and smiled with my mouth closed.

At school, at assembly, we all sat in the big common's room, and Fenway said a prayer for Albert and then we had a moment of silence. Nobody coughed or farted or burped. It was a first. Then old Fenface surprised me by asking me to come up and explain Albert's wishes about the park. He motioned for me to come up to the podium, and as I walked up, I looked at him and shrugged. He said, "Just tell everybody a little about it."

I turned around and faced the whole school. I swallowed hard, grabbed both edges of the podium, and held on for dear life. These kids came from all over the city. Most of them didn't know that much about the creek. Then, as I looked around, the only colored person I saw was the janitor, who was leaning on his broom at the back of the room. Then I saw one of the cooks look out of the serving window of the kitchen. This room was where we met, studied, and ate lunch. Everybody I was looking at was white. It was strange.

I think I told them I didn't know where to begin, and then somehow I just did. I told 'em that Albert had told me that he was interested in the kids of the Creekside area having a place to play sports, but also, I told them, there was more to it than that. I told them it wasn't even a sure thing that there was going to be a park, but that a lot of good people, both Negro and white, were working on it. That some people wanted this park to be in honor of the brave men of the Negro race who had never been recognized for their service to their country in World War I, World War II, and Korea, even the Civil War, I said.

This one kid stood up and gave a rebel yell, then screamed out, "*The South shall rise again!*" That started up some commotion, because some others started in, and I was amazed to see Hatchet

Head slither his bony self over and collar the heckler, who cringed. Hatchet Head looked around the room, and the place fell silent. He looked at me and nodded. I continued.

Some people, I said, wanted the park to be in honor of the Underground Railroad that had operated in that area, helping people to their freedom across the river. A few other colored faces poked out of the serving window. Some people, I said, wanted there to be a museum to honor these people, both colored and white, who worked together for freedom. And I said there are some people who didn't want a park at all.

I was starting to run out of steam. I paused. *What to say next?* I said, "Albert wanted a park. He wants to be remembered as your friend, your teammate, and most of all, he wanted, as his last act, to ask you to help him be part of making this dream come true, whatever its final shape might be. Please help," I said. "Thank you."

As I walked back to my seat, a couple of guys started clapping, and then the whole room burst into applause. The janitor waved his broom. After a minute, Fenway calmed them down. With eyes closed as usual, he thanked me for my remarks and then urged everyone to consider giving and that the money could be collected by the class treasurers and then held in a special account. The assembly was dismissed. Andy slapped me on the back. Ben punched my arm. Jerry nodded and grinned.

So that's how I got to be the school spokesman for the park. Throughout the day, kids would come up to me and want to talk about it. What did I think it should be? By day, I was a good citizen. Treasurers wanted to know who was in charge of the special account. I directed them to Mr. Fenway. Hatchet Head paid me a compliment. Said my delivery was strong, effective, and to the point. He complimented my poise. I suppose he hadn't been able to see my white knuckles.

But by night, I was a commando, sneaking the back way through the shadows of Creekside. I pretended I was an Indian. I walked as quietly as a panther. I stayed out of sight.

The night before we struck, I snuck over to the park, slithered and crawled down the creek bank past Sneed and down to Bill's. I didn't call out to him. I could hear him on the front deck drinking his beer. I could smell his cigarette. I slipped down to the waterline. I felt around. I found Mickey's eyebolt. The cable was there all right.

I snuck back to Creekside undetected. I knocked on the door. I wanted to ask Mickey about who was going to call the cops. How that was going to work. Mickey took one look at me and burst out laughing. Said I looked like I had been practicing for being a hog. I was covered with old black creek mud. He told me not to worry about the cop part.

"We'll have the bastards so friggin' crazy they'll call them their own selves." That's what he said.

I asked him when he was going to set everything up. He said part of it was already set up. He said he would slip down in a few hours and finish the job. He said Sneed never stayed there past two or so. Said he slipped in around ten, drank his beers, snoozed with his radio crackling. Parked in the exact same spot. Pitched his empties in the same spot. Just like a fat turd of a clock. "Regular as a bowel movement" was what he said.

CHAPTER 11

SNATCHED

As soon as it got dark, we set out. The canoe was a beat-up old wooden thing painted dark green. The current was slow and steady. We stuck close to the bank in shadows. There was a half-moon coming up. A breeze ruffled leaves, and that would have covered the sound of our paddles, but we just drifted mostly. Mickey in the rear steering. No talk now. Not until we were back to Creekside.

As planned, we were all in dark clothes. We each had two cherry bombs and a small box of wooden matches. We were so quiet that every sound stood out like red on black. A fish tail slapping the water. Ducks squawking and churning up the dark water, clearing out of our way. Out on the river, a barge was grinding upstream. The engines throbbed the air. The air horn sounded two long blasts. The last one seemed to hang in the air like a hand outstretched, and then the answer came from the barge headed downstream. Two answering blasts. The moon cleared the trees behind us, and the water before us glittered pale yellow on muddy green.

We put in on a broad curve right before Bill's road. We tied her up and slipped down the bank of the creek, just as I had the night before. The creek ran along the road about fifty feet away. Sneed wasn't there yet. We took our positions.

Mickey trotted down to where he figured Sneed was going to park. Tucker grabbed his hammer and his end of the cable and stake; he ran across the road and down into the ditch out of sight. Laura ruffled gravel over the cable, scuffing it with her foot, then joined me behind the brush pile. The battery was there, and the wire that ducked under the grass and stretched down the shore of the creek. I sure hoped Mickey knew what he was doing. He was the only one who knew where the damn things were. He had said we would be amazed.

There was nothing to do now but wait. Laura whispered in my ear.

"Are you afraid?" she asked. Her lips tickled and her breath made the hair tingle on the back of my neck.

"A little bit," I whispered back. She grabbed my hand and squeezed it.

"Me too," she said.

I could barely make out the outline of Bill's boat. In the dark, it seemed forever away. There was a very faint light goldish orange, a flickering dot, which I figured was his cabin's window. Between here and there, I thought I could make out some other shape, a darkness that seemed to blot out the leaf shapes jittering across the creek. A few minutes later, when Sneed crunched down the road, his headlights lit up a large black cruiser on the creek, then he backed, turned around, and drove toward us. He parked about forty or fifty yards away, right where Mickey said he would, underneath an old locust tree whose blooms in the tip-top looked like pale skinny lanterns. We could hear his radio crackling.

A couple of minutes later, a flashlight shined off the black cruiser onto the cop car and a voice yelled out, "Yo, hey! What's going on? Hello. Hello. Is everything okay here? Hello? Is everything all right?"

A light came on in the cop car. Sneed stepped out with his flashlight aimed on the boat. I could just barely make out this guy in a T-shirt; he was white and wore glasses. I could tell by the reflections. Sneed's voice sounded sort of wheezy and squeaky.

"We're police officers!" He said, as if that should settle everything. "Go back to bed."

The T-shirt replied, "Yes, well, I can see that, but why? Is everything all right?"

Sneed said, "Who are you, sir? And what is your business?"

T-shirt shouted, "I am Dr. Sol Weintraub. I don't see what my business has to do with anything."

Sneed shrugged and breathed heavily, a deep sigh. You could barely hear, too dark to see, but you could feel it, sort of like a heavy cloud bearing rain and thunder. Sneed said, "Dr. Weintraub, I am Major Roscoe Sneed. What is your business tonight on this creek? Never mind the rest of it. What are you doing here?"

Dr. Weintraub said, "I'm trying to sleep. Is that a crime? This is my boat, HMS *Chickenship*. I've docked here every year for seven years. I ask you again, is everything all right?"

Sneed sneered. "What did you call me? If you called me what I think you called me, everything sure as hell ain't all right."

The doctor calmly replied, "I called you nothing, Officer Sneed. I simply stated that I was sleeping at my dock on my boat called the HMS *Chickenship*. This is our first night here this season. Your radio is very annoying. I will tell you that. I am sleeping. I ask you once again. Is everything okay?"

Sneed said, "So far, but we've had gangs of niggers around here doing damage. Maybe you would feel safer at home in your bed, Doctor."

All of a sudden, a voice in the cop car called Sneed. He scurried over. When he walked back, he kept the flashlight aimed at his feet. He told the doctor that he was sorry the radio disturbed him. That everything was under control. To please have a good night's sleep. But there was no answer from the boat. Sneed walked back to the cop car. He closed the door quietly. You couldn't hear the radio.

A few minutes later, I figured out that the doctor was either Jerry's father or uncle. I didn't know which. I figured the deal was over. That they would leave. But they didn't. So we waited. There was nothing else to do. We couldn't have left if we had wanted to.

We waited for what seemed like forever; the crickets sang their songs, and way off from down on Bill's boat, came a lonesome sound of quiet harmonica playing. Real faint. Sort of mournful. It made me think of Albert. It made me think of a lot of things. It made me think of the little girl in Fred's church singing with all her might. It made me think of Hays in the balcony at the funeral. It made me think of Hawk in a jail in Alabama.

Laura put her arm around my waist. It made me think of the kiss, the light in the hayloft, the way her eyes had flashed and said what? What? The colors of her skin, warm up close. The light around her hair. I turned to her and kissed her neck and then a quick one on her mouth. The moon went behind a cloud and I could not see anything at all. The music stopped. There was only breeze, rustling leaves, and the metallic cricket chant. Off in the distance, a dog barked, another howled, almost as mournful as Bill.

I looked down the creek, wishing I was in the loft with Laura and none of this crazy stuff was going on. Bill's boat was dark. The grass was damp. It was getting cool. Laura whispered in my ear that she was hot and cold all at once. A tingle whistled up and down my spine. It blossomed behind my ears and on the back of my neck. It washed over the top of my head onto my forehead, down my face, and then through my whole body. I whispered back, "I know what you mean." Moonlight flickered. Her lips glistened. She winked.

Behind us on River Road, a car squealed through the curve, engine roaring, burning rubber the whole way. A bottle smashed against the entrance post. Yahoo! I figured Lieutenant Sneed would lay a patch of his own and chase after the crazy lunatics. But he didn't budge, and we listened to the growl of the engine shrink down to a purr. Over the next hour or so, a couple of other cars swooshed by. Then nothing. Even the dogs were silent. The breeze died down. The loudest sound was the ringing in my ears. The moon was starting to slowly slide down the other side of the sky. The clouds were coming in from across the river and it got cooler. Laura whispered that she was cold. I patted her knee and nodded.

Two clicks. One after the other.

I looked toward the cop car, but there was no inside light on. Next, we heard the gravel sound, real quiet, step, step, step, and then nothing. Now they walked through an area that was more open and I saw they were walking in the grass beside the creek. They looked like broken shadows moving slowly. We listened for the signal. Mickey was closest. My heart was pounding. My hands were sweaty. I wiped them on my pants and gripped the handle of the hammer to see if I could. I could. My mouth was dry. I thought I heard a gravel sound. I saw a man's shape against Bill's boat. The bastards were there.

Minutes went by. No sound at all.

I stared down the creek. I could faintly see Bill's boat, a bit of gray on black and then the gray was slowly swallowed up. I saw the dark shapes of trunks of trees, and then I heard Mickey. Three quick whistles. Sharp. *Now*! Laura looked at me. I slinked past her with my hammer. I nodded to her. I ran to my position. I scrambled with my hands, furiously searching the grass for my stake, found it, and I looked and saw Tuck stretching the cable. He about pulled me over and I tugged back and set the thing, just as this horrible explosion blasted through the air. Before I raised my hammer, I looked and there was a flash/boom and then a bunch of blasts at once. I was trying to hammer, and the stake kept jerking. I heard Tucker pounding and the thump, blam, blam, kerblam, and the creek was exploding one blast after another. Laura was coming toward me, and I still hadn't struck the first good blow, and then I connected, and again I connected. I sensed somebody running toward me, and out of the corner of my eye, I saw it was Mickey.

The cable was stretched pretty good. "We don't need that," he said. I gave him a look. He signaled for us to follow him. We jumped in the ditch on the Creekside edge of the entrance. Blam. Blam. A series of pops that must have been a hundred firecrackers. Then one huge blast! Mickey said that was his son of a bitch. Then it was real quiet, except for the sound of scuffling gravel, and the lights of the cop car came on and the engine roared. I started to run down the ditch toward the woods. I heard gravel spray and the Interceptor whine and then a horrible clunk crash and a screaming engine and then nothing.

"Son of a bitch! Son of a bitch! Son of a bitch!"

Suddenly the cop car lit up bright as blazes. A spotlight from the cruiser beamed right on it. Walking around it, if you could call it walking, was lard-butt Sneed, bent over and yelling "son of a bitch" and Hoyt was behind the car, holding his head with a pistol in his hand.

"Turn off that goddamn light!"

No answer from the boat.

"Turn off the light, goddamn it. Niggers is here! Turn off the light!"

The light just sat there steady as a star, a very bright star, and lit up everything except us down in our ditch, ready to slip out of there, I hoped, because I could see that Mickey wasn't kidding when he said he was gonna tear the ass out from under that SOB. Man, the car sure looked different. Headlights pointed up at treetops and taillights right down on the ground. The wheels were back a ways where the logging chain had snatched 'em. A good touch, but I was for blowing out of there quick. Sneed had his gun out now, too, and he was looking around. Not much more than a hundred feet away. It was quiet now.

"In the name of the law, turn off that light. Niggers is here. Turn it off or I'll shoot the bastard out!"

No answer from the cruiser. Hoyt aimed at the light and fired and I heard the bullet crack into a tree. Smack. But the light stayed put. Sneed knelt down and laid his arm across the hood of the car.

"This is how you do it. Gotta steady yourself."

Blam! Nothing but leaves.

"Turn off the light, Goddamn it. Nigger-loving commie bastard!"

Well, I guess that was just one two many "niggers" for Tucker. Scratch of a match and then a flicker of light in our ditch, and Mickey said, "What the fuck?" while Tuck flung a cherry bomb right at their backs. It landed right under Sneed, who was still leaned over the hood of the car. Tuck launched another one, but before it got there, the first one exploded and Sneed screamed and jumped straight over the hood. The second one bounced off the windshield and exploded right over the top of the car. Mickey said, "Oh shit," and he was right because, while Sneed was son-of-a-bitching and cussing up a storm, Hoyt walked out from behind the car and fired off a shot—blam! Dirt and gravel chunked down on us and now all of us were afraid to look. He fired again and we were inching toward the woods, but we were fucked.

"Sneed, the ditch! In the goddamn ditch."

"Hellfire!" A voice roared scratchy and gravelly as the road. "Hellfire! What in the name of God do you bastards think you're doing?"

It was Bill.

"You crazy bastards are shooting at children. Don't you know that? Put those firearms away *now*!"

There was some rumbling from both Sneed and Hoyt, but a siren was wailing out on River Road, and all I heard out of Sneed was, "Oh, dear God" and "son of a bitch." The sirens got louder and louder, and we squirmed down the ditch, but it was no good with the spotlight on. They would have seen us break into the woods. When the cop car roared up, it wheeled into the entrance and crashed into our cable, and the stakes yanked free and banged into the sides of the car. My teeth were clenched over that one. Now we had that one mad, too, and us in the ditch with the headlights right on us.

"Hands on your heads. Stand up slow."

"They're just kids, officer," Bill yelled.

"Stand clear, sir. All right, one at a time. Out."

So while another siren wailed toward us, we looked at each other in the crazy flickering light and climbed out like he said, one at a time. The next cop must have out-ranked all of them. You could tell. I almost felt sorry for Sneed. He was looking this way and that, like he wanted to run away and hide. I could relate to that. Bill stood there with his arms crossed, and what surprised me was, he wasn't carrying a gun. I mean, the way he sounded when he yelled at Hoyt and Sneed, I imagined he was carrying a big double-barreled shotgun. But he wasn't.

They rounded us all up in front of Sneed's car. Sneed started to talk, but the new cop just said, "Later!" and raised his hand. He walked around the car and back to the rear axle and wheels. The officer shook his head. Then he opened the car door and poked his head in. He slammed the door hard. The officer walked up to Sneed and held out his hand. Very politely, he asked Sneed for his weapon. Then, when Sneed handed it to him, he asked him if he had any more. Sneed looked at him like a fat baby, mad as hell and ready to bawl. He reached down and pulled a smaller pistol out of a holster down on his calf.

The cop walked over to Hoyt, asked him if he was armed. Hoyt nodded and handed him his gun. The man asked him, as he looked it over, if he had a permit to carry a concealed weapon. Hoyt started bullshitting. The officer turned his back on him and walked over to the other policeman and told him to secure the firearms in the trunk of his car.

The man walked over to us and looked us over one at a time. He looked at Laura and shook his head. She looked down. I think I did the same. Tucker looked right at him. The officer nodded. When he got to Mickey, he squinted his eyes. He asked us to empty our pockets. Cherry bombs and matches. Gum. Cigarettes. Mickey had a Trojan. The officer smiled and gave it back to him. He kept the cherry bombs. He asked us if we knew they were illegal. We nodded. He nodded, too, like he was bored. He looked at Bill and smiled and asked him how he was doing. Bill said just fine for a man whose boat had busted loose and who had woke up in the middle of a godderned shooting match.

About this time, Dr. Weintraub walked up in a bathrobe. He did sort of look like Jerry. Not fat, but the way his eyes twinkled, even when he looked serious, and he did look serious. He tried to speak, but the cop just raised his hand.

He said, "But I'm the one who called you."

The cop smiled, nodded, and raised his hand again. "What's this about your boat busting loose? What do you mean?" He looked at us after he said this. He looked at us hard, one after another. "What do you mean your boat busted loose, sir?"

"Officer," Bill growled, "with all due respect. How the bloody hell do I know? What I do know is that one minute, I'm sleeping and the next minute there is this jerk that wakes me up, and I sit up, take a peek out the window, and everything looks different somehow, and I go, son of a bitch. But before I can think, the whole place sounds like the Fourth of July, one boom after another for about a minute or so, and then a couple of minutes later, gunshots! The boat's hung on something, and I tried to tie off the stern, but the lines were both broke or cut."

He looked at Hoyt and Sneed when he said cut. Sneed looked up at the stars. Hoyt looked toward downtown, like he wasn't even listening.

"Lieutenant Sneed, how would you explain the current state of your assigned vehicle?"

"Can't explain it."

"Sir."

"Yes, sir. Well, see, we was chasing after these . . ."

"Lieutenant Sneed," the officer interrupted, raising his hand, "back up and think, unless all of the beers that you and your partner have consumed make that impossible. Think about how that chain there happened to become wrapped around the rear axle of your patrol car."

"I reckon they done it, sir."

"How?"

Sneed started to fidget. The cop raised his hand and looked our way. I shrugged involuntarily and cleared my throat like I was just stretching, but Mickey made a sound in his throat like he was holding back a laugh. The officer looked at him. Sneed glared. I expected the man to walk over, but he didn't. He walked up to Dr. Weintraub.

"You called us on your ship-to-shore."

"Yes, sir. Three times I called you."

"Why, the first time?"

"Major Sneed there . . ."

The cop interrupted and said, "Major?"

"Yes, he identified himself as Major Roscoe Sneed. I'm sure. I wrote it down so I could ask what was happening, because he told me there were gangs of . . ." He would not say the word aloud. He mouthed the syllables. Cop nodded. "And he was menacing in his deportment and would not say more than that I would be more comfortable elsewhere. Then he spoke to someone who called from the car—I suppose that fellow—and came back and suggested that everything was under control. 'Go back to bed,' he said. I asked him to turn off his radio and he did. The whole situation was strange. I called to find out what was happening. No one knew a Major Sneed. That troubled me as well."

"The second?"

"Could not sleep, so I watched to see what would happen and then I heard them walking and saw them go down toward Bill's boat almost on tiptoe. I could not see what they were about, but I did see the boat start to move, and when I went to my radio, the bombs went off. The last call was when I said 'Mayday, Mayday, help,' and went down below. They shot at my boat. They cursed me and shot at my spotlight."

"What do you have to say, Lieutenant Sneed? Did you fire at the doctor's spotlight?"

"No, sir."

"Your weapon has been discharged, Sneed. What did you aim at?"

The officer did not wait for an answer. He raised his hand and motioned for the other cop. The officer whispered in his ear and the guy hurried out to his car and we could hear the radio crackling.

The officer walked over to me and looked me up and down. Didn't say a word. When the cop trotted back and nodded at him, the officer put his hand on my shoulder and walked me out to the entrance.

For a few seconds, I had the powerful hope that he was going to tell me to run on home, but of course, he didn't. When we got out to the road, he spun me around gently and said that in a few minutes he was going to have to decide what to do with us. He said he didn't want to have to take us to jail, but that he might not have any choice. He said he hoped I understood. I nodded vigorously. He smiled and said a lot hinged on how we answered some questions. I was eager to answer. I nodded again.

"Why were you here tonight?"

I told him that Bill was a friend of ours and that we had found out what Sneed and Hoyt were going to do, so we figured we would make sure they didn't get away with it. I told him about the cable that Mickey attached to Bill's stern. He smiled. I told him that Tucker and I were the ones who put up the cable across the entrance. I showed him. He patted a pretty nasty dent on the passenger door. I told him that was an accident. It was meant for Hoyt and Sneed.

He scratched his head. "How did you do that without being spotted?"

"The fireworks distracted them," I told him.

He nodded. "And the girl? Where was she?"

I pointed at the brush pile.

"What was she doing?"

I told him she was in charge of the fireworks.

"All by herself?"

I nodded. I told him that all she had to do was touch a wire to a battery; it was all set up beforehand.

"Mickey?"

I nodded.

"And where was Mickey when the fireworks were going off?"

I pointed down toward the locust tree, which I noticed for the first time was leaning over pretty far.

"So who decided when the fireworks went off, the girl?"

"No," I said. "Mickey gave the signal right after Hoyt and Sneed had cut Bill's lines."

"So why the cable across the road? Was it to keep somebody out?"

"No, it was to keep them in," I said.

"But they could just step over it. The car wasn't going anywhere, obviously," he said, and his eyes sort of twinkled.

"No, sir," I said. "I guess it wasn't."

"You guess it wasn't?"

"Well, it sure didn't," I said, almost laughing.

"You didn't know about the chain, did you?"

"Not exactly," I said.

The officer shook his head and closed his eyes for a moment. When he opened them, he was still shaking his head. "Young man, that kind of answer can land you and your friends in jail. Be straight. It's going to come out anyway, believe me."

I told him we knew about the chain, but only Mickey knew what he was going to do. That was his job. "But," I said, "nobody would have thought . . ."

He raised his hand. Another cop car pulled up. He pointed to where everybody was standing. Two cops got out. He told them he would be over in a minute.

"Anything else you think I should know?"

"Yes, sir," I said. "Two things. Hoyt shot at us twice when we were in the ditch."

He nodded.

"Also, I'm pretty sure if you frisk 'em, you'll find oily knives and dirty oil on their hands and shoes."

"Mickey?" he said.

I nodded.

We walked back. He told me to stand with the others. Tucker asked me what was going on. I shrugged and said I wasn't sure.

"Come on, Bill," the officer said. "Let's have a look at that boat of yours."

Bill and the cop and Dr. Weintraub walked down to Bill's boat. A flashlight flickered.

Mickey whispered, "Know about the oil?"

I nodded.

They walked back slowly. Bill was walking ramrod straight. The cop was shaking his head. The doctor said, "What is this world coming to?"

"Sneed, Hoyt. Hold out your hands."

He put the flashlight on them. He signaled to the two cops who had just arrived.

"Cuff 'em, frisk 'em, and take 'em downtown."

Hoyt started struggling and screaming, "What's the charge?" He started kicking. The cop walked up to him and told him, "Resisting arrest, among a few other things." Sneed just held out his hands, but they made him put them behind his back. He just kept saying, "Oh Jesus, Oh Jesus." Hoyt told him to shut the fuck up and Sneed blubbered out, "You son of a bitch, you shut the fuck up yourself. This whole damn thing was your stinking idea." Hoyt tried to bump him over, called him a fool, and Sneed squealed like a pig caught up by one leg and butted back.

The officer just shook his head. "Get 'em out of here."

The four of us were looking at each other with big eyes. *What next?* The officer walked over to Bill, and they turned away from us and put their heads together. We couldn't hear anything. We just stood there. My fingers were crossed. *What are they doing?* After a few minutes, they both walked over, and Dr. Weintraub followed them. I noticed his spotlight was starting to get dim, but there was enough light to see that their faces looked damn serious. Laura looked at me and shook her head. I shrugged. I tried to cross my toes along with my fingers. Tucker stared straight ahead. I couldn't see Mickey. They stopped about three feet in front of us. Bill winked at me, but he didn't smile.

"I ought to run you in," the officer said and he looked slowly from one to the other. "How old are you, son?" Mickey said that he was eighteen. The cop shook his head and closed his eyes. "Destroying a police vehicle could land you in prison. You know that?" Mickey started to say something, but the cop raised his hand and Mickey shut up. That surprised me, and I was praying that he would stay shut up, for once. This was no time for cussing. "You three could go to juvenile detention. I could make it stick." He scratched his nose and shook his head. "What you did was crazy. It was dangerous as hell and stupid. Somebody could have been seriously injured or killed. You all realize that?" We nodded. I was praying like mad that Mickey could hold his tongue. *Oh, please.* "On the other hand," the officer continued quietly, "your crazy cockeyed scheme may have saved a man's boat and maybe even his life." He paused and looked at Bill.

Bill nodded and smiled. "Crazy little farts," he said.

The officer shook his head and tried to look real serious; I thought I saw a slight smile twitch at the corners of his mouth, but he tamped it down. He swallowed, cleared his throat, and continued. "Bill has urged me not to take you in. He suggests that we release you into the custody of your families."

I'm thinking, *Oh shit, can't you just let us go?* I was thinking jail might not be so bad. I looked at Laura and she was smiling. Tucker had a little grin. I couldn't see Mickey.

"Bill tells me that you three kids are good kids from good people . . . but you," he said pointing to Mickey, "Bill says you are one sorry, ornery, sneaky, low-down, not-worth-skinnin' varmint, so I . . ."

"Blast your rotten-ass, mother-humpin' son bitch . . ."

Now we're screwed. Damn it. Damn it.

"Just kidding, Mickey," the officer said, but Mickey kept right on cussing.

"Hush your mouth, boy," the man said. Bill was laughing his head off.

The officer took us home.

CHAPTER 12

LAW

I t was almost dawn before I got to sleep. At first, they were so angry that the kitchen seemed to throb. The officer had brought me home first. At the front door, knowing what was coming, I actually tried to stand behind him and use him as a shield from my parents' wrath. He put me in front of him with both hands on my shoulders. I was fucked. I had told my parents that I was spending the night at Ben's. What I didn't know was that Ben had called and asked to talk to me. They had been worried sick. And now there I was with Captain Moore.

"What's wrong? What's happened? Where have you been?"

The officer was good. He calmed them down. He told them there was no one hurt and no terribly serious infractions of the law. Possession of illegal fireworks. Trespassing. Minor damage to property. He said I was not being charged with anything at that time and that if we would appear at Substation Five in the old quarry at nine a.m., that I most likely wouldn't be.

My father had asked why we had to go to Substation Five if I wasn't charged with anything, and the cop calmly told him that the situation would take time he didn't have to explain. He said there were three more kids he had to take home.

"Be there," he said.

So it was up to me to explain, and it wasn't easy. For one thing, they kept interrupting. Why hadn't I been where I said I was going to be? You lied. You lied to us. I've been worried sick. What have you done? Who are the others? How did *you* get mixed up with this bunch? What kind of hold do they have on you? Are you on dope? So Hoyt was right? Sneaking around running with darkies? I raised my hands and told him that Hoyt was in jail.

"Hoyt's in jail?" my father asked, looking down and frowning.

I thought that might slow 'em down a bit.

"What do you mean in jail? For what?"

"For trying to kill Riverboat Bill, for shooting at Dr. Weintraub's boat, for cutting Bill's boat's lines, for shooting at us!"

"Shooting at you? Why? Who's this Bill? Dr. Winetrout?"

"Weintraub," I said. "Hoyt and Sneed tried to shoot out his spotlight after the rear end of their car got ripped out from under them when they were trying to make their getaway."

"What kind of foolishness is this? Weintraub? Weintraub, the eye doctor?"

"I guess so," I said.

"What's this about his spotlight? Who's this Sneed?"

"Sneed is Hoyt's cousin. He's a cop. He's in jail, too."

"Why? A cop's in jail? What's this about the car? The rear end torn off? Shooting at Dr. Weintraub's spotlight? What are you trying to tell me? What were you doing there? Why weren't you at Ben's? Have you been drinking? Why would anyone shoot out a boat's spotlight?"

"Well, see, after the explosions, they were trying to get away and the logging chain snatched 'em and tore the axle and wheels off, and so they were—"

"*Explosions*! What explosions are you talking about? Explosions?" My father shook his head and straightened his robe.

"All right," he said. "All right, just calm down. I am sure there is some kind of logical explanation for all this. Right?"

"I guess so," I said. "I mean, I think so."

"Just take a minute and think back to the beginning. How did all this get started? Start there and try to tell me."

He nodded. I nodded.

"Well, remember that Sunday I went to church?"

My father's eyes got big.

"Church?" he said and shook his head. "What does church have to do with it?"

"Well, see after the Bluebirds sang . . ."

My father started shaking his head impatiently, so I tried to speed up and fit in some more details.

"Well, see, outside before the picnic, I met Tucker—"

"Bluebirds?"

"Well, yes, the gospel group with the little girl who sang like an angel."

My father shook his head even faster. His eyes didn't look right. I swallowed hard.

"Well, see, actually, the way it happened was—remember the night of the big thunderstorms?"

My father held up both of his hands, signaling for me to stop.

"All right. Now, let's just forget about the little angel and the bluebirds and let's not discuss the weather. Unless you were at church tonight, let's leave church out of it."

He nodded. I nodded.

"Where were you tonight? Let's establish that. Where exactly were you when the police found you interesting enough to detain?"

"Well, in the ditch beside Bill's road. You know at the park."

"In a ditch? What park are you talking about? You mean the Green property? All right. In a ditch. Why?"

"I don't know. We should have just run back to the canoe."

"The canoe? What canoe? What? Are you . . ."

I think he was counting to ten. I was hoping he would count higher.

My mother suggested we all go to bed and discuss this thing in the morning. My father shook his head no. Said he wanted to get to the bottom of this.

He didn't.

I think what really baffled him and made all of the details so hard to see was that he couldn't figure out how I could get caught up in such a thing. He sort of got to the point where he knew the lay of the land, but then something like the punch line of a joke would go off behind his eyes, and he would shake his head and say, "I just don't get it. Why?"

To me that was a real big question with all sorts of possible answers. He wanted a simple explanation, or so it seemed, but behind every single one of my answers was one of his whys.

Also, there were other things in the way. For one thing, I had broken the law. No matter what, he couldn't get over that. Vandalism, hooliganism, setting off explosives, destroying property. In his view, there had to be some explanation for Lieutenant Sneed's behavior. Policemen weren't like that, and Hoyt had always seemed like an upright person—not bright, but not treacherous. When I told him that they thought they were going to get money from the real estate agent for moving Bill's old boat out of there, he laughed and said that was the most ridiculous thing he had ever heard. They couldn't be that stupid. Real estate agents weren't like that, and besides, he said Bill's boat had nothing to do with anything one way or the other. He said the whole thing made no sense at all.

"Well, they cut his lines, didn't they?"

He went up to bed scratching his head. Said he didn't know what to think. He told me to stay put. "Good night." A few minutes later, he knocked on my door and opened it. I was already in bed. All I could see was his silhouette.

"How do you get into these scrapes?" He shook his head and chuckled. "Kicked in the head by a dead cow. You sure you're not making all of this up?"

"I don't know."

"Try to get some rest. Good night."

He should have said good morning. It was getting light. The birds were cranking it up. I listened to one whose call seemed to be saying,

"What you need? What you *need*? *What you need?*" I put the pillow over my head and made it dark and quiet. *I don't know. I don't know! I don't know!*

———

The officer made it simple somehow.

We were all sitting around a big Formica table, all except for the officer, Captain Moore, who was standing in front of a blackboard. Laura was seated between her parents. They were dressed up like they were in church. Her mother was real pretty. She held her head high. Her father drummed his fingers on the table, until he caught her look, then he folded his hands in his lap. Laura wouldn't look at me. Hays was there with Tucker—Hays and this guy who turned out to be Tuck's older brother. He was huge. Tuck and Hays were dressed up, but the big guy was wearing overalls. Mickey was sitting next to a man who turned out to be his father, but he looked real young, had a flattop, and wore sunglasses. He was dressed sporty and casual. Mickey was wearing a clean T-shirt. Bill was there. I was slicked up and my father was wearing one of his business suits.

The cop passed a clipboard and made us all sign it, and after we had, he started by thanking us all for coming. Then he said he knew everybody was unhappy about having to be here. Everybody nodded.

"I am personally embarrassed," he said. He let this sink in. "A member of my force has brought disgrace and dishonor upon himself, which reflects upon me and all responsible, dedicated officers. Be assured that he is unhappy where he is. Dereliction of duty. Drunk and disorderly. Wanton endangerment. Criminal mischief and so forth and so on. His sidekick, a Mr. Damon Hoyt, is no better off, I can promise you. They will not be arraigned until Monday morning."

Then he went to the blackboard and drew the road, the creek, the ditch, the doctor's boat, Bill's boat, etc. Then he pointed to Laura and asked her where he should put her name in the picture. She told him, and he wrote it on the board beside a tangle of lines with "woodpile" written above it. He went around the table until he had placed us all.

"Now, right smack dab in the middle of this, we place Officer Sneed and Hoyt."

As he told what happened, my father looked incredulous. He looked at me like he couldn't believe his ears. I half expected him to ask the cop if someone had put him up to this. Laura's father put his hand over his mouth, but I could tell he was smiling by the look in his eyes. Everybody either looked like they couldn't believe it and they thought it was funny or else they just couldn't believe it. All except for Hays, whose expression didn't change, although she was shaking her head from side to side. Tucker was grinning and Mickey was too, until his father jabbed him in the ribs with his elbow. He sat up straight then and tried to look serious, but when Captain Moore got to the part where they cut the boat loose and the fireworks went off and the logging chain kicked in, Mickey started laughing out loud and everybody else tried not to. The cop even smiled. But when he continued, he looked real serious.

"We are all lucky to be here this morning," he said, and he looked at each one of us, one at a time. It made you swallow, knowing your turn was coming next. "You kids took the law into your own hands. Any one, or all of you, could have been severely injured or killed. Thank God, nobody was."

He pointed to Bill and nodded.

"Well," Bill said, "first off, I got to say thanks to you kids for maybe saving my life and trying to save my boat. I mean that. I think you all are pretty good kids. No telling what would've happened if that old wooden tub of a so-called boat had cleared the creek and got out in the open river. No lights, no motor. I had my skiff, of course, but a lot of good that would have done me bouncing along underneath a barge. So I thank you with all my heart. Now, hard to say,. You all just about sunk her your own damn selves! I woke up this morning and stepped into about eight inches of water that run in overnight from the plank that the cable jerked loose."

"Your boat didn't sink?"

"No, Miss Hays, it didn't—*hasn't*. Not yet, anyway, and I got a pump running, and this afternoon, she'll be back like she was. But anyway, thanks. But you kids better listen to Captain Moore."

"That's a terrible thing," my father said. Everybody nodded. "Captain Moore," he continued, "are you absolutely certain that Hoyt and this officer in question cut the lines to this man's boat?"

"Yes, we are certain. Ample evidence, and Sneed has confessed. You see, sir, this is my problem. I am in a bad spot. Bill has made it a little easier for me, for all of us, I hope. There has been damage to his boat, but he doesn't care to press charges."

"Nah, no way, never," Bill said. "Not against the kids."

"But you understand," the cop continued, "I have a destroyed police cruiser to explain. It is not an everyday thing. The rear end entirely torn off. Transmission mangled. Engine blown. You see, I can't just let this go. I, too, like Bill, think these are pretty good kids. But they got in way over their heads. So here we have a problem."

He turned his back on us and erased the blackboard and started writing. He wrote down all four of our names, then at the bottom put Sneed's and Hoyt's. He turned toward us and said, "options," then wrote "options" off to the right of our names. He said with Sneed and Hoyt, he had no problem. The court would decide. But he said, as of this moment, there was still some latitude that he had with how to proceed with the rest of us. He wrote "J. C." and said, "Juvenile court might be an option for three of you." He pointed at Mickey's name, "But you are not a juvenile. If I send you into the court system and you try to defend yourself, it will be a long, drawn-out, expensive process. Nobody will be happy during or after."

"I am sure everyone would like to put this behind us," my father said. "Believe me, everyone, we don't want this thing in court, if it is at all possible to avoid it."

"Thank you, sir," Captain Moore said. "Here are our options."

His chalk started screeching on the board. I watched the letters appear from beneath his hand. The letters became words and the words changed everything.

He started with Mickey. "Options: Court = jail time or military."

Mickey's dad was nodding in agreement. Mickey was shaking his head no.

The cop said that he knew that was how the judge would see it, if Mickey got lucky and the judge decided to be lenient. He said he would help if Mickey chose the military. Otherwise, he would have no choice but to be on the other side. "Think about it." He said he knew what he would do, if the choice were his.

He lumped Tucker, Laura, and me with one of those bracket lines that looks like a drawn bow}

"Probation Officer, evaluation, charges probated for two years. Parental oversight, prohibition of association."

He turned and looked at us.

"Let me explain myself," he said. "I don't want any more trouble for or from you people. If this thing goes to juvenile court and the premeditated nature of all this stuff comes out, I'm not sure but that the judge might find it in the best interest of the commonwealth to have you put in some sort of detention. Throwing explosives at a police officer, destroying a patrol car, etc, etc. I see you, Tucker; you want to say the cop was no good, a bad cop. Well, I agree. But what you did will not please a judge, I promise you. I will say it again. You took the law into your own hands. The judge will see it that way. You won't have a chance, no matter how right you might think you are, believe me.

"Now," he pointed to the words "Probation officer, evaluation."

"This is pre-trial. I can recommend in my report that there has been an incident involving juveniles that I am not sure is worth the court's scrutiny." He winked. "In effect, this means that, unless you meet with the probation officer and act crazy and say you can't wait to do it all over again, he will basically pat you on the head and tell you to be a good kid. You might have to see this person several times, but if you stay out of trouble, there will be no charges filed. There will be no record at all after two years."

He pointed at "Parental oversight."

"Your probation officer will want to know your parent or guardian. He will want assurance of cooperation. He will want to know that the parent or guardian is willing to accept the responsibility to assure him that nothing like this will occur again. Do you understand? This is teamwork.

"Prohibition of association may seem unfair. It means that, unless you are at an official function or in a situation strictly supervised by your guardians, that you are forbidden any physical contact. You can talk on the phone. You can write letters, but no hanging out for two years." He was afraid that was the best he could do. "Take a few minutes and think about it."

He looked at his watch, said he would be back in ten minutes, and left the room.

My father shook his head and said we really had no choice. That was that.

Out in the parking lot, we all went our separate ways. I tried to wave at Laura, but it was like her parents surrounded her. Mickey was having a pretty hot discussion with his dad. They roared off in a shiny white Corvette. For once, I was glad my dad didn't drive a fancy car. The truck that Tucker's brother drove was an old, beat-up farm truck that wasn't a whole lot fancier than Bill's jalopy, La Bomb Flambé. I waved at Tucker and he waved at me and made a fist. My father didn't see that. He was telling Bill that he sure hoped his boat would be shipshape soon. Bill started laughing.

"Not likely anytime soon anyhow," he said. "Say, you were in the fourth, weren't you?"

"Sure was," my father said.

"Me, too. Good to meet you."

I was expecting them to say something more. Saipan, Iwo Jima, or something, but they didn't say anything at all. They shook hands, nodded, and said, "Take care." When Bill fired up his car, it backfired a few times and then he roared off at about ten miles an hour.

As we were pulling out of the lot, my father said that sometimes life just didn't seem fair. I nodded.

"That man, Bill, is a casualty of the war just as much as the ones who never came back home. Some just never get over it."

I shook my head. I was going to ask my dad if *he'd* gotten over it, but something in his voice and in his look told me I probably shouldn't. I just nodded again.

———

When we had been leaving the conference room, Hays had come up to my father and in a low voice had said that these weren't bad kids, and this kind of thing showed the need for a park. She had patted me on the shoulder and squeezed my father's hand. He had nodded and told her it wasn't over yet. She had looked into his eyes intently, her eyes glistening.

"Do you think there will be a park?" I asked him.

"It's hard to say," he said. "These things take time."

———

I expected to be punished somehow, but on the way home, my father seemed almost lighthearted. He actually started whistling a happy tune, then he missed a note and laughed softly as he licked his lips.

"I think my whistle is dry."

"I'm a little bit thirsty myself," I said.

"I bet you are. You better get some rest, too, then maybe have a little talk with yourself."

He actually smiled at me and winked when he said that. I think I nodded and said I would. Then he took a deep breath and said that it was about time to put in the garden. He wanted to try out this new mulch paper he had read about, said it was supposed to hold in moisture and keep the weeds down. When we got home, he pulled into the garage, turned off the ignition, turned to me, and gave me a good long look. I was thinking *here it comes*, but he just shook his head and smiled.

"Listen, your mother is going to a luncheon at noon. If I were you, I would make myself scarce for a few hours. I'll tell her you're exhausted, so give her a kiss, and when I tell you to get up to your room, you just do it, hear me?"

I nodded, and that's exactly what happened. I was sure glad he had forewarned me of what he was going to say, because when he said it, the tone in his voice was such that I took the stairs two at a time and was halfway up before I remembered the wink he had given me. I think I sort of smiled, but I kept on going, closed the door to my room and, to my surprise, fell sound asleep.

I don't know what my father said to my mother, but I don't think she even tapped on my door. Still, I expected something to go wrong, at the very least a horrible lecture, but nothing like that happened. When I woke up, I was disoriented. It was mid-afternoon. I tiptoed around. My brother and sister were playing on the swing set in the backyard. Jean, our family's maid, was taking clothes off the clothesline. My father would be playing golf. I grabbed a chicken leg out of the fridge. Drank some milk, then hopped on my bike and took off. I thought about dropping in on Bill, but figured he was probably tired, so I ended up in the loft of the barn. I stayed there for the rest of the afternoon.

My father had advised me to have a little talk with myself, but I didn't know where to begin. I sat there on a hay bale and looked down on the park and smoked. Sneed's car was gone. I thought I could make out the rear axle, but it was hard to see through all the leaves that seemed to have doubled in thickness overnight. I could see Bill's boat, and from what I could see, it looked okay.

I realized that my hands were shaking a little bit. I tried to think of something funny like Tucker's cherry bomb. Instead I saw Hoyt's face right before he fired, and that made me close my eyes, trying to shut it out, make it go away, but it didn't work. "You're just lucky to be alive," was the quiet voice I heard. I think I answered out loud. I know I took a real deep breath. I wasn't quite ready to join Albert. It was funny. It was almost like I heard him laughing and saying, "Naw, not yet. You don't get off that easy."

For some reason, I felt sort of peaceful as I pedaled back home. Part of me was still dreading what I feared might happen, but then something told me that it might not be so bad. I knew I was hungry as could be. When I walked into the house, the first thing I heard was my father playing his ukulele. That was a positive sign. I knew already that he'd had a good golf game. He only played the ukulele when he was relaxed. Then I heard my mother's high heels clacking away upstairs, and that most likely meant she was getting dressed for a party, so I walked right into the living room where my father was singing and sat down. My brother and sister were singing along with him, and when he nodded at me, I joined in, too.

A few minutes later, my mother strolled in, looking radiant. We were singing the last chorus of "Jimmy Crack Corn," the part that goes, "I don't care, the master's gone away." My father took a little bow and smiled. My mother applauded. My father looked at his watch.

As they were leaving, my father suggested that I might want to lay low and stay home. He said this with a smile and that surprised me. My mother didn't say a word, just gave me a big hug. That surprised me even more. I said I would and meant it, then I asked my father how he had played, and he shook his head and said, "Lousy. I couldn't make a putt to save my life. You got to make your putts. Hit the ball pretty well, though. See you in the morning."

The next morning it was raining, and it rained all day. There would be no gardening. I figured I was screwed. Surely something was bound to come up, but nothing did. I was amazed. There was nothing about it in the paper either. There was nothing on the news. It was almost like it never had happened at all, like it was a dream. But then I would see Hoyt's face and hear the blast of his gun, and I swear sometimes I felt the dirt falling down on the back of my neck, and I knew it hadn't been a nightmare. It was real.

For some reason, I didn't talk about it at school either. I didn't want to. Seemed like there would be too much to explain, and I didn't want to face Ben's cross-examination. I didn't want to listen to any jokes about it either.

The entire week flew by. We lost our game. I guess that was the low point. We could have won it. But some good things were happening. Not just our class, but the entire school was donating money for the park. Midweek, Hatchet Head came up to me and handed me a note at lunch. He didn't look angry. The note said, "Headmaster's office, right after lunch." Mr. Hatch patted me on the shoulder before he walked away. I didn't even eat my dessert. I went straight to the office. The secretary wasn't in the room, but her perfume still was. I peered into Mr. Fenway's office. He was having his lunch at his desk. His eyes were open for a change, and he motioned me in and assured me that I wasn't interrupting anything. In fact, he cracked a joke about the food. He asked me if I could identify the source of the protein on his plate. I told him I couldn't. "Neither can I," he said.

He motioned for me to have a seat. He told me that the response to Albert's request, that monetary gifts be earmarked for the park, had far surpassed his wildest expectations. He smiled and said that he might have to hire another secretary to handle calls from parents who wanted to contribute. But there was more. Albert had played sports in several church leagues, and they had contacted Mr. Fenway and were raising money for the fund as well. I think I started to say something, but Mr. Fenway raised his hand. In addition to that, the kids who played in the church leagues were students from schools all over the county, and five schools so far had contacted him to tell him that they were raising money, too. He said it was a groundswell. He shook his head and closed his eyes. I wiped mine, then he squinted at me, eyes glittery, and said, "I thought you might want to know." I thanked him, he nodded, and I left.

By the end of the week, several more schools and at least a half a dozen churches had joined the effort. It was amazing. I spent more time in the headmaster's office that week than I ever had before. I spent so much time there I started to smell like perfume, but I got to know Mr. Fenway better. I found out that the reason he kept his eyes shut so much of the time was from some wartime injury that had to do with the North African desert sand; it had left his eyes permanently damaged and overly sensitive to light. Together, we signed lots of thank-you letters. I was listed as the student representative.

———

On the way home from school on Friday, Fred was in a jolly mood. He bought me a malt. As we were cruising out River Road, he told me it looked like things might be looking up. He had run into Mr. Traylor and Hays and they had just come back from a meeting with my father and the county judge. They had told him that things seemed a bit more promising, but he said from the way they were acting, he figured things must be going pretty good.

He passed our turnoff and I asked him where we were going. He just smiled and chomped his cigar. We turned onto his road and he allowed as how he was following orders from headquarters. We pulled into his driveway and before we had completely stopped, Lucky came out the door with a pan of brownies. You could smell 'em before she got to the car. She handed them to me and said, "That's the way we do it from now on." She gave me a beautiful smile and said, "I need a new range, so I probably should have sent Fred over with these, but I don't want to be too hard on the man. You can give him a taste if you want to. I don't want him pouting either." She put her hand on mine and squeezed. I thanked her and we drove on home. We could barely talk from chewing, but Fred's eyes were twinkling and mine were too, I bet.

Ben called and wanted to know if I could go see some monster movie with him and then spend the night, but my father said no. I was about to prepare myself for one of his talks, when he looked at me calmly and said that he needed me the next morning, so I told Ben I couldn't. Then I went into the study and asked my father what we needed to do. He said I needed to take him down to Bill's tomorrow right after breakfast. I asked him why and he looked up from the stack of papers in his lap and said, "I'm not quite sure yet. We'll cross that bridge when we get to it."

I read for a while, then surprised myself by doing my homework just to pass the time. I was real curious. My dad didn't seem the least bit angry. The next morning at breakfast, he told me he had done a little research on Bill. He asked me if I knew that Bill was a genuine war hero. I told him I had heard something, but that I didn't know what he had done. My father told me that he had saved five men's lives, dragging them to safety under enemy fire, until he had been wounded and had to be evacuated.

"Just like you," I said.

"Be that as it may, but I bet you, he's never told you a word about it."

"No, not a word."

"He won't either. He's a marine."

On the way over, my dad asked me if I knew what had happened to Bill's wife. I told him that Fred had told me after church on the day that the Bluebirds sang. I added that they were a gospel group, so he wouldn't get confused. He shook his head, said it was an awful thing.

I was surprised to see Bill sitting out on his deck drinking coffee like he was waiting for us. I asked my dad if Bill knew we were coming. He said he didn't know how he could have. My father said that's one of the reasons he had wanted me there, to make introductions and smooth things along.

My father actually saluted. Bill, with a puzzled look, saluted back. I said, "This is my dad." Bill nodded and asked us aboard. My father got right to the point after apologizing for being so rude that pitch-black evening on the driveway. Bill told him not to worry about it, that he would most likely have done the same, given the circumstances.

"Bill, you want to stay here, don't you?"

Bill nodded, but didn't say anything.

"Bill, there's nothing in the contracts between you and the Greens about any of this. Not about the docks, the gas pumps, or your berth here. However, I found this," he said, holding up a sheet of paper. "It was among Sam Green's papers, and it suggests to me that, at one time, there might have been some kind of written agreement between you two. This is like a first draft. It mentions the boat, moving it, a fellow by the name of Marcus, who it states will help you with repairs. It also says something about what he calls the dock operation, slips, pump, ramp, then it says a dollar a year as long as you want it. It also says something about stock, IBM and his company's stock, then something about a truck he offers to buy and a plot of land on Shirley Avenue, which I have the deed transfer on. Trouble is, this is a crummy carbon copy that you can barely read, and it's not signed or dated. I was wondering if you might have one of these, hopefully signed, because if you do, it'll help us both a lot."

"With all respect, sir, this is my home, and if I do have such a paper, what will it mean?"

"Bill, you are just going to have to trust me on this. The Green family is about ready to donate this land to the county for a park, and if you have a copy of this paper signed by you and Sam Green, I can guarantee you'll be able to operate here as you have for as long as you want."

Bill looked us over for almost a full minute, then went into his boat. He came back out on the deck with a metal box. He rifled through it. Postcards, letters. Then pulled out an envelope. He took out a paper, studied it, and handed it to my father. My father got a great big grin. He almost seemed to glow.

"Damn it, marine, you've hit the bull's-eye."

"It'll do some good?"

"Hell yes, it will. Hang on to this. Can you come into my office on Monday morning?"

When we were leaving, my father reminded Bill to bring that paper with him and, in the meantime, to guard it with his life. Bill said something like, "Yes sir, captain" and did a salute that turned into a wave as we rolled away. My father said he couldn't believe Green had actually dated the thing, said Bill was in luck, that most of Green's personal papers were worse than a maze to get through.

"One thing I still don't understand; why didn't you just tell Bill, or why didn't you tell me?"

"Would you have believed it?"

Halfway out to the river road, my father stopped the car. He said he wanted to get the lay of the land. I pointed out where everybody had been positioned that night. The rear end of Sneed's car was still there. He was easy to place. I pointed out the brush pile where Laura and I had been, then my father started rolling forward, where Tucker had hidden. My father started chuckling as we approached the stone fence posts and the black gate that opened into the drainage ditch. Craziest thing he'd ever seen, said he would never for the life of him figure out how that fiasco had ever happened, and he wouldn't have ever either, if I hadn't started laughing.

He surprised me when he started laughing as well. He just shook his head.

"That's what started this whole thing?"

He looked at me like he couldn't believe his eyes.

"Keep it to yourself," he said quietly. Then he smiled. "I'm proud of you, son."

ABOUT THE AUTHOR

Ed Middleton was born in Louisville, Kentucky, and with the exception of exploratory years, has mostly always been blessed to live there. Aside from publishing poems and short fiction in mostly forgotten rags, he has worked in many capacities to pursue his quest to be forever learning and studying about and from the timeless world that surrounds us and the courageous ones who bear witness.

ACKNOWLEDGMENTS

The author would like to thank Susan Lindsey of
Savvy Communication LLC for her tireless and astute editing.
Further, Shellee Marie Jones deserves praise for
thoughtful and sensitive design work.

www.ingramcontent.com/pod-product-compliance
Lightning Source LLC
Chambersburg PA
CBHW071333250626
47159CB00004B/1579